Bucket of Tongues

DUNCAN MCLEAN was born in Fraserburgh in 1964 and brought up there and elsewhere in Aberdeenshire. He now lives in Orkney. He has had several plays performed and is the author of *Blackden, Bunker Man,* and *Lone Star Swing.*

Also by Duncan McLean

Bunker Man

Lone Star Swing

Duncan McLean

Bucket of Tongues

W. W. Norton & Company
New York • London

ISBN 0-393-31897-4

W. W. Norton & Company, Inc., 500 Fifth Avenue, New York, NY 10110
www.wwnorton.com

W. W. Norton & Company Ltd., 10 Copic Street, London WC1A 1PU

1 2 3 4 5 6 7 8 9 0

For Vicky Masson
Thanks for the typewriter

Contents

Acknowledgements

Stories from this collection have appeared in:

Edinburgh Review, Hippo, Iron, London Magazine, Lost, Minion Opinion, Onionhead, Out From Beneath The Boot, Panurge, Queensferry Free Press, Self Determination and Power, Setting Forth, Tales from the Clocktower, West Coast Magazine.

'Lurch', 'The Druids Shite It, Fail to Show', 'Thistle Story' and 'The Big Man That Dropped Dead' have appeared in pamphlets from the Clocktower Press.

When God Comes and Gathers His Jewels

They came home from the pub to find their flat had been fucking done over. She noticed first, through in the bedroom hanging up the coats.

Shit, she said.

He was ben the kitchen making tea, he didn't hear her.

Shit! she shouted.

He came out into the lobby. What's up? he said.

Come and look at this, she said. I think somebody's broken in.

He looked where she was pointing. The big window at the end of the room was open slightly, and the folded newspaper that blocked the gaps around it had fallen to the floor. The strips of paper were lying on top of jags of broken glass. The middle of the five panes had been burst in, the one next to the catch.

Fuck! he said. Why us? Why fucking us? Jesus . . . He put his hand up over his eyes.

Robbie, she said, Do you think they're still here?

He didn't say anything.

She took a step backwards. Robbie, look under the bed will you?

He dropped his hand to his side. They're more likely to be in the cupboard, he said.

Robbie, please! Will you check under the bloody bed? Don't muck around now. I don't want somebody under my bed!

Alright, alright, he said. I'll check the cupboard first. He took a couple of steps round her, leant forward to hook his fingers over the handle, and yanked open the cupboard door, leaping back as it swung towards him. It was empty except for a couple of suitcases and some binbags of unsorted stuff.

Under the bed, she said quietly. She was still holding the coats, pressing them against her chest, pulling them right up to her chin.

He cleared his throat, then said in a loud voice, If there's anyone under the bed, you better come out now, right? Fucking right now!

Silence. Through in the kitchen the kettle started to whistle. She looked at him, then back at the bed. He lifted the corner of the top blanket with the toe of his shoe, and flicked it up on top of the bed. He cleared his throat again then knelt, his side against her legs, well away from the bed, and lowered his head down to the floor. He gazed into the dark, narrow space. After a few seconds he crawled closer, reached out, and lifted the whole side of the blanket clear of the floor and up onto the bed. He looked under again.

There's no one in there, he said. There is something though. He lay flat down, shoved his arm in up to the oxter, felt around for a few seconds, then dragged himself back and sat up, holding a small radio-cassette. He grinned. Here it is! he said. God, I was looking all over for this last night, couldn't find it anywhere. How the hell did it end up under there?

She flung the coats past his head and onto the bed. I put it there when you were cleaning your teeth; so you wouldn't put on a bloody tape and then fall asleep five minutes later, leave me listening to bloody Hank Ballard all night. It always happens! You go off to sleep and I lie there listening to your bloody tapes.

He sniffed. I bet they give you sweet dreams though, eh?

She looked around the room, across to the window, then back down at him. What are we going to do? she said quietly.

He got to his feet. Well, we have to . . . what have they taken? I mean at least they didn't smash the place up. What have they taken though?

We should phone the police.

Aye, I suppose. I mean probably.

We have to. Whoever it was might be hanging about out there; they might come back, while we're asleep or something!

Aye, okay, you're right. We better get the pigs. He looked around. So what do we tell them's gone? He narrowed his eyes. How about your books?

My books! Oh no! She stepped over to the mantelpiece and ran her fingertips along the spines of the paperbacks lined up there. Half-way along she stopped and cried, Where's my . . . oh, no, I lent that to Bunk last week. She came to the end of the line, let her fingers rest for a moment on the alarm clock there. No, they're all here, she said. She flicked a finger out at the bell on top of the clock. Ting . . .

What's the fire doing there? he said, looking at the calor-gas heater that was pulled out from under the mantelpiece, at an angle to the blocked-up grate. Did you move it?

No, she said. Unless maybe when I was leaning over just now . . . Wait, the back's open . . . She bent over the heater, made to close the back. Robbie! It's empty! Where's the canister?

He stood up from the bed. The canister? He frowned. Oh no . . . You're not telling me they've took our fucking gas canister?

She looked at him, shrugged, then shifted her gaze over to the open window. Maybe they chucked it out, just for badness, maybe it's down on the back green . . .

He crossed to the window and looked down. I can't see anything. It is dark right enough, but you'd think I'd see it.

Shit! That was new in two days ago! She banged her hand down on top of the fire. It clanged.

When the ringing stopped he said, I was just thinking, love: see when you hid the radio last night, did you hide my tapes as well?

She shook her head. No need, she said. She looked over to the floor at the far side of the bed. They were down there, as usual . . .

They're gone.

Och Robbie, your tapes! I'm sorry . . .

He looked down, shook his head. I'll go and phone now, he said.

No! Don't leave me here!

Well you go then.

No, they might be hanging around . . . Why can't we both go? Let's both go.

Aye, that's a good idea, he said. He picked up the coats and held hers out to her. Come on, let's both go and phone the pigs right now.

On the way to the front door she nipped into the kitchen and switched the gas off under the kettle. The whistle had popped off the spout and was lying on the floor by the stove. The kitchen was full of steam and the kettle was boiled dry.

Come on! he shouted from out in the stair.

Back again, they opened the front door and stood with it open for a few seconds, listening. Nothing. She stepped in and waited till he'd closed the door behind him before leading into the kitchen.

We can still have some tea, she said. Heat us up a bit.

It is cold out there, he said.

It's cold in here, she said. I'm keeping my coat on.

He nodded, topping up the kettle at the sink. He turned both gas rings on full, depressed the igniter button, and lowered the kettle onto one of them. Flames spilt up round the blackened edges. He adjusted the gas till they died down, then rubbed his hands in the heat from the second ring.

She was looking in the cupboard at the other side of the sink. We could have a bit of toast, she said.

He sniffed. That's just the drink talking.

What, a bit between us even?

We better not, really; that loaf's meant to last till Monday. After a moment he looked at her. But we could. He bit the corner of his lip. I mean it would heat us up, eh?

She shut the cupboard. No, no, you're right: we better not. She walked away from the cupboard and over towards the stove. Let me in on some of that fire, she said.

There was a battering on the front door. Neither of them moved. More banging. Then the bell rang. That'll be the pigs, he said.

Keep your voice down! she said.

He looked at her. The bell rang again. I'll get it, he said, and turned and walked out of the kitchen.

The kettle was hottering. She picked up the teapot from the draining-board, splashed some hot water in and swirled it round, then emptied it down the sink. She heard the front door being opened, a voice in the stair saying, Break-in? and Robbie replying, Aye, aye, come in . . . She dropped a teabag in the pot and was starting to pour in the boiling water as footsteps came into the kitchen. Robbie cleared his throat. She turned.

Well here we are, said Robbie.

The pig nodded, and moved his head around, taking in the whole room. This is the kitchen, he said.

She looked at Robbie, and their eyes caught. He looked down. Eh, aye, said Robbie, The kitchen.

So is this where the break-in occurred?

No, she said. Through in the other room, the bedroom; they've broken a window and lifted the latch and . . .

Could you take me to the bedroom? said the pig, already turning and heading for the lobby.

Aye, sure, said Robbie, and followed. She put the teapot down on the stove, turned the gas away to almost nothing, and went after them.

The pig had on a dark coloured rain-jacket of some thick crackly material that rustled and creaked as he moved along the lobby; when he brushed against the door-frame going into the bedroom it crackled loudly, covering up something he was saying.

What? said Robbie.

The pig stepped round the bed and over to the window. Nothing, he said. The two of them watched from just inside the door as he pushed the window open wide, stuck his head out and looked left and right, then down at the back green.

What about fingerprints? she whispered.

Robbie shook his head. Gloves, look, he said.

The pig drew his head back in and shut the window firmly. A large shard of glass dropped out of the frame and smashed on the lino at his feet. He paused, then slid the catch to, and turned to face them. He nodded, looked from one to the other. Right, let's get some details, he said, and sat down.

Aye, details, said Robbie. Well, we came in about . . .

The pig held up a hand, shook his head. He ripped open the velcro on his rain-jacket and reached inside. The jacket crackled. He pulled out a small notebook; from the ring binding at the top he extracted a pencil, then flipped over a few pages, checked his watch, and began to write. After a few seconds he looked up.

Name? he said. You first, sir.

Robert London, said Robbie.

Address?

Here.

The pig stared at his notebook. Are you trying to be smart?

What? No! I just thought . . . eh, sorry. Twenty-five Peter Street.

The pig started writing again. First floor right is it?

Back right it gets called, she said, First floor back right.

Shh! said the pig, without looking up. Now. Age?

Twenty-eight.

Occupation?

None.

Unemployed?

Eh, aye.

The pig nodded, wrote for another second. Now then. Your name please?

Jackie Bruce.

The pig looked up, half smiled. My name's Bruce, he said.

Oh. Good.

He looked down again. Now is Jackie short for anything? Jacqueline maybe?

No, just Jackie.

Address?

The same as him.

So you both live here?

Aye, said Robbie.

But you're not married as such?

No, said Jackie. Co-habitation, that's what it's called.

Fine, said the pig. I don't need to know that actually. Now your age is . . . ?

Thirty.

The pig looked up at her, put the end of the pencil to his lips for a second, then wrote. And your occupation?

None.

Will I put housewife?

You will not! She snorted. I'm unemployed, that's what I am.

The pig wrote on for a few seconds, then brought the pencil down sharply to mark a full stop. Right, he said, Let's get the story now. I'll do you both at the same time. You'd been out – where? – and you came back – when? – and what did you find?

You do it, said Jackie.

Robbie cleared his throat. We'd been out at the pub, he said, the Rosemarkie, just round the corner.

So you'd been drinking?

Well . . . two rounds . . . a pint and a half each. It is Saturday night!

And when did you return home?

After the football results, said Jackie.

Aye, said Robbie, We never stayed for the match. So I suppose it was about quarter past ten we got in. And found the place had been done over.

Fine, said the pig. Now, did it look just like this, or have you moved anything?

No, this was it, said Jackie. I mean we just went out and phoned you lot straight away, and then you came quite soon.

He nodded. I was in the area, he said. He looked around the room. You came in, found the window open, and one pane broken? They nodded. And what's been taken? Can you tell me everything that's missing?

Well the main thing is the gas canister from the fire, said Jackie. And it was new as well: we only put it in the day before yesterday!

A calor-gas canister. He sniffed. Anything else?

Cassette tapes, said Robbie. All of my tapes are gone.

How many would you say?

Och, twelve or thirteen.

I see. Can you give me a description of the tapes, what was on them and so on?

Well, they weren't bought tapes, ken, just ones I'd made up myself. Soul mostly, a bit of blues.

Home-recorded tapes, said the pig.

Eh, aye.

Anything else? Any money, valuables, jewellery?

God, I forgot! said Jackie. My diamond necklace is gone!

The pig sat up. What's that? he said.

Jackie laughed. It was a joke . . .

The pig shook his head, sighing.

Just the gas and tapes, said Robbie, That's all we've noticed so far.

The pig stood up. So not much really, eh? He looked around, then frowned. Hold on. Your telly: where's that? Have they taken that?

There was a pause. We don't have one, said Jackie.

You don't have a telly?

No, we don't. Haven't had one for a while.

Oh. Why's that?

Robbie and Jackie looked at each other. What's that got to do with anything? she said.

The pig shrugged. Och, nothing, nothing. I was just interested. He made for the door. They parted to let him through. Well I think that's about all I can do at the moment. I'll have a quick look down round the back on my way out, but I don't suppose there'll be much there. And I'll keep an eye out as I'm driving around, stop anyone I see lugging a calor-gas thing about, eh! He laughed. He put his notebook away, and his jacket crackled as he fastened it. Apart from that I'd suggest that you get some good locks fitted to your windows; this would never've happened if you'd had those. He unlatched the door and turned to them. Well, I'll be off then.

Robbie raised a hand to the side of his head. Eh, hold on, he said.

Yes?

Well are you not going to check for fingerprints or anything?

Aye, what happens now? said Jackie.

The pig smiled. Fingerprints are nothing to do with me, he said. That's CID you're talking about there. They'll definitely get given a copy of my report, so there's a chance they might come round to see you the morn. But to be honest, they probably won't bother with a job like this. I mean nothing of any value's been taken really, so . . . He shrugged.

So what does happen? said Robbie, as the pig stepped out into the stair again.

You'll get a letter in two or three weeks, just to tell you nothing's happened, said the pig. Unless of course the stuff turns up, in which case we'll have you in to identify it. But I wouldn't hold my breath. He shrugged again. Now I really must get going, he said. Good-night to you. He went off down the stairs, two at a time.

Robbie and Jackie looked after him.

Good-night to you too, said Robbie.

Well at least he didn't say, Evening all . . .

He was over at the window, sellotaping some sheets of newspaper over the broken pane. I wish we'd done this earlier, he said, Before the rain started up. It's making the wood all wet and the tape won't fucking stick.

We should probably just go to bed as soon as possible, she said.

We'll soon warm up then. I mean we'll always be cold as long as we're sitting about here with no fire.

I'm well aware of that Jackie, but someone has to block this fucking hole up, unless you want a fucking gale of rain blasting in all night. Jesus!

Don't get ratty at me! I'm freezing too you know!

Aye, aye, I'm sorry. He tore a long piece of sellotape off in his teeth, and struggled to line it up down the edge of the newspaper as it flapped about in the wind. After a few moments he said, What are you doing, anyway?

Ah-ha! Just you wait and see. Something that'll warm you up good and proper!

What? You haven't found my secret Deep Heat stash in those binbags have you?

She laughed, and stood up from where she was kneeling in front of the cupboard. A clinking sound came from the black bag she was holding.

Whisky! he cried.

Just you finish fixing that hole, she said, and went out the door.

He went back to taping the paper down, humming something, smiling to himself. After a few seconds he took a step back and looked at his work. The paper heaved in the middle whenever the wind gusted strong, but the edges were fixed firm and weren't moving. He threw the sellotape roll onto the unit by the bed, and was stretching out to draw the curtains when there was a sharp bang and a scream from ben the house. He moved.

Jackie was standing by the sink, elbows pressed into her sides, one hand clenched into a fist against her chest, the other gripping the handle of the kettle. Steam was trailing out of its spout and hanging around in the cold air of the kitchen. There was broken glass on the tiled floor all around her feet.

As he paused in the doorway, her eyes closed, her lips curled back, and she blirt out crying, no tears at first, just the noise from her mouth; then tears did appear, streaming down her reddened cheeks and dropping off her chin . . . and all at once she was greeting and roaring, her shoulders slowly moving up and down as she slorped in air and grat some more. And he was stepping over and opening his arms, saying her name, telling her to shoosh, when, Stop! she shouted, and he stopped.

What is it? he said.

There's broken glass between us and you've only got your socks on, she said, crying, but as she spoke her girn turned into a smile and she laughed, laughed loud on the out breath, then cried some more as she breathed in.

He started laughing too. You're a daftie, he said. There's nothing to greet about, nobody's hurt.

Ach . . . I know . . . I just feel so stupid . . .

He reached out from where he was standing, took the kettle from her, and let it drop on the stove-top. Then he moved his hand over and wiped some of the wetness off her face with the sleeve of his jersey. What were you doing anyway? he said.

She looked at him, blinking. Ach . . . She sniffed. I found a couple of old Irn Bru bottles in the cupboard, and I thought I could fill them up, kind of hot-water bottles, use them to heat the bed before we got into it . . .

Och Jackie, you didn't pour boiling water into a glass bottle did you?

No! I might be daft, but I'm not stupid Robbie. The water was getting hot, but nowhere near boiling, and I filled one bottle and that was alright. And I went to put the top on that so it wouldn't cool down, before I filled the other, but something happened, I don't know what, I think I didn't thread it right; it was sticking,

and when I tried to undo it I must've caught the other with my
elbow or the kettle. And I saw it kind of toppling on the edge, and
I made to catch it and then I knocked the full one too and then
they both fell on the floor and smashed. Now we don't have any
hot-water bottles at all!

Her face tightened as if to greet again, but he smiled at her,
reaching his hand to her shoulder, and after a few seconds a smile
came over her too.

Jesus Christ, she whispered.

Jackie?

What?

I thought you were asleep. Did you wake up?

No, I never got to sleep, I just pretended: closing my eyes and
breathing slow, trying to trick my brain into letting me really
sleep.

He rolled over to face her. Did it not work?

It's the weight of all these coats and stuff. I feel like I'm getting
crushed.

We need those layers, like extra blankets. Otherwise we'd be
freezing.

I am freezing. *And* I'm suffocating!

You don't have to put your face under you know . . .

She jabbed her elbow into his stomach, and chuckled. He
laughed too. Silence.

Robbie . . .

What?

What time is it?

Are you asking me to put my arm out into the icy wastes to
look at my watch?

Aye. No! Have you not got a light on it?

So I do. Hold on. He pulled his head down under the covers

and curled up slightly, bringing his arms round in front of his face so he could press the light button and read the time. Twenty past two, he said, and sighed.

Is that all? Jesus! Are you sure your watch hasn't frozen up?

No, but I'll tell you something Jackie, he said, still under the covers.

What's that?

A fart at this stage of the game could be fatal . . .

Och Robbie, you big kid!

It's the view down here, it just put it into my head somehow.

Come up then. And stop wriggling about down there.

You don't usually mind me wriggling.

Aye, but you're lifting up the edges of the blankets, letting all the cold in. Come on, cut it out!

He straightened out, and his head emerged from beneath the covers onto his pillow. Jesus, it is cold out here, he said.

It is cold, she said, But I think we'll be okay once we get off to sleep. We won't notice the cold once we're sleeping.

I bet that's what Captain Scott said, said Robbie. Famous last words.

She chuckled, then yawned. Outside the wind was getting louder, and there was the smattering of rain on the window again. If they hadn't broken the window it wouldn't've been so bad, she said. I mean the room would've taken years to heat up without the fire, but it would've got warmer in the end, just with our bodies and that. But with the window put in too it's just impossible: as soon as we breathe out some heat it just gets whipped away and a blast of cold comes in instead.

He sighed. As long as you can see your breath, at least you know you're still living. Mind you, it's too dark in here to see fuck all; where does that leave us?

The only thing I'll say is this, she said. I hope whoever it was had a bloody good reason for nicking somebody's gas at this time of year, in this weather.

I'll tell you what I hope: I hope whoever it was blew himself up when he tried to fit the canister into his own fire.

Och Robbie . . . But you know what I mean: it might be okay if it was for a bairn's room or an old granny or something.

Spare us Jackie! Do you think it was Robin Hood screwed the place? Aye, and I bet he's given my tapes to the bloody starving Ethiopians too!

She didn't reply. He didn't speak either. For a while there was nothing but the two of them breathing, and the wind and rain at the window. Once she sighed. Then there was another long silence. Then she sighed again and said, Maybe we should go through to the kitchen.

I was just thinking that, he answered straight away.

We could light the rings and heat the place up in no time. We could even have some tea while we're waiting for our limbs to thaw out. Some toast as well, eh? We could call it breakfast.

We couldn't do that.

Yes we could. Why not? Breakfast. It is the morning you know.

Ah, but we haven't been to sleep, have we? And that's the important thing: you're fast asleep and then you break it by getting up and eating: breakfast!

Silence.

I don't think that's right, she said.

Actually, I'll tell you what I was thinking, he said. I was thinking that we should move through to the kitchen permanently, move the bed through there, take the table out. And just sit eating on the bed. It would make sense: we'd only have to heat one room. In fact we probably wouldn't have to heat it at all: I mean with the cooking and the kettle and us being there all the time – plus with it being a smaller room – well, it would more or less heat itself. The problem with this room is those windows, they're so fucking big. The cold just comes knifing in through all that glass. And as if that wasn't enough, you've got the gaps all around where the frames are warped! Jesus, we should've thought of this before. It's common sense really. Don't you think? He paused. Jackie? He turned to look at the shape of her. Jackie?

Hmm . . .

Jackie, don't you think?

Hmm, what?

He leaned over and shook her slightly. Do you not think, Jackie?

What? What is it? What're you asking me?

What! Were you not even listening?

I think I must've been dozing a bit, you know, just dropping off . . .

Christ, here's me spouting great ideas and you're not even listening.

But I was listening. You were saying we should go through to the kitchen, eh no? Is that not right? He grunted. Aye, well, let's not bother though, cause we're more or less falling off to sleep now, aren't we? At least I was till you woke me up, you bastard.

He sighed. Sorry, he said. After a few seconds he spoke again. Jackie, I've got another idea. Mind how you said I always fall asleep when I put on my tapes? Well, go and put the radio on, see if we can find some decent sounds, and we might fall asleep listening to that.

Oh no . . . *You* always fall asleep, but I'm aye left lying awake!

But you were just getting off there anyway, weren't you? Come on. It's just going to get colder and colder forever unless we get to sleep, and the longer we argue the longer we put off sleeping . . . come on!

Oh God! Alright then . . . She poked an arm out from under

the blankets and layers of clothes and groped around on the floor beside the bed. After a moment she found the radio and lifted it up on top of the covers. There was a click, and a burst of loud white static noise. She turned it down, and started adjusting the tuning knob, running through several sets of voices talking in different foreign languages, some classical music, and a lot of static and burbling, whining noises. She paused at a station speaking in an American accent; it was reading out scores of baseball or gridiron football. That's all we need, she said. She moved the tuning knob some more.

After a few seconds more static, there was a countryish song coming through, quietly but clearly. I think that's about as good as we're going to get, she said. She turned the volume up slightly, leant over to place the radio on the floor by the bed, then pulled herself back under the covers and drew her arms and legs in tight around her body.

The guy singing had a whiney kind of voice, and he was singing about his girlfriend dying. To start with he was upset and crying, but then the minister came over and told him he'd meet his girlfriend in heaven, when he died too. What the minister said was, You'll meet her up there, up in heaven so fair, when God comes and gathers his jewels. This cheered the lad up, and from then on he was quite happy; he went on with his life, and whenever he was starting to get depressed, he'd just repeat the chorus to himself and get cheered up immediately: When God comes and gathers his jewels . . .

Hey Robbie, said Jackie as the song was finishing, How do you think the girl died? Maybe she froze to death, eh?

He didn't reply.

I suppose it must get cold in Texas sometimes, mustn't it? Or wherever it is. Country-and-western land. She sniffed. What do you think?

He didn't reply.

Robbie, she said quietly, Are you asleep?

He didn't say anything. The radio was playing an orchestra version of a seventies pop song. She reached out into the cold and switched it off.

Robbie?

Silence from his side of the bed. Then he breathed out. She waited. He breathed in again.

She waited.

Cold Kebab Breakfast

It was the night before Christmas, and we'd been drinking for two days solid. Now this big bastard in a bow tie was bearing down on us, rolling up the sleeves of his dinner jacket, mouthing words involving lots of fs and cs as he strode towards our table. I turned to the body slumped next to me. It was Martin Jugger.

Hey Jugger, I said, Let's shoot the crow.

Can't, he said, I've gone blind.

You've just got your eyes closed, I said.

Nah, he said, I'm going to have to stay here till closing time. Or till I die, whichever comes first.

Across the table was my brother Ivan. He was shaking his head at my suggestion. I like it here, he said. It's friendly, ken . . .

Just then two big red hands landed on his shoulders, dragged him up off his chair, and shoved him towards the door. Ivan tripped over his feet and knocked into the next table along. Some drinks went over him as he fell to the floor, and four women sitting there jumped up and started kicking him, sticking their stilettos into his ear and his arsehole and twisting.

The bouncer reached across our table, grabbed me and Jugger by the throat, and tried to bang our heads together. His aim was crap, and my head smashed down on the table in front of Jugger, sending his ashtray skiting and a big pile of doups and fag-ash flying up into the air then down onto my pash. I started to fight back, punching out and landing a wild swing on something soft and juicy.

Aiya, my cock! shouted Jugger.

The bouncer pulled both of us up by the hair and held us in front of his big red face. Fucking language! he shouted. Out of my pub!

What, are you the owner? said Jugger. Cause if you are, I've a complaint to make: your beer's pish! It's watered to fuck! Ten pints and I'm still not unconscious!

The bouncer wasn't listening. He was dragging us across the floor towards the door onto the street.

I'm leaving this place right now, shouted Jugger as he was pulled along. It's a shitehole. Hey everybody! Come on, a boycott: all out of the fucking pub now!

A few folk looked round, but nobody really moved, except for one of the dames who'd been kicking in Ivan. She turned and spat a mouthful of dark rum in Jugger's direction. Some of it sprayed in his face, and some of it went over the bottom of the bouncer's trousers. He stopped and looked down at the spit and drink dribbling across the shiny leather of his shoes.

Fucking gobbing! he shouted. Out of my pub! He let go of mine and Jugger's hair and lunged over towards the woman who'd spat.

After our heads had bounced off the floor a couple of times, me and Jugger scrambled up and out of the place. Screams and the sound of breaking glass followed us out the swinging door as we tumbled onto the pavement.

We got up again and looked around. At first I couldn't see Ivan anywhere, but then I deeked a pair of feet sticking out from under a car parked a wee bit down the street. I ran along, grabbed the ankles, and started to pull. The body seemed hell of a heavy, I could hardly budge it, so I turned back and waved on Jugger to come and give me a hand. He came running up, and we took a foot each and pulled hard, leaning back and shoving against the side of the car with one knee for more leverage.

There was a shout from under the car. Fuuughyouwha . . . We pulled some more. Fuck off! came the shout. Leave a man to sleep! We pulled harder. There was the sound of rusty metal tearing, and suddenly the two of us staggered backwards and Ivan was out and lying half on the pavement, half in the gutter, clutching a ragged piece of exhaust to his chest like it was a teddy bear. Goodnight, sleep tight, he sang, Don't let the buggers bite. Then he started to pretend to snore very loudly, then burst into laughter.

Jugger crawled over and slapped Ivan round the puss a couple of times, then the two of them got to their feet, kind of hauling themselves up by holding on to each other's clothes grip by grip. They straightened themselves out a bit, then set off up the road. They seemed to have forgotten about me, but I followed the bastards anyway. I went as fast as I could, but they were definitely pulling away from me. Also, my knees were beginning to hurt. I decided I'd have to get up and walk. Soon I caught up with them.

Hey Pockie, said Ivan, Where've you been? It's all decided.

Eh? What is?

It's terrible, said Jugger, I haven't spent all my dosh yet: Christmas fucking bonus, man!

Aye, we're going to go for a massive curry, said Ivan.

There's a load of Indian places down Lothian Road. It's just as well. The first one we passed was closed; the second one had two big bouncers that shook their heads and flexed their biceps at us; but the third one came up trumps. As we walked in the door, a waiter came running up to us.

Table for three, I said.

No, he replied.

Table for three, *please*, said Jugger.

Sorry, said the waiter, We're full-up.

There's an empty table over there, I said.

No, it's booked! The waiter looked at his watch. Party arriving in ten minutes.

Well, we'll eat quick, laughed Jugger. I'm fucking starving pal: could eat a horse!

So that's one tandoori horse, said Ivan, And a couple of nans as well . . .

Look, said the waiter loudly, his arms out to stop Ivan and Jugger breenging past him, You can have a carry-out, but there's no tables at all. Carry-out only. Here's the menu, please take a seat.

He waved us over onto a row of plastic chairs in an alcove by the door. We sat down and started looking at the selection.

Do they do anything vegetarian? said Jugger. Cause I'm a vegetable myself, and I'm not into being a cannibal . . . He laughed, then hiccupped, bouncing up off his seat slightly. When he landed it was right on the edge of his chair, and he started to slide off slowly away from us. Suddenly he tipped right over and thumped onto the floor.

Me and Ivan looked at him. Should we get him up? I said.

No, he's safer there, said Ivan. As long as nobody trips up and spills red-hot vindaloo over him.

We looked back at the menu. After a second I found I couldn't concentrate on the reading cause I was bursting for a pish. I'm off to the bog, I said, and weaved away across the restaurant. It was fucking packed, but I only bumped into a couple of elbows on the way.

When I came out of the lavvy, I paused for a second, trying to

22

remember where I'd been sitting. As I was looking round, I spotted somebody I kent at a table over by the window. She was beautiful, absolutely beautiful. She'd been beautiful when I'd met her before – at a party I'd crashed in Fountainbridge somewhere – but she was even more beautiful now. I don't know what it was, whether it was something she'd done to her hair and her eyes, or whatever clothes she had on, or maybe something I'd been drinking, but I felt myself drawn towards her, sucked across the restaurant, my eyes glued to her face and the forkful of chicken korma she was lifting to her mouth. At that moment my greatest wish in life was to be a lump of chicken korma.

I knelt down beside her, wobbling a bit. I put my hand on her leg to steady myself, and looked up, smiling: smiling and almost greeting as well, she was that beautiful.

Christ, Dilys, I said, It's great to see you again! My God you're looking barrie! It's a Christmas present seeing you here, that's what it is: bloody magic! I just . . . Christ, I love you Dilys, I just do, I love you.

She looked down at me. My name's Nicola, she said. I think you've got the wrong person.

Nicola, Nicola! Of course! What did I say? Dilys? Christ, what a fucking numptie, eh! It's just I was so carried away there: you're so fucking beautiful! Even more than before!

I don't think I know you at all, she said, taking a grip on her fork and hovering it over my hand on her leg. I must've been gripping her knee too hard; I leant against the edge of the table instead.

Nicola, come on! That one night! We were getting on great. Down by Marco's, mind? I loved you then even, I just couldn't say it: I was kind of shy, mind, cause you'd caught me smuggling that bottle of bleach out of the bog and I was going to put it in the punch!

Oh aye, said Nicola. I remember you now.

Sure you do!

Aye, I do. So could you just get out of my sight right away?

But I love you Nicola, I really do! I know it's short notice, but come on, let's get married: now! We'll get the head waiter to do it.

It's impossible, she said. I'm married already. This is my husband here, and my mother-in-law.

I looked at the other folk sitting at the table. I'd kind of forgotten they were there, I was that carried away. Hello! I said. Christ, you're a lucky man, married to Dilys here: fucking gorgeous! Here, if you're ever getting divorced, let me know, eh! Ha ha ha!

The husband had a funny look on his face, as if he was about to go totally fucking radge at any second for some reason. And the mother was looking a bit stunned as well: maybe she'd just bit into a chilli or something. I looked back at Dilys, no, Nicola again. She had a grain of rice stuck to her top lip right at the corner of her mouth. I reached up with my pointy finger to brush it off, a friendly kind of move, but something went wrong, she jerked herself away, and I got a jolt off her chair and my finger went out of control and poked her in the eye. She yowled.

Oh Christ, I'm sorry! I jumped up, grabbed a napkin off the table and tried to push it against her eye as a kind of pad. She shrieked again, started swinging her arms at me. Her husband stood up. I think it's time you left pal, he said. His mother was shouting, Waiter, waiter, waiter! And I was beginning to get the feeling that I'd offended somebody in some way. Eh, maybe if you put some water on the napkin it'll cool it down, I said, picking up the jug from the middle of the table. Then somebody shouted my name.

Pockie! Come on you bastard! It was Ivan across by the door. He was pointing at Jugger, who was just walking out with two carrier bags of foil boxes of grub.

I turned back to the table. I'm afraid I'll have to love you and leave you, I said.

Piss off! said Nicola, no, Dilys.

I caught up with Ivan and Jugger outside. That's a hell of a carry-out, I said to them.

Aye, I went for the set meal for six in the end, said Ivan.

But there's only three of us . . .

Aye, but I wanted onion bhajis, you see, and you didn't get them with the three-person thing. Anyway, I'm fucking starving!

Jugger stopped. I'm fucking starved as well, he said. Come on, let's have a bit of it now, there's plenty for later.

Best to get it hot anyway, I said, and took one of the carriers off him.

We sat down on the doorstep of a shop, and spread the boxes out on the pavement in front of us. The problem is how to know which is what, said Ivan.

Only one way to find out, said Jugger. He picked up the container nearest him, started to peel the lid off, then screamed, Aiya fucker! and flung the box away from him, red sauce and steam streaming out. Fucking burnt me you bastard! he shouted, and started blowing on the back of his hand, which had splashes of sauce over it.

That looked like a bhuna to me, I said.

What! Jugger, you dopey cunt, said Ivan. I was looking forward to the fucking bhuna, that's my favourite you bastard!

Well tough shit! I'm probably fucking scarred for life cause of your fucking bhuna.

I'll fucking scar you! said Ivan, jumping to his feet and kicking a couple of containers away across the pavement. I'm going to have to eat some of your creamy Persian prawn shite now: milky fucking skitters you bastard!

Look, settle, settle, I said. Let's get stuck into what we have, eh? I opened a couple of boxes. Look, here's pilau rice. Who's got the forks?

Silence.

Somebody must have them.

I thought Jugger was getting them, said Ivan, stepping from one foot to the other.

I thought Ivan was getting them, said Jugger, looking down at the rice steaming away in its boxes.

I sighed. Ach, fuck it. Look, we've still got the bhajis. Let's split them and get a taxi home. I'm shagged out with all this to be honest.

Ivan nodded slowly. Aye, I suppose so. I've got to get home and wrap up Diane's present yet . . . He started off down the road.

I got up and headed after him. In a second, Jugger came alongside me, clutching the wee bag of onion things. Hey guys, he said, Great idea! We can get the joe baxi to stop in by the shopping centre, and we'll get a kebab to take home with us. I think there's a bottle of Grouse under our tree. Well, I fucking ken there is: I bought it for my old man. He won't mind us having a wee sup for the festive season.

I yawned. Well, I suppose it is after midnight probably . . .

Aye, fucking magic! Merry Christmas here we come! Jugger walked out into the road and started whistling through his fingers, waving down full taxis as they skiffed by him at top speed.

Then an empty joe appeared and stopped, and we got in. It was a woman driving. Where to? she said.

All the way darling! shouted Ivan, and him and Jugger started laughing and carrying on: kissing the glass partition and stuff.

After a minute the driver looked in her mirror and said, Okay, one last chance lads: where to?

Jugger and Ivan were still laughing and mucking about, trying to get each other's trousers down or something, and they paid her no heed. So I leant forward and told her where we were going.

Before I'd finished speaking even the taxi pulled away with a lurch and I was flung backwards and onto the others; they shoved me off, shouting abuse, and I was tumbled onto the floor of the cab as it zoomed round in a U-turn right across Lothian Road, and sped off northwards.

There was a faint smell of sickness down on the floor, and also something else, a kind of burnt oil smell, but on the whole it wasn't too uncomfortable. It even had a carpet. I decided I might as well just stay lying there for all the time it would take us getting home.

So I lay there, looking up at Jugger and Ivan fighting on the seat, seeing streetlamps and lit-up buses passing by the back window. There was a bit of a rhythm to the bumping of the road and the grinding of the gears, and soon it was lulling me off to sleep.

And there as I lay, half-dozing, half-waking, I saw a vision of Christmas future, a premonition of what was surely to come. Clear as day I saw me lying in my bed on Christmas morning, still in my clothes under the covers, a pint of water on the bedside unit. And as I struggle awake, rubbing open my eyes, a strange strong smell prickles my nostrils. I look round. My right hand is clutching something on the pillow, a large-sized doner, one bite out of the end, lettuce and onions and strips of greasy meat dribbling down onto the sheets: cold kebab breakfast.

A/deen Soccer Thugs Kill All Visiting Fans

In Kenny's Fish Bar at the top of Bridge Street, there's a lad sitting by himself. He stretches his legs out under the table and kicks the bottom of the empty chair on the other side of it. He drums his fingers on the orange plastic table-top, glances at the clock on the wall above the coke machine, drums his fingers some more. There's an empty coffee cup in front of him; the lad picks it up, looks in it, swirls the dregs around, then replaces it on the saucer. From a bowl at the end of the table beside the sauce bottle and salt, he picks out six packets of sugarcubes, packed in twos: He unwraps these, not tearing the wrapping, but unpicking the stuck-down flaps with his fingernails and unfolding the paper and smoothing each piece out on the table-top, before dropping eleven of the cubes into his cup. He chucks the twelfth cube into his mouth and crunches it as he lets the others fall into the cup one by one; as each one is dropped in, he murmurs a name:

Goram, Hunter, Collins, Weir, Kane . . .

When they're all in, he stirs them round and round with a teaspoon, round and round, the cubes clinking against the sides of the cup, round and round, till they start to soak in the coffee dregs and disintegrate and form a sludge at the bottom of the cup. Then he tips his head back, lifts the cup to his lips, and empties the contents into his mouth in a oner, shaking the cup to make sure he gets the last few drops and granules. He puts the cup down and chews the mouthful. But in fact there's more than a mouthful, for as his jaws are moving, he lets his lips open slightly for a second, and a slaver of brown liquid runs down the side of his chin and drops between the open halves of his tracksuit top onto the front of his tee-shirt, which is white.

Aw FUCK!

He looks down, frowning, puts the cup down with a clatter on its saucer, and immediately reaches over and yanks a handful of paper serviettes out of the dispenser at the end of the table. He folds one of these double and wets it by spitting on it, holding it close to his mouth; but the spit comes out slightly brownish. He chucks that serviette to the floor, works his cheeks and jaw for a few seconds, and spits onto a second serviette. He studies the clarity of the saliva, then spits again on the same place, and starts to wipe at the coffee and sugar stain on his shirt. After a while he stops, pulls the shirtfront out from his chest and looks at the stain: it is slightly lighter, but also slightly bigger than before. He gets a fresh serviette, spits on it a couple of times, starts rubbing again. After a minute he stops: the stain is still there.

Jesus fucking Christ! Twenty-two quid!

He drops the serviette, fastens his tracksuit and zips it right up to the neck. He folds his arms, leans back in his chair, balancing it on its back two legs, and shuts his eyes.

He stays that way till there is the sound of the bell above the street door jangling, then he lets the chair fall forward and it cracks loudly on the floor tiles under his weight. Two girls about the same age as him have just entered; he glares at them for a second, then slumps forward and lays his head on his arms folded on the table, facing away from the counter where the girls are now standing, ordering chips and tea. When they've been served, they walk back past him, slowly, saying something about his clothes as they go by, and laughing; they sit down at the table nearest the door, and start eating and looking out the window at the folk passing in the street. Now the lad looks up again and checks the clock: it is half past five. He stares at the table-top, then shoves his hand into his pocket and takes out some money; he puts this on the table and starts to arrange it into two piles, a tall one of copper coins, and a small one of silver. The doorbell jangles loudly again, and he looks up.

Check the clock man! Where the hell've you been?

The man who has just come in drops his big shoulder bag to the floor and pushes it across the tiles towards the lad with a kick. Aye, good to see you too, he says, grinning, then walks to the counter and talks to the girl there. She laughs, then goes to the fryer and starts digging out some chips; he turns, leans back with his elbows on the counter and says, You needing anything?

Aye I'm needing my bed: have you seen the time?

Settle, settle, says the man, There wasn't any taxis at the airport; I had to wait for one, right? Now cool the fucking beans.

The girl puts his plate down on the surface behind him with a bang, and he turns back round immediately and starts talking to her in a quiet voice, leaning forward towards her across the counter. The lad looks at his back for a few seconds, then away: he pulls a green-and-white scarf out of his pocket, smoothes it out and re-rolls it. The man comes over and puts three cups of coffee down on the table, then goes back to the counter and returns with a plate of fish and chips, another of beans on toast, and knives and forks.

Get that down you, he says, pushing the beans over to the lad, But mind and blow on them first.

The lad looks at him for a second, then sits up, leans over the plate and starts to eat. The man drinks one of the coffees down, watching him, then reaches for the sauce bottle and squirts it onto the side of his plate.

Aw shite . . . Hey! Excuse me! he shouts across to the girl serving, Have you not got any brown sauce?

What? she says.

Brown sauce. There's just this red stuff here . . .

Aye, tomato, tomato ketchup. She looks at him. I could give you some tartare if you were having fish.

I am having fish.

Oh sorry, hold on . . .

No, I don't want that though. Only if you had some brown.

Well . . . She shrugs, shakes her head, and goes back to wiping the metal counter-top.

The man turns back to his plate and starts eating, avoiding the chips with red sauce on them. After a while he says, So how's my wee baby brother then?

The lad stares into the man's eyes, at the same time as reaching his fork out across the table towards his plate; suddenly he lunges, spears a big piece of fish, and transfers it onto his pile of beans. He laughs and his brother grins. The lad tears a bit of the fish off with his fingers and rams it in his mouth, at the same time saying, Do you ken if there's a launderette about here?

What, shat your pants about the game?

Aye very droll Davy, very fucking funny. He unzips his tracksuit top. Look: spilt my coffee down it. About five minutes ago. And it was your fault as well: that's twenty-two quid you owe us!

Right away pal, right away!

Too fucking right man: if you'd been on time you would've been here when I did it, and I would've been talking to you instead of playing around with my cup, and I wouldn't have done it, see?

Davy shakes his head. Tch tch tch. He looks at the lad through eyes narrowed to slits. Where's my bag gone?

Under your seat.

Davy leans over and pulls his bag out and up onto his knees. He unzips it and starts rummaging around in the tangle of clothes and books and trainers inside. The lad looks at the cloth badge stuck to the side of the bag: there is lettering saying SUBSEA ELECTRICS and a picture of an eel with sparks coming out of its tail.

Here you go then. Davy hands over a light yellow tee-shirt. Don't say I'm not good to you.

The lad holds it up to his face and sniffs. Is it clean? I'm not wearing anything you've been digging oil up in for the past fortnight.

I never had it on you ungrateful wee bastard. Look, you can borrow that, and I'll take yours and get Sheila to stick it in the machine in the flat.

I'm not sure that's a good swap.

Too right it's not a fucking swap: I'm needing mine back. You can get Mum to post it up to me, right? And I'll send yours away the minute it's dry. And I *am* needing that back: you can't get them anymore, rare as a proddy in Paradise those.

The lad takes off his tracksuit top and pulls the dirty tee-shirt over his head. He picks the yellow shirt back up, and is sorting out which is the front, when the girl shouts from behind the counter.

Hey man, where do you think you are! He starts pulling on the new tee-shirt. Any more stripping and you're out!

Och, come on over and join in, says Davy, He wouldn't be so embarrassed if you took yours off as well . . .

And you behave yourself as well; you're not over big for me to . . . to get the boss to chuck you out.

Aye, sorry, sorry: look, can we have another couple coffees please? She says something under her breath. Pretty please . . .

She goes and pours two coffees, and Davy walks over and gets them and pays for them. Back at the table the lad has the tee-shirt on and is smoothing it out across his chest; on the left side there is a small badge of an electric eel like the one on the bag.

Hey this is a mental shirt! Barrie! Exclusive as fuck, eh? Wait till Mivvy sees this: he'll be tearing it off my back man!

Here, he better not be, or I'll be tearing the skin off his back.

Nah, only joking Davy, he's okay really, the Miv: he's just a bit radge as far as clothes are concerned, ken, a total trendy: he's already been had three times for lifting.

Davy sips his coffee. So the trendy scene still going strong is it?

Strong as ever man, can you not tell? He has put on his tracksuit top again, leaving it open so that the eel is visible as the top swings open.

Hmm. Well I'm a bit out of touch myself these days to be honest. When I was on the casual scene we were all into Fila sports gear and side shades and that.

Side shades! The lad laughs, and Davy does too. I'm meant to be meeting the lads at the back of six actually. That's how I was pissed off at you being late.

Where you meeting them?

Eh, a bar called the Star and Garter; I think it's in the next street along from here.

In the bar eh?

Aye! The lad goes a bit red in the face.

Eh! Come on . . . !

Well . . . you ken . . .

Aye young Francis, you'll be in the under-fives for another couple of seasons yet. Despite that fluff on your top lip, you *man*!

Francis laughs, and starts to get less red in the cheeks. Aye, Herbie's Under-Fives, that's our team, mental as fuck.

Batter folk to death with your rattles do you?

Away to hell! I get served in loads of places anyway.

Aye in Edinburgh maybe, but not up here matey; they're pretty fucking tight-arsed up here, I'll tell you. And the Star and Garter? Jesus, even I got the knockback there once.

Aye?

Aye, it was when I first came up here and started at Altens and college and that, and I went in there with a guy called Grassick, Ian Grassick, and me and him must both've been seventeen I suppose.

Just chancing it eh?

Och, me and Ian would probably've been all the way, but he had his wee brother with him – can you imagine eh? His wee fucking brother! Fourteen or something! – and as soon as we went in the door the guy behind the bar just started in laughing: Ha ha, he says, sorry boys, ha ha, away you go afore I hurt myself.

What a bastard.

Aye, but that's Aberdeen pubs for you.

Well, to be honest, the Herbies are meeting up outside, and the SNS just'll be inside. When they come out they'll let us in on the plans like.

Here, hold on, what's all this SNS stuff? What's happened to the good old CCS? The famous Capital City Service!

Och, the CCS is still on the go Davy, but it was getting too big, ken, a bit out of hand, so it usually splits up into different wee groups these days. You ken, there's the Southside Mob, Young Leith Team . . .

So what's SNS stand for? Where are they from?

I'm not right sure to be honest. All over.

Hey, come on!

Well actually it's the, eh, Stanley Knife Squad.

Aw Jesus, you're joking? Blades! Fuck's sake.

Aye I ken, I mean I'm not that keen on it myself really, but what can you do? I mean everycunt's carrying blades these days.

Och that's just . . . They're just a bunch of stupid wee laddies.

No they're not, not just laddies: there's one guy who's a doctor, there's another owns his own shop: he must be, Jesus, twenty-five at least . . .

Just stupid fucking kids. Davy shakes his head.

Aye it's okay for you to say that now: we didn't see you shaking your head five or six years ago.

Aye fair enough Frankie, but listen: it was the old Fight For Fun thing in my day, you ken: hands, heads and feet. No fucking blades! The most you got would be an Irn Bru bottle chucked at you or something.

Aye well, times change.

But it's plain fucking daft man: somebody could get killed! How can you go in and enjoy your fighting if you ken you might be killing somebody any minute? Or even taking their eye out for fuck's sake! I mean, it's only a game.

Frankie smiles. Nah Davy: football's a game, fighting's more than that. Football's something you just do, or just watch, but a casual, that's something you *are*.

Davy shakes his head again, breathes out loudly. He goes to say something, then stops, looks at his watch, turns to check it against the clock above the coke machine.

I'm meant to be meeting Sheila here at six.

Well it's six the now.

I ken. She's maybe got held up at her work.

Where's she work again?

Markies.

Oh aye.

They sit in silence for half a minute, then Davy says, Mum still working at that printers down the Walk?

Aye: turning and folding, turning and folding. Hih!

Davy sniffs, looks down. After a few seconds he says, Look, as soon as Sheila arrives we'll just fuck off, okay? We'll come round to Crown Street with you, show you the Star and Garter. We'll not embarrass you by going in, we'll go to the Grill across the road maybe: have a drink then go for a curry or something. While you're kicking somebody's head in. Tch.

Are you coming down for Hogmanay this year?

Jesus, never mind the kicking: you'll probably be slicing somebody's face open!

I said, are you coming home for Hogmanay this year?

Davy looks at him, turns round and looks at the door to the street. No one is coming in. The street outside is dark. He checks his watch, clears his throat. Don't know for sure yet; might be offshore for Christmas and New Year.

Good bonuses, eh?

Aye, not bad.

Was it not last New Year one of the other rigs on your field nearly blew up?

Platforms, aye. A couple of folk who should've known better got blootered. Booze is banned usually, but seeing as it was New Year they'd been turning a blind eye.

Bet they won't be doing that this year.

Nuh. Mind you, it could happen any time really. I mean if folk get drunk then they won't notice a problem building up, but problems like that happen all the time, ken. It's just they're usually spotted before they get dangerous. So you lot never hear about them. The public!

So, has it happened when you've been out there like?

Aye, sure it has. Not this time, but the last time I was offshore, there was a build-up of gas in this chamber, this thing called the rich oil heater, gas was feeding back into it from the main pipeline, you see: it should have been going the other way round. Anyway, the pressure was way up; it could've been serious. But it was spotted within minutes, the gas was shut off and various escape valves opened and that. I didn't even ken anything had happened till about three hours later. But when you saw inside the chamber room . . . Jesus! These inner bulkheads had just disintegrated, and the feeder pipes had buckled from the pressure, bent like they were made of Plasticine.

For fuck's sake Davy! Were you not feart? One spark surely and . . . fuck's sake.

Aye, it's surprising it didn't go up actually, but there you go. Anyway, I would've been okay whatever: I was a couple of hundred feet under water at the time.

What!

Aye. Davy laughs. Down one of the legs like, inside!

What the fuck were you doing there?

Och it's routine man. You can go down from the platform into any of the legs; there's steps round and round all the way down: it's like a lighthouse, except it's under the sea instead of at the edge of it.

Davy puts down the cup he's been playing with, looks at his watch, and round at the door once again. He turns back, frowning, then the frown eases up off his face and he talks on.

There was a couple of divers doing some maintenance on the outside of the leg; they have this hatch they can go in and out of you see. Anyway, me and this other spark were down just giving them back-up, keeping an eye out for anything going wrong. That's what I do ninety per cent of the time, to be honest, just sit waiting for something to go wrong.

How long were you down there for?

Hih, the whole fortnight. At least we got to come up and sleep in our own beds at night though; the divers had to stay down there non-stop, their whole stint, night and day. In case of decompression sickness, you ken. Poor buggers; good pay but . . . tch.

Davy shakes his head and runs his finger through the cup-rings of spilt coffee on the table. Frankie looks at him; he frowns; he goes to speak then stops, keeps his mouth shut. He looks at the top of Davy's head as he bends over the table.

The door opens. Frankie looks up, and Davy turns and looks at the woman who is coming in, pausing to brush some water off her hair and the arms of her coat.

Sheila!

She looks up with a start, then smiles. Oh, hiya David. She comes over and stands by the table. I didn't see you; thought you maybe weren't here yet.

Not here yet! I've been stuck here all afternoon talking to this boring bugger!

Hello, says Frankie.

Are you not going to introduce us then?

Frankie this is Sheila, Sheila this is the youngest of the tribe, Francis P. Cormack.

Frank.

Sheila holds out her hand. Hello Frank. His face is starting to go red again. Have you not learnt shaking hands yet? Suit yourself . . .

No, sorry, eh . . . Hih!

Come on She, wee Frankie's never held anybody's hand before, don't embarrass the lad!

Away to fuck Davy.

Aye, away to fuck Davy; you're only jealous cause you're past your prime, past your bloody sell-by date.

Frankie laughs, and Davy does too.

Come on and budge over then, says Sheila, I've been on my feet all day already.

Davy drags his bag out from under his seat, stands up, and says, Actually She, we won't bother hanging around here: Frank's got to meet some mates, and I thought we could have a drink or two and then go for an Indian.

Oh I fancy an Indian, says Sheila, and winks at Frank.

Don't get the boy all worked up now. He'll need a cold shower before he goes to Pittodrie.

Well he'll get one on the way: it's bucketing out there.

Ach shit . . . Never mind: we'll just go round the corner to the Grill. Come on Frank.

Davy gets out from between his seat and the table, and suddenly grabs Sheila round the waist inside her coat and gives her a short kiss. Frank looks away and under the table.

Okay Frank, says Davy after a second, the coast's clear.

I was just looking for something actually, says Frank. He slides out of his seat, holding a tightly rolled green umbrella by the wrist strap.

Well you'll be okay, says Sheila. Come on.

Sheila and Davy walk to the door and Frank follows. Outside, Davy shifts the bag up onto his shoulder, and Sheila puts her arm through his.

Put the brolly up then, says Davy, as Frank comes out into the street behind them.

Eh, I won't bother actually. But hold on, I'll just put this on. He takes his scarf out, unrolls it, then winds it several times around his neck and tucks the short loose ends down the front of his top, which he then zips up almost all the way. Right oh, he says, lead on.

They set off walking along the street, Frank lagging slightly behind the others. At the junction with Union Street, they wait for the green man together. The rain is coming down hard.

Your hair's going all spiky, says Sheila to Frank.

It does that when it's wet, says Frank.

I like it, it's like a hedgehog. Can I feel it?

She reaches out her hand and touches Frank's head. Frank pulls away slightly, and Davy laughs, Leave him alone you cradle-snatcher! Here we go look . . .

I wish you'd just shut it, says Sheila as they're crossing the road, You're so cruel!

Davy was telling me about how he nearly got blown up a couple of weeks ago, says Frank. There was a build-up of gas, it was a miracle there wasn't another Piper Alpha.

Ih!

Shut your face, says Davy, She doesn't want to hear that.

You never told me . . .

Och, I'm sorry love, it was nothing really, I was only gabbing . . .

The pipes were bent like Plasticine.

Shut the fuck up Frank! Jesus! You yap on about your mates and their fucking blades, you're swanning about carrying a brolly with the fucking point sharpened – I know all the fucking tricks pal – and then you stir up the fucking barney rubble for me ! Jesus *Christ* I wish you'd grow up and leave people in peace you wee bastard!

Sheila is marching on ahead; Davy runs to catch up with her, takes hold of her arm. She shakes her head, keeps walking fast. Then they stop at the top of Crown Street. Frank comes up behind them a second later. He clears his throat.

Eh Sheila, I'm sorry about saying all that. I was just making it up to get at him. Anyway, I thought he would've told you himself.

Sheila turns to him; she is holding her face up, so raindrops are hitting it and running down over her cheeks and down off her chin. I'd rather not know these things, she says. But don't worry, I'm not angry with you.

Well I'm sorry anyway, I just . . . He shrugs.

Look Frank, says Davy, There's the Star and Garter; that'll be your mates in the door I suppose. You better be going over to them. We'll just nip into the Grill here.

Aye. Okay. Well, see you then.

Aye, okay. Hey, listen Frank. No sweat, eh? It's just one of these things, you ken?

Aye, don't worry about it Frank. It was good to meet you anyway.

Frank looks over towards the Star and Garter. Aye, good to meet you too. And eh, see you again, eh Davy?

Aye, sure pal.

Frank goes to the edge of the pavement and looks up and down the road. Then he turns back to Sheila and Davy and says, Eh, would you like this umbrella? It looks like it's going to be bad for a while yet.

Sheila looks at Davy. No it's okay, he says, you need it more than us.

But thanks anyway, says Sheila.

Och . . . Frank kicks the tip of the umbrella as it rests on the ground. He shrugs. He pulls the scarf up from round his neck, so that it covers his mouth and nose. Thanks to you as well, he says.

Have a good game, says Sheila.

Aye, give the bastards one from me, says Davy.

I will, says Frank, and turns back to the road. Over the top of his scarf, his eyes watch for a gap in the traffic.

The Big Man That Dropped Dead

I had this pal that knew about poetry, he was in the mental asylum. He could speak poetry really good, in fact he couldn't speak anything else. He'd see it up there and he'd just pull it down and speak it. On and on. He dropped dead though. I was standing there and he fell down right in front of me. Aye he was a big man, but he just dropped dead. So there you go, eh, poetry . . .

The Doubles

He was sitting up in bed when she came into the room.

Who are you? he said.

She put a pile of ironed clothes down on top of the dresser. Do you want me to lay you out a shirt for tomorrow? she said. He looked at her. Or do you think the blue one'll do another day?

He turned his head towards the door and shouted, Sarah!

What? she said.

I'm not talking to you, he said, I'm shouting on my wife. Sarah! Where are you?

She walked to the foot of the bed and stood there, looking down at him.

Sarah!

I'm here, she said, Right in front of you.

You're not Sarah. He smiled slightly. Oh you look like her, I'll give you that. Not an exact match but not bad. You even sound like her. But you're not her.

She laughed for a second, then sat down on the end of the bed and leant towards him. Peter, she said, What are you playing at?

He pressed himself back against the headboard. Keep away from me, he said, Just keep your distance you. I don't know what you want from me, but you're not getting it. He glared at her. And what have you done with Sarah?

She moved her hand over the duvet and went to lay it on top of his. He snatched his hand away and thrust it under the covers. Then he did the same with the other arm.

She gazed at him, frowning. When you said you were feeling tired, she said, Did you mean you weren't feeling well? Or has it just been a hard day?

It hasn't been a hard day.

So are you sick then? Are you worried? I mean why are you acting like this?

Hih! He snorted. I'm not acting like anything. You're the one that's acting. I'm just being myself. It's you that's acting: acting like Sarah. But you're not her.

Come on! She stood up, laughing but frowning. So who am I then?

I'm damned if I know. That's what's worrying me: who the hell are you? And how long've you been here?

Six years Peter.

Don't give me that! That's Sarah you're talking about there! And that's something else that's worrying me: what have you done with my wife? She took a step towards him again, and was away to say something, but he cut in: I've been onto you for a while, he said. You think you're clever, you think you're really bloody clever, but I'll tell you this: you're not fooling me! I've had my doubts for a couple of weeks, but now there's *no* doubt. I don't know why you've done it, but I know what you've done: you've taken my wife away from here, you're keeping her shut up somewhere no doubt – you or some accomplices – and instead of her there's you, you're trying to take her place. Some clever make-up, a wig as well maybe . . . you've learned up the way she talks and that . . . but it's not good enough. I'm onto you!

She folded her arms and looked at him. Then she said, Look, I reckon you should maybe try to get off to sleep.

What's in it for you?

For me? Nothing! Nothing's in it for me! You said you were tired Peter, you said you'd have a lie down. Now when I talk to you you're being all strange.

It would seem strange to you, he said, Seeing as you don't fucking know me. Of course it's strange: you're a stranger.

She walked quickly over to the door, paused, and said, I think you should get a good night's sleep. You can stay at home tomorrow if you want; I mean I could get the doctor round if you're still not feeling yourself.

Hih! Don't worry on that score: I'm feeling *my*self alright. What about you though, eh? Who are you feeling like?

There were a couple of twitches in her face, up around the eyes, then she turned and walked out of the bedroom, pulling the door to with a bang behind her.

He sighed, slumped down in the bed a little. After a few moments, his eyelids started to flicker and close.

Some time later, he was wakened by the sound of her opening the door again. She came in carrying a mug of something and a small plate with some biscuits on it. Immediately, he sat up straight in the bed.

Thought you might like some supper, she said. He stared at her. His eyebrows were trembling slightly, and the skin of his face was moving, ticcing, tightening then relaxing. He said nothing. Well, do you want it? she said. He kept his eyes on her, but moved his head to the side slightly and nodded towards the bedside table. She nudged a book clear with the mug then let it rest, the handle pointing towards him. She put the plate of biscuits down beside it. How are you feeling now anyway? she said. Did you get any rest?

Get out of my house, he said, very quietly, staring at her.

She breathed in. Her lips moved. She breathed out. She stepped across to the wardrobe, opened it, and started taking out some sheets and blankets. I'm sleeping ben the house tonight, she said.

Too fucking right you are, he said suddenly. What if I let you in here and then my wife came in the fucking door?

She left the room, her face set.

He smiled, took his arms out from under the duvet and stretched them up into the air, fingers clenched against the palms. He let his arms fall and for a few seconds they lay on the covers, and his fingertips scrabbled at the fabric. He pushed himself up to a sitting position again, reached over to the table, and lifted the mug towards him. He stared at the contents, then raised the mug to just beneath his nose, and sniffed. Steam swirled about below his nostrils.

That's not coffee, he said. Jesus Christ, would you credit it? He sniffed again. It looks like coffee, it smells like coffee, but it's not fucking coffee. Jesus, they must think I'm daft! He stretched over and put the mug back on the table beside the plate of biscuits. Suddenly he laughed loudly, then shouted out towards the closed door, And I'm not going to fall for the so-called fucking biscuits either! He laughed again, whacking his hands down on the covers by his sides as he did so. Suddenly he stopped laughing, and brought his head forward and down towards the duvet, just where his left hand had landed. Slowly he brought his right hand over and lifted part of the cover towards his eyes, holding it at an angle to the light. He stared at it, frowning for a few seconds, then let it drop. For another moment he sat motionless in the bed, then he threw the duvet off his body, clear off the bed, and leapt to the floor.

He shouted again, Where's the duvet? What have you fucking

done with it? Take this one away! Bring back the real one! He looked around the room, glancing at all the furniture, then up at the framed photos on the wall, then the ceiling and the light-shade. His eyes dropped to the floor. He shrieked. The carpet! Where's the proper carpet? I can tell, I can fucking tell you know, don't think I can't! He was breathing quickly, and almost dancing around as he yelled. He turned to the window behind him, tugged the heavy curtain across to one side, and leant forward, resting the palms of his hands on the glass and his forehead there as well. After a moment, he lifted his head slightly, and looked out the window. Jesus Christ, he said, That's not my car out there. And those trees: those aren't the trees that are out there.

After Guthrie's

Apparently there was an accident and business fell away drastically. Apparently the old blind guy who used to come in and get slowly paralytic every night had been making his way to the bog towards closing time one evening, when he fell down into the cellar. This was possible because the hatch down to the cellar was just outside the door to the gents, and somebody had been down changing over a barrel and had forgotten to close it. And of course the old guy couldn't see the hole in front of him. Apparently he died more or less instantly.

It wasn't easy to drink in there after that. Harry and Bella sort of lost heart, as did a lot of the regulars; the old guy had been coming in there for years. So the place was closed down for a while, and now it's re-opened there've been some changes.

In fact the only thing that hasn't changed is the name, Guthrie's; in every other way the pub is different. Before everything was brown; light-brown vinyl chairs, dark-brown wooden bar, yellowy-brown grease on the ceiling and walls, and everyone's face brown in the shadows and light from the two bulbs in the high ceiling. Now everything seems blue: dark-blue leather covering on the settee things and chrome bar-stools, greyish-blue marble stuff on the bar top and the tables, and the light from the rows of cone-shaped lamps on the walls seems cold and blue on the faces and clothes of the people who drink here now.

The people are the most different thing about Guthrie's, we noticed as soon as we walked in. They're definitely younger – and this is not just because we're older than when we used to come here, they're younger than we were then, even – and there's also a lot more women than there used to be: this isn't necessarily a bad thing, but it does make a difference. Often when we came here before I would be the only female in the place, but that didn't bother me; I used to think I got treated better because of it. Folk used to be very friendly, especially the older ones, and I have the idea that Ronny used to like me getting that attention.

And of course Harry and Bella are gone from behind the pumps. They were getting on even then, right enough, but three or four years ago it would just've been impossible to imagine the place without them.

What the punters are drinking now is different too. It's all this real ale. But everything else is unreal. That's what Ronny said. He said, Carol, I can't stand this place any more, I'm away home. And he slung down the bottom half of his pint in a oner. I said, What about me? I'm only just started mine . . . He said, You just finish up in your own time, it's just, I can't . . . He shook his head, picked up his jacket, and made for the door. On the way out, he stopped at the bar and bought a couple of cans and a half-bottle of Grouse. I waited for him to turn and wave or nod as he went out, but he didn't. Sod you then, I thought.

I finished my drink slowly, then went up and bought another one.

About twenty minutes later last orders was shouted. I checked my purse. I had just enough cash for another half, but decided against it in the end. This was me being responsible, saving enough for some milk and a couple of rolls in the morning; he'd have next to nothing left, after getting that carry-out.

I left the pub and started home. There was a bit of a drizzle, and I'd half forgotten the length of the walk; I must've been thinking that I'd just nip out of Guthrie's and round the corner into the square like we used to. But no. We looked in there a couple of days ago: there was scaffolding up on most of the houses, and the noise of sandblasting. Instead I had this great long walk down the hill then along past the football pitches before I would finally cross the old railway line and turn into the terrace. The drizzle was turning into actual rain as I walked, and there was always the worry of being followed in this part of town, the streets were that empty and dark.

I don't know if we'd've bothered leaving the town if we'd known we'd be coming back so soon, especially to live in this neighbourhood. Especially if we'd known we'd be even worse off and worse-tempered than when we left. But we were happy when we lived in the square: happy not working, happy just sitting around smoking and talking, happy going out for a pint or two in Guthrie's now and then.

Or maybe we weren't happy, maybe I just like to think we were cause I know for certain that we were one hundred per cent pure miserable after we left here. For three years. And if we'd known then that we'd be coming back and everything bad would be the same and everything good would be changed . . . we'd have left anyway. We had to. Just the same as we had to come back.

I came level with the B&B and looked up: the light in our room on the second floor was on. I hoped there was some carry-out left, the damp was seeping into my bones and I needed a heat.

There was the noise of the telly coming from the TV lounge

when I opened the door, but as I went up the stairs everything got quieter. By the time I was outside our room, there was silence.

I unlatched the door and pushed it open. Ronny was lying on the bed with all his clothes on, except for his shoes, which were nowhere to be seen. The lamp on the floor by the bed was on, but Ronny was completely asleep, his mouth open and his fingers twitching slightly in some dream. It looked like he'd polished off all the drink himself. I walked to the sink in the corner of the room and checked the bucket. Sure enough: two crumpled cans and the empty half-bottle.

Then, out of the corner of my eye, I noticed something that shouldn't have been where it was. He'd taken the suitcase off the top of the wardrobe and propped it up against the wall at my side of the bed, and there were some things arranged on top of it. I went over and sat down on the bed, slowly so as not to wake him. On top of the suitcase was the glass from the sink with what looked like Grouse in it. Beside that was a long serrated bread-knife with a white plastic handle, like the handles of the cutlery we got to eat our egg and slice of toast with in the morning. Beside that there was a piece of paper with writing. I picked it up.

> Dear Carol,
> Drink the whisky then cut my throat
> with the knife. Be sure and make a
> good job of it.
> Yours Ronny.
> P.S. Keep this note to show to the pigs.
> They won't be able to touch you.

I looked round at him; he was still asleep. I put the note back down on the suitcase and picked up the knife. I was seeing everything very clearly. There was a gathering of some kind of brownish gunge around the blade just where it went into the handle; I picked at it with my nail and it came away in flakes. I cleaned it all off and gave the blade a rub up with a corner of the bedspread. Then I put the knife back down and picked up the whisky. I toed my shoes off, then stood up slowly, not bouncing the bed, and walked to the far side of the room. I turned and looked at him sleeping; his head was thrown back on the pillow and his neck arched out slightly, pulling the top of his tee-shirt tight against his chest. I lifted the glass to my lips and drank half of it straight down, watching him.

The dirty bastard! Nine-tenths of this was water! I took another sip. No doubt at all: there was some whisky in there, but it had been watered down beyond all recognition.

I could just see him. He'd have got down the suitcase, laid out the knife, written the note, and filled the glass with the last of the half-bottle. Then he'd have chucked the bottle in the bucket and lain down on the bed. But the bastard would only have been lying there for half a minute before sitting up, getting to his feet, walking round the bed. And he stands there thinking for a moment. Then he snatches up the glass and gulps down three-quarters of the whisky.

And then to fill it up out of the tap and hope I wouldn't notice! It was pathetic. I drained the glass. If he thought I was going to kill him under these circumstances he had another think coming.

New Year

David woke up with a start: somebody was ringing the doorbell. The room was in darkness, except for a blade of yellow streetlamp light that cut through the gap between the curtains and fell across the foot of his bed. It was the middle of the night; who could be ringing at this hour? He listened: the house was in silence, but he could hear quiet voices outside the front door, immediately below his bedroom window, and there was a scrunching noise as someone moved from foot to foot on the packed snow. The doorbell rang again. The noise was loud in the still house, and it came right up the stairs and up against the door of his room. Should he answer it? He looked at the chair by the tallboy, where his jeans and the jersey he got for Christmas were laid out; he was meant to put them on in the morning because his gran and granda were coming out for dinner, New Year's Dinner. Then he remembered: tomorrow was New Year's Day, that's why they were coming out, and this was Hogmanay . . . how could he forget?

The voices grew louder for a moment, then he heard footsteps going down the front path, and the gate being unlatched, opened, then shut with a clunk. The footsteps faded off down the street into the quietness. The village was very quiet, silent almost. David held his breath and could hear people laughing somewhere, and then there was a rushing whisper and a thud: snow falling off a tree out the back of the house.

For a second he wondered about getting up and quickly looking out to see who'd been at the door. But no, he was probably too late already; they'd be half-way back to the square by this time, walking in the middle of the roadway. It wasn't that there were no pavements, and it wasn't that they were drifted up – they'd been cleared in the afternoon by a guy with a kind of combination snowplough and lawnmower, and no more snow had fallen since then – it was just the way folk went about out here. They'd never get away with it if they lived in the town, they'd get run over in a second. But there were cars in the country too; it was just that everybody ignored them. What a way to carry on . . .

David tried to stop his brain thinking so much, and get back to sleep. He didn't want his mum chasing after him for not being up and ready when the visitors came. He closed his eyes and listened to the quietness of the house again. His mum and dad would be out first-footing somewhere themselves; she'd said they'd probably go out, it'd be a good opportunity to meet folk.

They never used to go out when they lived in town, and they definitely wouldn't've left him by himself. Of course he was older now, but still. They must've been away for hours now, and him all alone in the house. Or it might not have been that long, he couldn't tell; his watch was in the pocket of his jeans, and there were no clocks with bells in the village: nothing you could listen for if you woke up in the night and wanted to know what time it was.

Suddenly he remembered the exact feeling of Hogmanay in the town, thinking of the bells had brought it back to him . . . It was being woken by your dad late late at night, and him taking you down to the back door, giving you his jersey to put on over your pyjamas as you stood on the doorstep. Maybe there would be folk in ben the living-room, some kind of party going on, but your dad would always remember, always be there to wake you up, a minute before midnight. And then the bells would start, not exactly at the same second, but almost: they'd start ringing, you'd hear them clear in the quiet night air, as if the whole town was stopped in its tracks, holding its breath to hear them better, the bells from every clocktower and spire in the town, ringing in the new year. And as soon as the bells started there would be the sound of the hooters from the docks too, all the ships sounding their foghorns and hooters, the whole harbour full of noise and it echoing up through the streets. Then it was straight back to bed again and straight to sleep almost immediately, because you were happy, you'd seen the new year in, been part of the whole town ringing and hooting and cheering and being awake.

It was different in the country: the only bell was in the church, and that only rung on Sundays and at funerals, and there were no ships at all for miles. But still, it would've been good if his dad had been there. Just to wake him up at the right time. Just so he could see the hands of the clock pass midnight and keep on going, to check they didn't stop dead in the last minute of the old year, or bounce against the number twelve and start going backwards . . .

There was a noise outside, a voice raised. Then another voice too, louder, both voices speaking loudly, then fading away to silence. Then one voice spoke again, and straight away they were both shouting. They sounded angry. There was a pause, then the whole thing started again: the talking, the silence, the angry shouting. But this time David could hear that there were two other noises: just before the silent spell there were two thumps, the second bigger but duller than the first. And now the same pattern was repeating yet again, louder than ever: they must be in the street right in front of the house now.

He lifted a side of the blankets and slid his legs round and out into the cold air, then jumped down and crossed to the window. He put his eye up to the gap in the curtains, careful not to move them at all. Out in the middle of the road, walking away from the centre of the village, were two men, and they were arguing. They were just at the stage where both of them had started to speak at once, and they were trying to talk each other down, and getting louder and angrier with every word. David didn't know their names, but he'd seen them passing before; they were brothers, and both lived in the cottar houses a mile or so down the back road out of the village.

They were both yelling now, almost screaming – then suddenly one of the men swung his arm round in a half-circle and punched the other in the chest; the second man tottered for a few seconds, then fell with a thud onto the snow piled up at the side of the road. David blinked: the punch had been really slow coming, he must've seen it a mile off! He could've ducked it easily, but he just hadn't: another funny carry-on . . .

The man struggled in the snow for a few seconds, seemed about to settle there, then tumbled back onto his feet again, and came face to face with his brother, who was standing waiting for him a couple of metres away, swaying slightly. They started to walk on up the road again, till the man who'd been knocked down said something in a low voice; his brother answered, then they both started speaking and shouting. Then the one who'd been punched before lunged round and hit the other on the shoulder. And he fell backwards into the snow. He struggled, muttering to himself, then got up, and they both carried on out of the village.

David watched them knock each other down till they were out of sight. Then he stayed standing for quite a while longer, staring at the empty street.

Headnip

As well as washing the dishes and the pots and that, I had to make up the sweets when the orders came through. All the bits were in the fridge, I just had to chuck them together in the right order. This one time I was stacking glasses in the dishwasher machine when Andrea the waitress stuck her head round the door and shouted, Hey Conn, strawberry meringue nests!

I kept on racking up the glasses. What? I said.

She came a bit further in and leant on the edge of the door. Can you make me up two, she said, Two strawberry meringue nests for table four. And they finished their meal a while ago, so could you do it now?

I looked at her. I can only do it when you ask me. You should've asked me before if you wanted them before.

I know, I know, it's just that I kind of forgot. I mean I got involved in making out somebody's bill, then another table wanted more drinks . . .

All right, okay, I said. I looked away and back at the glasses I was sticking in the machine. And you can stop grinning at me like that.

Like what? she said, her eyes looking out at me from under her fringe.

I looked away again. Okay, I said, I'll get them in ten seconds.

She smiled. Thanks Conn, she said, and swung out the door and away out front. I could hear her singing along with the restaurant sound system as she went past the stores and the toilets, then the music burst louder for a second, then nothing, just kitchen noises.

Kitchen noises are mainly the noises of the chef clattering pans about on the cooker. He doesn't use a wooden spoon to stir the grub like any normal person; instead the bastard just lifts the pans and shoogles them about a bit then bangs them down – *bangs* them on the metal grills over the gas flames, *hammers* them down – which is a right pain, especially if you're trying to sleep, as I usually am when I'm doing the dishes. Banging about and shouting at the waitresses to get their fucking arses in gear, that's what the chef does, but him and his wife own the place, so who's going to tell him to wise up? Only her, and she's fucking worse.

I went over to the fridge and took out the bowl of strawberries, the trimmings, and a couple of meringue shells. I laid the stuff out on a work-top, then got down dessert plates and started putting the things together: a layer of cream stuff from an aerosol in the bottom, then a layer of strawberries, then more cream, more strawberries, big good-looking ones this time, a dod of cream on top, in a swirl shape if possible, then a sprinkle of chocolate flakes and a few green leaves of some chewy substance round the edges for decoration. Easy: each one would take me about three minutes, what with getting the berries in circles and that, looking good. Still, three minutes of my time, my time at one-sixty an hour, that's eight pence manpower costs for the making of a meringue nest. And how much do they cost out front? Two fucking seventy-five! I tell you, somebody's doing well out of this game.

I had just finished the first layer of cream on the second

meringue and was picking out some strawberries from the bowl, when there was a scream from the far end of the kitchen: GET MY STRAWBERRY OUT OF YOUR FUCKING MOUTH!

I jerked round, knocking my elbow on the edge of the fridge and sending the handful of berries I'd selected scattering over the floor. Down at the far end, Robert the chef had turned from the cooker and was standing there, glowering at me, a big wooden tattie-basher in his hand. Slowly he lowered his gaze to where the strawberries were lying around my feet. He took a pace forward.

I wasn't touching your strawberries, I said. Well, except for making up the sweets like.

Pick those bastards up NOW! He took another step forward, thrusting out the basher to point at the berries on the floor, his hand trembling with the weight of it. I went down on my knees and scrabbled around, quickly picking up all the strawberries I could see, except for a couple that were squashed and burst. I stood up. Robert was right in front of me, looking down. What's wrong with those? he said.

Eh . . . I must've stood on them.

Aye, but what's wrong with them?

Well . . .

PICK THE BASTARDS UP!

I reached down and scraped up as much of the remains as possible. Suppose we'll have to chuck these, I said as I straightened up.

Chuck them out? Aye, sure, sure . . . MY ARSE! He lifted the tattie-basher up in the air and began to scratch the top of his head with it. Give me them here, he said. I emptied the berries into his hand, he gave me the basher in return. Stand clear, he said. No, on second thoughts, fuck off.

I went over to the dishwasher, put the tattie-basher inside, closed the door, and switched it on. As the water started to scoosh in I remembered to click the control round to the glassware cycle.

You should've done that ages ago, said Robert. I mean what's the fucking point in filling the fucking dishwasher if you don't switch the fucker on? You think it's going to work its fucking self?

Well actually I was going to just then, but Andrea came in and she was in a hurry and . . . Robert, what are you doing? Actually I could see what he was doing: he was jamming down the strawberries, the ones off the floor, he was jamming them on top of the cream in the meringue shell. But he was doing it all wrong, pressing them in too hard so the cream was squelching out over the edges, smachering them down any old way, not in proper snug rings.

What does it look like I'm fucking doing? he said.

Eh . . . hih! I shrugged.

He picked up the cream aerosol. I'm doing your fucking job, amn't I, that's what I'm fucking doing. He squirted a lump of cream onto the middle of the strawberries, and went to pick up the chocolate-shaker.

Eh, the chocolate doesn't go on yet, I said.

What?

There's another layer of strawberries to go on yet, a dose of cream on top of that, then the trimmings at the end.

He banged down the chocolate-shaker. I do know that, he said. I am the fucking chef here am I not?

Aye! God aye!

Well don't come the cunt then. Here, take the cream and finish the bastard off: I'm not doing your fucking job for you.

He snatched up the cream-aerosol and threw it at my chest. I caught it as it bounced off. Thanks, I said, but he was already half-way back to the cooker and there were footsteps running along the corridor from the restaurant. The door opened and Andrea came in.

Where's the . . .

What the fuck do you want? shouted Robert.

She stepped sideways past him and came over to me. Meringue nests, she said, Have you got them Conn? Table four's giving me gyp about them. Come on, I asked you years ago . . .

Just coming, I said. Robert was helping me with them.

Oh, I see, she said. From the far end of the kitchen came the sound of a bottle being prised open and the top hitting the floor. Andrea was still talking. Well, can you take them through to the bar when they're done? I'm run off my feet. That Bridget's hopeless: she asked somebody if they wanted ice in their prawn cocktail. Will you do that for me?

I'll just be a second if you wait . . .

Thanks Conn, bye! She pushed out the door and away down the corridor.

I sighed, glanced up the far end. Robert was brushing a tray of very small chickens with some oily bree, at the same time drinking out of a big bottle of Czechoslovakian beer. There were already three empty bottles on top of the extractor hood above the stove.

I turned back to the work-top and quickly finished off the nests, sticking extra strawberries and cream on the one that Robert had half fucked-up. Then I wiped round the edges of the plates with a corner of my apron, picked them up and headed for the door.

Oi! Where are you off to shitepants?

I turned and backed open the swinging door. I'm off out front with these, I said, nodding down at the plates.

Aye, well, no fucking skiving, he said. I'm needing you to do something for me, special duties.

I let the door swing to behind me and went off towards the restaurant. Robert was a fucking chancer. Here it was getting on for eleven, my finishing time, and he was wanting me to do extras. The last time he conned me into that it was cleaning out the deep-fat fryer, a hell of a clart: my hair was filled with grease for a week after. But it was probably just chopping up veg for tomorrow's lunches: not so bad, but still not one of my official jobs. And I still had some writing-up to do for college when I got home. Maybe I should just tell him where to stick his special duties.

I passed through the second door and into the restaurant. It was emptying now; Andrea was getting a party of five into their coats over by the door. Janice, Robert's wife, was doing something behind the bar, and looked up as I came in. She glared at me. I walked over towards her and put the plates on the bar-top.

What are you doing through here? she hissed.

I was bringing these through for Andrea. She said she was rushed off her feet.

Janice banged a liqueur bottle and two glasses down on the bar-top. Look at the bloody state of you! she said. Your apron's filthy; what've you been doing with it, washing the floor?

I shrugged. These are for table four, I think.

God! Janice turned and looked at the slips of paper hooked to the board beside the coffee machine. They're for table four, she said. She scowled at me again, pursing her lips so I could see sweat on the top one gleaming under the bar-lights, then picked up the two dessert plates, switched on a smile, and walked away to the far corner of the restaurant.

I watched her go for a few seconds, then was away to turn back towards the kitchen when Andrea came up beside me and jabbed her elbow into my guts.

Ya beauty! she said.

What?

See that lot that just went out? Six quid of tips! Six quid! She reached into the pocket of her apron, took out some folded notes and waved them in front of my face.

Very good, I said. Lucky you.

Lucky you too, she said, and stretched over to drop the money into a glass beside the till.

What do you mean lucky me? I said.

Two quid each from one table . . . can't be bad!

What do you mean two quid each?

You, me and Bridget, three into six goes two.

But I don't get a share of the tips.

Eh? Aye you do.

No I don't. I should ken.

Don't come it, Conn. Janice always takes away a share for you: a share each for the waitresses, and another one for you. She always does.

Christ, I've never seen a penny of it!

I reckon we'll get at least a fiver each the night.

Jesus Christ . . .

Andrea! Janice was shouting from half-way across the restaurant. Andrea, would you bring over the Tia Maria please, and another glass too. I'm sitting with the Abercrombies. She paused. And, oh, Conn . . . She jerked her thumb in the direction of the door to the kitchen. I gave her a big cheesy grin. She went back to the far corner, and a few seconds later Andrea followed her with the bottle and glasses.

I quickly glanced around, then nipped in behind the bar, took the tips glass down from beside the till and emptied it out on top of a pile of wine-lists. I started counting.

Hiya Conn! How's it going? It was Bridget; I hadn't heard her come up on me.

Och fine. Pretty busy you ken, but not too bad . . .

No, the tips, how're the tips doing? Oops, hold on . . . She took out a handful of coins and threw them down on the rest of the money. I started counting again.

I make it twenty-seven pounds and twenty pence, I said.

So how does that come out? she said, looking up from the coffee she was pouring. Seven each, no, nine each . . . not bad eh? Brilliant actually.

The most I've ever got, I said. In fact, I reckon I'll just take mines the now.

There'll be more though . . . scuse! She squeezed past behind me, making an effort not to spill the coffees.

This'll do me, I said. She was away.

I counted out a fiver, three singles and a pound coin, stuck it into my pocket, shovelled the rest of the tips back into the glass and replaced it by the till. I glanced around. Andrea was coming back towards the bar. Bye, I said, and waved to her as I walked quickly to the door and through into the passage.

I paused. I could hear Robert singing through in the kitchen. He had a not bad voice, but he only ever sang when nobody else was about. I took a couple of slow steps towards the kitchen. The singing stopped. There was the sound of a throat being cleared, then, Is that you Conn? Where've you fucking been?

I sidestepped into the storeroom. For a second I listened. Robert started up singing again. I undid the ties on my apron, lifted the loop from around my neck, and flung it down on top of one of the chest freezers. It slid across the lid and fell down the back. Fuck it, I said to myself. I got my jacket down off its hook and put it on. At the door of the storeroom I stopped and listened, holding my breath, then nipped straight across and into the staff toilet. I didn't bother to lock the door, but just quickly reached up and pulled out the paperback that someone had hidden behind the cistern. I reckoned it was more than likely Robert's; the idea of one of the women wanking in the lavvie just seemed impossible, for some reason. I could be wrong. I jammed the book into my inside pocket, buttoned up my jacket, and walked smartly out, down the corridor, into the restaurant, and out the front door. I stared straight ahead till I was outside, catching only a glimpse of Janice gowping at me open-mouthed from behind the bar as I passed. Out on the street, I walked quickly away to the left, crossed the road at the drinking fountain, and strode up one of the lanes that led up the hill towards our estate.

After a few minutes I was passing Hong's Garden, and I realised that I was hungry. I decided I'd get a carry-out with some of my tips. I went in.

Hello Mrs Hong, I said.

Hello, she said. Yes?

Eh . . . let me think. I looked up at the menu, then back at her. I shook my head. Do you ever get fed up of working here? I said. She looked at me. Right . . . I'll have special fried rice and a thing of curry sauce please. And a fork. She took my money, then leant round a doorway and shouted something through the back in Chinese. Sizzling noises began. I rested my elbows on the counter.

Mrs Hong reappeared. Late nights, she said. People fighting. Too much drink. I don't like working then. It nips my head.

I laughed. I ken what you mean, I said. But you own the place, eh no? You and your man? That must make a difference?

She shrugged. My husband's family own it. That nips my head too.

There was a shout from the kitchen. She went through and came back almost immediately with my order in a carrier bag. She handed it over.

Good-night, she said.

Good-night Mrs Hong.

As I started up the lane again, I saw somebody coming down towards me on their hands and knees, moving fast. It was a guy in a shell-suit. He passed me. It was my wee brother. I blinked and turned to look after him. He was already twenty metres down the lane, still crawling.

Oi, Bizzer!

He slowed to a stop, but didn't look back.

Bizzer, it's me, Conn.

Slowly he crawled round in a semi-circle till he was facing me. What are you doing up there man? he said.

What am *I* doing?

Get down!

I looked behind me. The street was empty. Then something clicked. Bizzer, I said, Have you been nicking my mushrooms?

He crawled towards me a few paces, and grinned up at me. Well I was looking through your records, ken, and I found this shoebox . . .

You bastard!

I only had a few man, don't lose the rag, just a few of the wee scrotty ones . . .

There was only scrotty ones left! All the big meaty ones were finished! Christ, those were meant to last me you bastard!

Hey, I only had a couple, just a few! And I'll tell you this, I had to eat a fucking lot of the few to get any effect, a lot of the few: they're weak as shite. They've just about worn off already!

I sighed. So why the fuck are you crawling around on your fucking hands and knees?

He looked up at me, laughed. Everything's tipped up, he said, Everything's on its side. If you don't get down you're likely to fall off.

I shook my head. Why do you have to go around eating my mushies? I said. Why can't you just get pished like everybody else?

He had picked a piece of grit up off the ground and was holding it to his nose, sniffing it. After a second, he put it in his mouth. He grunted. No cash, he said.

I looked at him. They're needing a new dishwasher down at Guddler's, I said.

Is that right?

They'd probably give you an hour now if you went down there.

He frowned. Here, is that not the place you work?

Used to. Not any more.

Aw, right. I reckon I'll give that a go then. He started to crawl round till he was facing down the lane. He paused. So is it an okay place to work then?

Oh aye, it's fine. But I reckon you should go there right now.

He nodded, his head nearly hitting the cobbles. See you man, he said, and started crawling away, slowly at first, then faster and faster, till he almost skidded turning into the street at the bottom. He disappeared in the direction of the restaurant. I smiled to myself, then turned and started up the lane.

At the top of the lane was a small area of grass with a couple of empty flower-beds in it and a bench on one side. I went and sat down on the bench. I took the foil carton of rice out of the bag, got the lid off, and laid it on the seat beside me. It smelt magic. I poured the curry sauce out of its tub over the rice and mixed it in. I forked some up to my mouth. It was still burning hot. I put the fork down for a minute, got up, and dropped the curry tub and the carrier bag into the litter bin at the end of the bench. I sat down again. Then I remembered Robert's book. I got it out of my jacket pocket. It was called *Adventures of a Victorian Mesmerist*. I'd known for a couple of weeks that it was jammed in behind the cistern, but had never had the time to have a proper look at it.

Robert would be worried sick when he found it was gone, worried maybe Janice had found it or something . . . I smiled to myself again, started reading.

It was all about this young guy, Lord somebody-or-other, who'd inherited his father's estate. He'd then went away to Paris on the proceeds and learnt various things, including how to hypnotise folk. Anyway, now he was back in England putting this to good use, and within three pages of the start he'd hypnotised a housemaid and shagged her, hypnotised his own sister and shagged her, then hypnotised them both at the same time and got them to shag each other. It was terrible really. I mean it gave you a hard-on, but there was something really depressing about it as well, the whole set-up was just rotten.

I closed the book. I was away to put it back in my pocket but then stopped, leant over, and dropped it into the litter bin instead. I gave the bin a bit of a shake, and the book fell down into the middle of all the rubbish. I lifted the carton of rice onto my knees. There was still steam coming off it, but not at such a rate as before. I picked up the fork and started to eat.

Doubled Up With Pain

John came back from the kitchen with two cans of beer and sat down along the settee from the boy. The first time I met your mother, he said, I was doubled up with pain at the foot of Leith Walk.

The boy looked up from the football comic he was reading.

I hope you're not going to embarrass the laddie, said Freddy, leaning out of his chair to take the can John was offering him.

Not at all, not at all. I never did embarrassing things in these days.

Not like now, eh!

John sighed, tapping the bottom of his can. Give us a break will you Freddy? I'm telling the boy his family history here, let me get it out, eh?

Aye John, go on there, sorry, on you go. He peeled the ringpull off and lifted the beer to his lips.

John looked at his can for a second, then put it down on the floor at the end of the settee. Well, he said. He looked at the boy. The boy shut his comic and put it on the floor. This was outside the Central Bar at the foot of the Walk. I'd been struck by indigestion, see, like a spear through my guts. I was getting it all the time in these days, the grub I was eating and that. And if I'd had a drink the night before as well, ken, that would bring it on in the middle of the next morning, without fail. Anyway, this one morning it had come over me bad, really biting into my belly, like the acid was going to burn right through to my backbone, and I had to stop in the street, stop in my tracks, and I was holding my guts with one hand, leaning with the other on this post-box there. I was staring down at the pavement just, doubled up with pain.

Freddy laughed. And there you saw your bride-to-be, lying on the ground in front of you!

John glared across at him, then quickly grinned along at the boy and kept on talking, looking down at the rug in front of the fire. I was in a wee world of my own there, he said, Just concentrating on this ball of pain, keeping it down in my belly, stopping it from spinning up my throat, ken, waiting for it to pass, and I wasn't hearing the traffic at all, or aware of folk passing me by . . . and it was a hell of a busy place in these days, with the station still on the go and that. But then something did break through the haze and into here. John tapped the side of his forehead with a finger, glancing from the boy to Freddy and back again. Voices speaking in a deliberately loud kind of way, right behind me. So I straightened myself and looked up, and there were two lassies standing there, a big stack of letters and packages each which they started to stick into the post-box as soon as I moved out of their road – not even looking at me any more. And then I heard one of them say, the one that wasn't your mother . . .

So the other one was Agnes was it?

Aye Freddy, that's the point, that was Agnes standing there, sticking letters in the thingmy, and there's me bent over like a half-closed knife beside her!

A touch of the old gutrot, eh? Freddy screwed up his face and grimaced across at the boy. The boy looked away and back to his dad.

The one that wasn't your mother, said John, Well, I heard her saying, And at this time of the morning too! It's a damned disgrace!

The boy smiled at the pan-loaf voice his dad had put on, then listened again to the story.

I saw the both of them looking over their shoulders at the Central, ken, and I thinks to myself, Aye aye, they reckon I've been on the bevvy, enjoying myself, and really I'm chopped in half with the bloody indigestion! And I don't know what came over me to bother, but I just reckoned I'd set them right. I mean nine times out of ten I wouldn't've given a toss, but this particular time for some reason I just stood straight up there, thumbs down the seams of the breeks, looked them in the eye and said, Ladies, excuse me for butting in here, but I fear you're misconstruing me . . .

Misconstruing! said Freddy.

That's what *they* said, said John. And I said, Aye, you've been construing the fact that I'm hytering about here as proof that I'm half-cut, when the fact is I'm sober as a judge and sick with a stomach complaint! Well, the two of them made kind of oh-ing noises, still sticking mail in the slot. So don't be so quick to condemn, I went on. I could've been dying with an exploded ulcer and you'd be standing there tut-tutting!

The boy laughed and Freddy did too, then said, Aye John, you had a sharp tongue on you that day right enough.

John grinned. Well I had had my mid-morning pint ten minutes before, you see, I reckon that's where all my smart comments were coming from. Hih! Anyway. Agnes, your mother, she looks at me, kind of biting her lip, and begins to say, Sorry . . . But the other one grabs her by the elbow saying, Come on now, don't pay him any heed, let's get back over the road. And she starts to pull her off towards the crossing. I look after them, ken, and I'm just about to spit some acidy spit after the back of them when Agnes looks round and sees me watching her rear. So quick as a flash I whip off my cap and nod to her, a big smile across my chops. And sure enough she pulls away from her mate and walks right back towards me.

Here comes the juicy bit, said Freddy.

The boy sighed and leaned forward, elbows on his knees, listening to his dad.

She walks right up to me, a nice-looking lassie she was, she walks up and says, I'm sorry about my friend, her man takes a bucket, she's touchy about it. I felt I had to say something, but I couldn't think what to say, so I just kind of shrugged and said, Ach, and waved my cap at her. Then I stopped waving my cap and put it back on my head and said, Ach, again. She kind of cocked her head on one side and looked me up and down and said, You were telling the truth were you? I mean you weren't in there drinking? Not at this hour? I shrugged again then shook my head – cause I hadn't been in the Central at all, I'd had my pint in the Spey up the road – and then I decided that I really better say something. Anything! So I said, No, not at all, I was in the Job Centre there, looking around the vacancies and that . . . John paused, frowned, then said to the boy, Except I didn't say Job Centre, it wasn't called that in these days. I was in the Labour Exchange, that's what I said to her. John cleared his throat. She looked me up and down again, her head on one side like a bloody bird, and she said to me, So you're out of a job, eh? I nodded, tried to look sorry about it. I was sorry about it! Hmm, she says, Come with us then. So I came with them. Or at least I went with Agnes: the other one walked off ahead with her nose in the air when she saw me coming. Hih. We crossed the road and went down Kirk Street. We're in a shipper's office down here, said Agnes. They've been looking for a man for the stores for weeks now, what do you think? Ho ho, I said, Tell them to look no more!

There was a silence. John looked along the settee at the boy, who smiled briefly, then frowned. John looked across at Freddy.

So that's how you met her, said Freddy. I never knew that one.

John reached down and picked up his can. He tapped the bottom of it. And that's how I got that job as well. I was there for more than a year, it was a fine job. He opened the can and played about with the ringpull for a few seconds, slipping it on and off the fingers of his left hand. Then we got married and got the house out in Porty and the both of us found work out here. Then after a few more years you came along, then after another few more . . . well, that's now. John took the ringpull off his pinkie and flicked it away towards the bin by the fireplace. After a second he lifted the can and took a long drink.

The boy sat back into the depths of the settee, frowning. Dad, he said.

What son?

Where's Mum gone?

John took another drink, then lowered the can and held it in both hands in his lap. She's gone, he said. It doesn't matter where.

Freddy half stood up, then sat down again on the arm of his chair. Here, he said to the boy, How about you taking me out the back for a bit of penalty practice?

Dad . . .

A silence.

Dad!

What?

When's she coming back?

John gazed at the boy for a moment, then shrugged. Ach . . . He looked at the top of his beer can, then bent over and put it on the floor between his feet. He stayed bent over for quite a long time before straightening up.

Bod is Dead

The three of us are hanging round the back of the chippie keeping busy doing f-all when there's this roaring noise and Buzby tanks round the corner, trucks cracking like guns off the paving gaps of the precinct, him bent over like he's riding some west-coast tidal wave, muscles hunched, hurtling . . . then the board's skiting out from under his Adidas and he times it fucking perfect and leaps off right in front of us, thick sliced flat soles plopping on the concrete like flyman suckers while the board flashes on and smacks its nose on the giant stone flowertub of cans, condoms and carry-out cartons across the way, and Buzby's looking like a public enemy or nigger with attitude with his sweathood pulled up and the floppy fucking hat on top of that, and the way he stands with his legs apart, and his arms out, fists clenched, eyes staring over his wound-round paisley scarf, staring at us – me, Jeg and Artic standing there, standing against the chippie's back wall, leaning and smoking – and we lean there and smoke and look at him, stopping speaking, waiting for him to come in and get out of his system as usual all the shite bubbling up there.

Go cut creator go, I say.

He grabs off his hat, crumples it up, flings it to the floor, kicks it, toe-pointing, lifts it, whips it against the wall to the side of

Artic. He shouts through his scarf, The cunt's done it this time! Artic looks at the hat flopped in a stain on the ground.

I for one look at the Buz: he's tugging his scarf unwound, reaching inside somewhere, coming out with a softpack . . . before anything more he bends double, knees together, stomps his feet, screams BBBAAASSSTTTAAARRRDDD!!! This is a bad one all right, something's got into him, something bad, and he's off on one of his radge attacks, brain boiling over or something, coming out his ears in steam, out his mouth in fucking fury . . . but Buzby's like that, getting in a rage he does all the time, it's a waste of time, a waste of heat, it leaves you feeling cold when you've burnt it all off, aye but he's like that, quick to rouse, quick to freeze, he'd punch some bugger's lights out or give them a fucking hug depending on his mood, how his feelings felt that day, that minute, and all for nothing at all. His dad killed himself a couple of years ago, jumped in front of a bus, but Buzby was a hot-and-cold cunt before that anyway, that wasn't the reason, there was no reason, it was just his nature: Buzby the madder.

He stalks away over, boots the skateboard back towards us, stams a fag in his face, lights it with his fancy fucking US Navy Zippo, cow's-arses it . . . aye he's bad all right.

Crash us a fag, says Jeg, but Buzby doesn't reply. I said crash us . . .

FUCK OFF! shouts Buzby, then he digs in his pocket, flings the tabs across at us. Jeg picks them up, sticks one in his mouth, then passes them to me. The Buz isn't looking, he's walking up and down, glowering at the ground, so I take one also, hand them on to Artic. He grabs one too then holds out the pack, and when Buzby stops to snatch and stuff them away, Artic takes the chance to say, Hey Buz, eh, something bugging you?

No thing, he says, No fucking thing, no THING is fucking bugging me: someONE, somefuckingONE, by Christ, he is dead,

Bod is dead, he is fucking finished by the way, I'll fucking kill the fucker dead.

We all take a drag, hold the smoke down . . . Jeg lets his out first, says, Thought Bod was a mate? A good mucker like?

So did I, that's what I thought, but I'm a stupid bastard, see? It's obvious now, he's a traitor, a judas, a mojo by Christ!

We look at each other, and back at Buzby, and back at each other again. So what's Bod done? I ask him.

He's fucked my mother, the cunt!

What?

He's fucking fucked my mother. Buz throws down his dowp, it goes out, he treads on it, smears it across the wet concrete.

What, says Artic, You mean he's killed her?

No no, fucking no, says Buzby, It's fucking worse than that: he's screwed her, he's stuck it up her, he's sticking it up her now!

But I saw your old dear just half an hour ago, says Jeg, just coming out of the Gunner. Right enough, she did have a grin on her face, but I thought that was cause she was pished, not cause of, eh, anything else.

Buzby twists up his face then says, Aye aye aye, she was blootered, but this's all happened since then. Me and Bod went back to my place after school, see, to watch some videos and that, and I was just away to make some toasted cheese for my tea and he was just about to go home when my mother comes in, flings off her coat, chucks herself down in the armchair beside us.

What, the three of you on the chair? says Artic.

Don't be fucking dense, says Buz. Me and Bod on the settee, her on the fucking seat next the fucking settee.

So is this where the sex comes in? says Jeg.

Shut up, says Buz, And listen. She holds out this tenner to me, ken, says, Here's your family allowance son. So I take it, right, I take it, but the thought's running through my head, By Christ we better get out of here fast: she's acting *fucking* strange, doling out tenners like this . . . So I jump to my feet, kick off the video, say, Come on man, I'll stand you a poke of chips. And he gets up too, and I'm making for the door, when my mother speaks again, she says, My God, I've got a real nippy pussy . . . Fuck's sake Mother, I go, stopping with my hand on the door, Don't say things like that! Her eyes are closed, and she's leaning back in the chair rubbing the front of her skirt with the palm of her hand. I can't help saying it if it's true, she goes.

Well, I say, while Buz takes a breath, She's got a good point there, you ken.

Stop interrupting, says Jeg, He's just coming up to the porn bit.

I'm away to say something else, says Buz, when I notice Bod's looking at her in a funny way, this creepy smile on his face, just standing there with his hands on the back of the settee. Let's get the fuck out of here, I shout, and I open the door. Bod doesn't seem to hear me, he's just staring there, and he's leaning against the settee-back now. Come on, I shout, and go over to grab him and rug him away, but he turns right then and says to me, Well, fair do's, Buzby. What? I say. Nippy pussy . . . says my mother. Bod goes round and sits down on the settee again, Well there's only one cure for that, he says. She opens her eyes, And what's that? she says. Well you're obviously a bit dry, need some lubrication . . . Oh aye, she says, looking at him, And who's going to give me that? I'm only seeing the back of his head now, but he must make some face or smile or something, cause right away she stands up, walks out into the lobby. Well are you coming? she calls back. Bod jumps to his feet, makes for the door. I take hold of his arm, I say to him, What the fuck are you doing man? That's my fucking mother out there! This is my big chance, he whispers, Let go! Jesus, I've been waiting sixteen years for this . . . Get a fucking grip, I say, My old dear! She's fucking twice your age! And she's a mauchit old bag as well. He shakes his head: I'm sorry, he says, But . . . And he gets out of his jacket, me still standing there holding the sleeve, he walks out. I hear the door of her bedroom bang shut, then my mother saying something, then . . .

Buzby stops, turns away from the three of us standing there – me, Jeg and Artic – and he's reaching inside his top, then lighting another fag.

Jesus Christ, says Jeg, Jesus . . .

Fuck's sake . . . I say.

What happened next? says Artic.

Buzby looks at us through a breath of smoke that hangs in front of his face till he blows it away with a shout: WHAT THE FUCK DO YOU THINK HAPPENED NEXT?

Artic shrugs. Eh . . . is that when they had the shag?

Buzby says something under his breath, blinks slowly, then says, What happened next was I walked out of the house, and I came here. You ken what like the walls are in our place – thin as gossamer fucking durex – I wasn't going to hang around and fucking LISTEN, listen to various noises and try to work out what was going on! Jesus Christ!

Oh, right enough, says Artic.

He's a fucking sicko if you ask me, I say, I mean no offence Buz, but your ma's no spring chicken, eh?

I hope he turned the light out, says Artic.

FUCK OFF, shouts Buzby.

He's sick, says Jeg, I mean with you in the house and that . . . We're all needing to get our hole, but Jesus, that's a bit fucking much.

Buz is standing with one foot on his board, looking down. How long have I been here? he asks.

I look at my watch. Eh . . . fuck . . . ten minutes?

Right, he says, They'll be finished by now, I'm going over there, I'll wait outside, and when he shows his face, I'll fucking have his balls, the cunt.

We all nod, spout shite like a man's got to do whatever the fuck, and watch him boiling up again.

Buzby pulls his scarf up, tugs his hat down, turns and says, I fucking well mean it, Bod is dead, then pushes off and boards down the precinct and away, weaving about, really nashing it, leaning the board into swerves for speed.

We watch him go, then Jeg gets out his JPS and passes them round. Well well well, he says.

The girls of the world ain't nothing but trouble . . .

If it was a girl it would be okay, says Artic, but an old fucking alkie, dearie dear.

I ken, I say, I was just quoting.

Buzby's certainly pretty pissed off about it, says Jeg.

Are you surprised? I say.

No, it's fair enough I suppose. But he did go on a hell of a lot, eh?

So?

I reckon he's jealous.

What! shouts Artic, You reckon he wants a go himself?

I never said that, says Jeg, looking about, But still . . .

Me and Artic look at each other, burst out laughing. Now you come to mention it Jeg, I say, I think it's you that's jealous!

Aye, says Artic, You've always fancied older women: look when you were going out with that lassie in sixth year!

We all have a laugh, Jeg as well: it's all a load of shite.

Pretty soon after this we split up, Jeg and Artic making off for the Medway on the far side of the shopping centre, me on down the precinct in the same direction as Buzby went. I go out onto the main road, look back at the crowd of kids yelling outside the chippie, then cross over and start to walk down my street. When I get to my stair though I keep on walking, go right on by and to the end of the road and stop there by the lock-ups . . . I can see across the big roundabout to the high-flats, the nearest one with Buzby's house on the ninth floor. I look up, there are lights on and off all over, I can't work out which is his ma's bedroom at all, and I'm just turning back when there's a move at the foot of the block and I see a figure lurking there, floppy fucking hat on top of it: Buzby, leaning on the wall by the flats' main door, arms folded, looking down, and I can't see his face, can't make it out, but he keeps on looking down at the ground.

I think for a minute about going over and helping him kill Bod, or stopping him killing Bod, but then I think, Fuck it fuck it fuck it, and head off home for my tea.

Bed of Thistles

Down in the main hall Margaret and her two bridesmaids were moving about amongst the dancers; one of the two was holding the long tail of the bride's white dress, and yanking it to one side or another now and then, trying to keep it out of the fag-ash and puddles of spilt drink on the dance-floor; the other one was carrying a big basket with flowers round the edges, and little rolls of paper tied with ribbon inside. As they passed through the crowds, the bride was sticking her hand into the basket and giving out these pieces of paper to folk who were dancing, or sitting drinking and watching at the long tables pushed to the sides of the hall. It seemed to be mostly females who were being given these things, and they all seemed to be very happy about getting them.

Up in the balcony, Ewan turned from looking down to pick his pint up from by his feet, and also to take a glance at Shareen at the same time; she was still staring down at the band on the stage, and her lips were still pressed together in a straight line.

Look, I never meant never, said Ewan, I just meant . . .

Shareen jetted breath out through her nose.

The point about Margaret and Norrie is, you know, they've been going out for ages . . .

No longer than us, Ewan.

Aye, but they seem so well suited and that.

Oh and we don't, is that what you're saying?

No! Och, aye . . . Jesus! He sighed and looked back to the dancers.

Let's just forget the whole thing eh?

Ach no Shareen, that's not what I want, I mean not what I meant, it's just . . . now isn't the right time, you ken?

She looked at him. I'm starting thinking it'll never be the right time for you and me.

No, look, shut up, all I'm saying is that now isn't the best time to talk about it, with all this racket and that going on. Can we just talk about something else the now, eh? Can we?

Shareen watched the bride going around giving out the rolls of paper. It's meant to be good luck if you get given one of those off her, she said. I don't suppose I've much chance of getting one sitting up here, have I? But there you go, that's the story of my life, is that not right Ewan?

So that's what that's all about is it? I thought it was maybe trick or treats, ken? Put your pants on your head and say the alphabet backwards, and all that.

At a wedding! For God's sake Ewan, don't be fucking pathetic.

He said something under his breath.

What was that?

I said don't fucking swear at me you fucking bad-tempered cow.

I'll swear if I fucking want!

If it's swearing you want, I'll fucking give it you, you fucking sour-faced bitch! You're okay if that's all you're wanting!

She was looking at him, but immediately he stopped talking she turned and stared down the length of the hall, and her eyes were filmed over.

Go away, she said, Go away and leave me alone, that's obviously what you're wanting.

Don't you worry, don't fucking worry on that fucking score. He jumped up, kicking his pint over. Aw . . . shite! He bent and snatched the glass up, swallowed the tiny amount that was left in it. Then he set the glass down, balanced it on top of the metal railing that stopped folk falling off the balcony, turned and walked towards the door at the far end. He passed a couple he didn't know, but who were staring at him anyway, and then was reaching to open the door onto the stairs down. He stopped with his hand out about to push and looked back: Shareen wasn't looking after him, she had her eyes on his glass balanced on the railing: it seemed to be tottering slightly, almost swaying there on its perch, but this was maybe just an effect of the disco lights the band had on stage. He shoved the door open and went through and down, pausing half-way when three boys about ten years old came bombing up towards him, all of them giggling like crazy, the biggest one clutching something under his jacket, probably a can of lager pinched from under the nose of some uncle who was pretending not to notice. They froze when they came up against Ewan, and looked guilty for a few seconds while he glowered at them. Then he said, Okay lads, just hope you're not planning on driving home the night, and winked at the one with the bulge under his jacket. They burst out laughing again, squeezed by him and went on up. He heard the balcony door swing shut behind them as he reached the bottom of the stairs and looked up and down the corridor.

There were folk buzzing about, men in kilt rig-outs or suits, women in long bright-coloured dresses if they were young, or matching jacket and skirts if they were older, and there were waitresses in black and white going past in one direction with stacks of empty glasses and the other way with tinfoil trays piled with small slices of wedding cake. An elderly waitress passed by right in front of him going towards the hall, and he reached out and lifted a couple bits of cake off the top of her tray. Wait your turn laddie, she said, without breaking step. He held the pieces in the flat of his palm and peeled off the layers of icing and marzipan; he looked around, then balanced these on a kind of narrow sill that ran along the walls, marking where the wood panels below changed to painted plaster above. He stuck one of the slices into his mouth, and chewed on it as he walked along towards the room that was being used as a bar. Just before he reached there, he dropped the second piece of cake into the pocket of his leather jacket, wiped some crumbs off his moustache and lips, and then dug around in his trouser pockets and took out all the change he had. In the queue to be served he spent the whole time counting his cash, very slowly, three times, head down.

It worked: nobody talked to him. He didn't want to talk to anybody, he just wanted to find somewhere there was a bit of peace and quiet, for five minutes even. There had been nothing but noise and annoyance all day, and not a chance to think at all, and the thoughts were still sluggish and poisoned after the night before, his brain still staggering about all over the shop though his body wasn't anymore. More than could be said for Norrie's body actually. But surely this was one of the Great Scottish Traditions, that the groom should be half-pished and three-quarters hungover from his stag do right through the ceremony and the reception and all the other shenanigans.

For some reason the bar was being run by the staff from the local golf-course clubhouse. Norrie wasn't a golfer; maybe the father of the bride played. Or maybe they were the cheapest, full stop. Ewan scanned the bar staff as he got close to the trestle table that was being used for a counter: Mrs O'Leary the clubhouse manager was there, and so was her son, whose name was . . . something or other. He had been behind the bar the last few times Ewan had been up at the clubhouse, up there playing snooker: they had the only table in the village, and it saved the journey into the town centre, if you could put up with the stupid bastards in their tartan trousers and pink Pringle jerseys with green fucking diamonds on them, and all their talk about birdies and bogeys and God knows what. Golfing casuals: fight for fun on the fairway, clubbed to death on the ninth green . . .

The boy was talking to him.

Eh what? Eh, pint of lager tops please.

Sure thing Ewan, here we go . . . And how are you keeping this weather – one pint of tops – very fine I hope?

Och middling to be honest eh young Mr Leary-o; yourself?

Fair to middling Ewan, as you say. Now that's one pound exactly so far – just like that eh! – and anything else to go with it, for Shareen at all?

No.

Was it not Shareen Ewan?

Aye, but I'm not buying her a drink the now, okay? Ewan put a pile of coins into the boy's hand, picked up his pint, and walked out the room; O'Leary was still shouting goodbyes after him, fucking annoying friendly bastard.

Out in the corridor there was still a hell of a bustle: folk rushing about in excitement and in tears and of course in various stages of inebriation. A wedding reception isn't the best place to come for a quiet night out, right enough. Ewan stood in the doorway of the bar-room, took a long sup of his pint, getting the lager safely down from the rim of the glass; he looked up and down until there was nobody much coming and stepped out, started walking smartly towards the main door of the building. Half-way down the corridor, he came to a stop: there was a great racket coming from just outside the front door, a crowd of folk shouting or singing. And then a bunch of guys jumped up the front step and into the corridor; they had their arms around each others' shoulders and appeared to be completely blootered, although the reception had only been going an hour or so: these guys must've been chucking the bevvy back all through the meal, full steam ahead from the start. On the end of the front line of the crowd was Norrie's younger brother Ian, and as they approached Ewan up the corridor, still singing – dancing three steps forward then two steps back – Ian spotted him and stretched his arm out as if to join him onto the end, to grab Ewan round the shoulders and dance him off with the rest of them.

Ian was shouting on Ewan to join in, but Ewan just pointed to the nearly full glass in his other hand and then raised it to the lads, going two steps back. He pressed himself against the wall of the corridor to let them past, and found he was actually standing in a doorway; he reached quickly for the handle, twisted it, and almost fell back through the door as it swung open in the way, just as the dancers were passing. He slammed the door shut, and there was the noise of the lads banging on it with their fists as they went past, still singing and shouting. Then the door was no longer shaking, and the uproar was fading away down the corridor and into the general hubbub of the music and thumping feet in the main hall, and there was almost silence.

Then a burst of laughter from behind him, and Ewan turned quickly to see two naked men, Norrie and his best man, his step-brother Alasdair, the both of them just in Y-fronts, Norrie with his kilt around his ankles, Alasdair bent over rummaging in a big hold-all on the floor.

Feared of being trampled under the stampede? said Alasdair.

He stared at the two of them, not able to say anything yet.

Come on man, said Norrie, You're not entering into the proper spirit.

Ewan checked his pint for spillage, took a drink, and then raised his eyebrows at Norrie. So is this what you call the proper spirit, is it? Buggering the best man in the boiler-room while your bride greets her eyes out in the arms of the fucking vicar?

There was a pause.

You dirty cunt, said Norrie, This isn't the boiler-room!

Everybody laughed. Norrie stepped out of the kilt and lifted a hangerful of clothes from the back of the room's other door; he pulled a pair of grey suit trousers off first, hung them over his arm, then took off the jacket that went with them and laid both bits of the suit on one of the piles of chairs that half-filled the room. Finally he took a blue-and-white-striped shirt off the hanger and started putting it on, having a bit of difficulty getting his arms into the proper holes. Alasdair was getting into a suit as well.

So how does it feel? said Ewan.

That's a rather personal question, said Alasdair.

To be a married man, said Ewan.

Norrie shrugged, doing up the collar button on his shirt.

He doesn't ken fuck all about being married yet, said Alasdair. Ask him in three years' time, then he'll tell you what it fucking feels like.

Three years, take as long as that does it?

Listen, said Norrie, I'm under no illusions, right? I'm not sweet sixteen and never been kissed by any manner of means.

Aye and neither's Margaret, said Alasdair. Everybody laughed.

I think comments like that'll have to stop, said Norrie. Otherwise I shall have to ask you to step outside for besmirching my wife's good name.

You think Margaret's a good name? said Ewan.

Come outside with you? said Alasdair. God, illicit snogs on the fire escape, nobody's asked me out for one of those in years!

What do you expect? You're a respectable married man!

Well now Ewan, you'd be surprised what some respectable married men get up to . . .

Right enough: it's not because you're married nobody'd kiss you, it's because you're such an ugly cunt! That beard! Jesus, you'd be as well kissing the cat!

Better than kissing a dog, said Norrie. They laughed again.

Ah but, said Alasdair, You don't look at the mantelpiece when you're poking the fire.

Norrie groaned. I think we're all a bittie beyond that stage Alasdair, we're all doing all right eh no? I mean Margaret, Anna, your Shareen Ewan: she's all right eh? More than all right!

Aye Shareen's all right.

She's a big girl eh? Norrie laughed, pushing the knot on his tie up towards the collar.

Ewan drank at his pint. Aye she's a big girl.

Well stocked in the tits department, said Alasdair.

Ewan sighed, looked down.

Fuck's sake man, said Norrie, Here's me trying to be tactful and non-fucking-sexist and you blunder in with your big tits you cunt!

You saying I've got big tits? said Alasdair, frowning and puffing his chest out. But Norrie was looking away now, so Alasdair turned, chuckling to himself, and went to finish dressing.

Listen: I think you two are doing absolutely the right thing by the way, said Norrie. He was kneeling on the floor tying his laces, and he looked up at Ewan, talking quickly. You and Shareen, biding thegether like.

When I'm onshore.

Aye, aye; I'm right behind you there; I mean just cause I'm getting married and that . . . I mean I think it's fine. In fact if I was younger, that's what I'd be doing, ken: I'd be sharing a flat or something, definitely, I definitely wouldn't be getting fucking married anyway, not at your age, no way. I mean what are you these days Ewan, twenty-three is it?

Twenty-two.

Twenty-two, well aye, all the more fucking reason. I mean it's different for me, I'm past thirty now, and plus Margaret being a bit of a church-goer and that ken? But you young ones, you've got the right idea: find out the score before you commit yourselves; I admire you for that. Is that not right Alasdair?

Absolutely Norrie, the same goes for me and all: test the water before you take the fatal fucking leap Ewan.

Norrie was standing up now, brushing the lapels of his jacket and straightening his tie. I'll tell you something else pal, I'm jealous as well, aye, for being able to do that, for having the guts I suppose, I envy that.

You youngsters, you've got it fucking made, Alasdair came in. I tell you: the good job, good wages, that flat you done up, and a tasty fucking bird waiting there for you.

And not just that, she's a fine lassie as well, fine to get on with, said Norrie.

Aye, I'm jealous and all, said Alasdair, And do you ken why? I'll tell you: because you've fucking cracked it you wee toe-rag, you've cracked the bugger! I mean not that I'm not happy myself, with what I've got myself like, but still and all, you're a jammy young fucker right enough.

Aye aye aye, said Ewan, Don't lose the head though lads, I mean there's disadvantages as well you ken.

Alasdair stood with his legs apart, wagged a finger at Ewan. Well there's disadvantages in everything son, you'll find that out.

Ewan looked at him over the rim of his glass as he finished his lager. That's life pal: as you'll find out some day.

Aye thanks, but when I need some lessons about life I doubt I'll be coming to you for them! Twenty years with the water board! What do you know about the North Sea for instance? Fuck all! Alasdair went to speak, but Ewan kept on. I mean two weeks on is bad enough, but the three weeks off is fucking worse: boring! It would drive you mental! And living with somebody, I mean it's not exactly a bed of fucking roses, ken?

Aye, but neither's being married to someone, said Alasdair.

But nocunt's saying it is! said Ewan, That's the whole fucking point!

It's a bed of thistles if anything, said Alasdair.

Oh for fuck's sake . . . ! Ewan cracked his empty glass down on the window-sill at Alasdair's shoulder.

Oi, hold on a minute lads, hold on! Ewan and Alasdair turned to look at Norrie standing there. Do us a favour lads: no punch-ups on the wedding day, eh?

It's this cunt here and his smart fucking comments! He's done nothing but spout shite since I came in that door . . .

Ewan! Shut the fuck up! And Alasdair, you can it and all!

Ach . . . Alasdair sighed, rubbed his beard and his face with both hands. Sorry Norrie. And sorry Ewan, if I was going on a bit and that . . .

Ewan shrugged, said quietly, Sorry Norrie.

Norrie shook his head. Anyway, it's time you and me were out of here Al. He looked at his watch. The car'll be here for me and Margaret just the now, and there's a few folk I want to say cheerio to and that.

Aye, I suppose, said Alasdair. He was checking his reflection in the dark glass of the storeroom window. Well I'm ready, he said, and rifted.

Well . . . Ewan looked around the room. There were piles of chairs, and nothing else. The wee painted-shut window, the door to the corridor through which there were occasional noises of running feet, music, and folk talking and laughing. And the other door. Various bits of the highland outfits Norrie and Alasdair had been wearing for the wedding were scattered about the floor, and they were beginning to separate these out and put them into their bags. Well, enjoy it, said Ewan.

Ho ho ho, said Alasdair.

Married life, said Ewan.

Norrie had picked up his sporran and was winding the chain and leather belt around it. He grinned up at Ewan: Don't worry about me, I . . . He stopped, banged his forehead with the palm of a hand. Jesus, that was close. He unwound the belt, opened the sporran, and took out a small flask of dark wood and a silvery metal. The old man gave me that. Smart eh? He placed the sporran back on top of the folded kilt, the skean-dhu beside it, then zipped up the hold-all. He stood up. Actually Ewan, you could do me a favour here pal.

Aye, sure. What like?

Margaret doesn't ken about this, my da just slipped it to me up at the house. She doesn't want me drinking overmuch the day, see?

Secrets already, said Alasdair.

Norrie raised his eyebrows slightly at Ewan, carried on talking. So I don't want to take it with me, and I can hardly give it back to the old man, so eh, would you look after it for me? You'd have to be careful with it like . . .

No bother, sure Norrie, I'll be real careful. I could zip it up in my inside pocket till I got home, then I'd just leave it there someplace safe till you got back.

Just the ticket. Norrie clapped Ewan on the shoulder, giving him the flask with the other hand. He winked, and said in a quiet voice, And it's half-full still of the old Scotmid Deluxe. I won't be needing that back.

Fuck's sake, hih, thanks.

Just be careful with it eh?

No worries, Norrie, I'll guard it with my life.

I wouldn't go that far, said Alasdair, It's not Glenmorangie or anything. He opened the door.

Well that's us off, said Norrie, See you in ten days then.

Right, eh, as I say, all the best, and to Margaret and all. And I'll see you when you get back. They shook hands. Alasdair was already out in the corridor, making cheeooching noises and pretending to dance with a passing waitress.

Are you coming out the now too?

Eh, no, I'll be out in a minute.

It's just I'll have to shut the door now. My da's going to pick up the bags of gear afore he leaves, take it back to the hire shop for us the morn. I wouldn't want it nicked before he comes for it.

I'll keep an eye on it the now, and then when I leave I'll put the lights off and make sure the door's shut, okay? I'll just have a few minutes' peace afore I return to the fray though.

Come on Norman! Here comes the bride! Alasdair was shouting out in the corridor.

Norrie said to Ewan quietly, He's too pished to be trusted with remembering the flask or the kilts or fuck all.

Aye! It's a good job you got the ring off him before he got wired in to the bevvy!

Norrieman!

Norrie seemed to be yanked from behind, and he disappeared out the door, slamming it shut behind him. There was cheering out in the corridor. Ewan stood by the door for a minute, but nobody opened it or came in, and soon the noise outside was subsiding, and the storeroom was quiet. Ewan sighed, patted the breast of his jacket which was bulging with the flask in the inside pocket. He walked across to the other door, opened it, and stuck his head through: there was a short passage and then a fire-escape door, presumably to the outside world, the back of the hall somewhere. He let the door shut, paced across the storeroom and turned the knob in the other door. But he didn't pull the door open, just held the knob for a few seconds, stood there, eyes on his hand, gripping. Then he loosened his fingers. He stepped back into the centre of the room, swivelled round, then crossed to the other door in two strides, pushed it open and walked into the passageway.

After the storeroom door swung shut behind him, it was almost dark, the only light coming from an illuminated sign saying EMERGENCY EXIT at the end of the passageway. He examined the door under the sign: it didn't seem to be fitted with an alarm at all, so opening it wouldn't bring half the population of the hall screaming after him. And to be out in the quiet of the night . . . There was a metal bar across the door which would pull in the bolts at the top and bottom when pushed: he gave the bar a shove; it sprung back; he shoved it again, maintaining the pressure this time, till the door opened slowly out the way, the bottom bolt grating across the concrete floor.

There was a short ramp down to a chuckie path which led away to the right, along the length of the building and onto the main street of the village. There were some small windows high up in the wall above the path, probably from the kitchen, where the caterers had heated up the grub and the bar-staff were washing their empties; there was some light spilling out of these onto the path and the wall that divided it from the fields beyond, and occasional noises of clinking glasses or raised voices, but apart from that there was silence, and nobody and nothing in sight.

Ewan closed the door almost to, leaving it a wee bit open with the bottom bolt still scraping the ramp and not sliding on into its securing plate.

He went down the ramp and leant with his elbows on the wall. He looked over the dark fields, the black hills in the distance, and the clear sky streaming with stars. He sighed. There were sounds floating over the roof of the hall now, from the parking space in front of the main entrance: shouts, laughter, cheering, a car revving up and driving off through the village and away. He sighed again, reached inside his jacket, and took out Norrie's flask; he examined the polished wood and the engraved lines on the metal, then screwed off the top and stood up to pour some whisky down his throat.

Is this a private party or can anyone join in?

He turned. There was a woman standing in the doorway, or a girl maybe. The light was behind her, her head was back; she breathed out smoke, lifted a cigarette to her lips.

Well are you going to give me a drink then? Or are you waiting for me to offer you a drag? She held out the fag.

No, I don't smoke.

She laughed. Neither do I! As far as my ma's concerned anyway. That's how I'm out here, see? What a carry-on! God, you'd think I was ten the way she keeps pulling me up.

Ewan drank some whisky, looking at her. She was one of the bridesmaids, the one with the basket of lucky messages. She was wearing a long dress of some shiny material; it left her shoulders bare and her neck and the beginnings of her breasts. He passed the flask over to her. She took a draw on her fag, then tipped her head back, put the neck of the flask to her mouth, and took several swallows of whisky.

What age are you anyway? he said, taking the flask back, and screwing the top on.

She wiped her mouth. Old enough.

Oh, like that is it? he said. Sneaking about following innocent young men into dark alleys so you can pounce and have your wicked way with them?

She blew smoke out through her nose. Chance would be a fine thing. All the men here are somebody else's. Either that or over sixty. She threw her fag down onto the path.

And have you not got, eh . . .

Nah. There was a guy, but we split up, he was a right prick. Except he wasn't, if you know what I mean. A boring bastard in fact, always sweating over his homework. Jesus. She shook her head. Christ I could do with another fag, have you got one?

I told you I don't.

I'm gasping.

So am I.

She looked at him. You should try it you ken, it tastes good. See. She lifted her arm and held out her hand, extending the first and second fingers, the ones she'd been holding her fag with. Ewan moved his head forward slightly, sniffed her fingers, then moved again, took her fingers into his mouth, closed his lips round them. Immediately she pulled her hand away from his mouth, put it round the back of his neck and pulled his head towards her, at the same time taking a step forward. They were standing up against each other, they started kissing. Ewan put one arm round the back of her shoulders, the other hand down to where her arse would be under the dress. She moved her head about, turning her face, kissing him. After a few seconds they moved back so that he was leaning against her and her back was pressed to the wall.

After a while they broke apart. See some whisky, said the girl.

It's not whisky.

Aye it is.

No it's not, it's Glenmorangie, malt, classy stuff.

I'm impressed! She took a drink, wrinkled her nose. Tastes the same though. She handed the flask to Ewan again. Do I?

Do you what?

Taste the same?

As what? He looked at her. Taste the same as what?

As a girl that doesn't smoke.

He shrugged, took a slug.

As Shareen for instance.

Ewan stopped drinking, put the top back on, slipped the flask into his inside pocket. Shareen does smoke.

No she doesn't.

Aye she does.

No she doesn't, cause her sister's in my class at school and she was always coming in with fags she'd nicked from Shareen, but not any more, cause she gave up after New Year. Am I right?

Fuck me.

Okay.

You're a right wee know-all, eh? Fuck's sake. In Meera's class? Eh, so you'll be . . . sixteen?

Or thereabouts. She smiled.

Christ. Too young to be drinking this stuff anyway. He took the flask out again, swallowed most of what was left of the whisky, all the time looking at her. What did you say back then?

When?

I said fuck me and you said . . . what?

Give us a drink and I'll tell you.

He held out the flask, but when she reached out to take it he snatched it away and grabbed onto her wrist with his free hand. That's not what you said. She made a slight movement of her arm, he tightened his grip. You said okay! I might just have to take you up on that.

She opened her mouth and pouted her lips out, ran her tongue across them. She was looking at him through her eyelashes. He breathed out slowly, relaxed, let go of her wrist and let his arm drop, then circled it in round her waist and pulled her against him.

And what'll Shareen think about all this?

Shareen won't think nothing cause she won't know nothing.

But you'll know.

So?

So you'll feel bad . . . guilty!

He let her go again, took a step back. Look, me and Shareen, we're not fucking married you ken.

You'll look at her and she'll catch your eye, and you'll wonder if she suspects you; you'll be chawing your nails, shitting bricks, she'll go to speak and you'll jump in: I'm sorry Shareen, it wasn't my fault, I was drunk and she led me on . . . And she'll say, I was just going to ask you the time Ewan, but WHAT THE HELL'S ALL THIS?

Ewan took another step back, shaking his head. Look, forget it, eh . . .

There were footsteps, a grating noise, and the door from the hall was pushed open. Jesus, who's that? Ewan raised his arm to shield his eyes from the light that was shining down from the lighted sign just inside.

Och it's only you son. It was Norrie's old man, one hand on the push-bar, the other on the door-frame: he seemed to be holding himself up.

God's sake man, you gave me a scare there! I never heard you coming.

I was just checking Norrie and Alasdair's outfits were all right, and I saw the door was open . . .

Aye, I just thought I'd get some, eh . . . Ewan glanced across at where the girl was standing, in the dark shadow behind the open door.

And then I thought I heard voices you see . . .

She was looking straight into Ewan's eyes, smiling, and she was pulling her dress down, she was yanking the top down over her breasts, they were sticking out, and up at the ends there they were, there were the nipples up at the ends of them.

FUCK'S SAKE, no there's only me here, I must've been talking to myself. He shifted and leant against the edge of the door, directly between Norrie's da and the girl. Just getting a breath of fresh air, you ken. He forced a laugh, pretended to take a big gulp of air.

Aye, clear the head son, clear the head, good idea. I've had one or two myself, but why shouldn't I? It's my son's big day, why should I not have a drink? But I'm not drunk, no!

Quite right, said Ewan, slowly starting to swing the door shut. In fact I think you should have one right now. I mean it's your big day as well: go on, celebrate!

I think that's exactly what I'll do. The old man took his hand from the push-bar and held it out to Ewan. Now can I bring you out anything?

No thanks, nuh.

A wee nip maybe?

No, no, not at all. He was gradually closing the door in Norrie's da's face. I'll just bide here a wee bittie longer, then eh . . . There was a rustling noise behind him, and he said more loudly, I'll maybe see you inside, you can get me one there, okay?

Alright son, fair enough, if you're sure. At last he was leaning off the door-frame and starting to walk backwards up the passageway. If you're sure . . .

Ewan closed the door all but a couple of inches and watched till the old man was opening the storeroom door, then he closed it completely. He turned back to the girl. She was still standing with her back to the wall, and her dress was pulled down almost to her hips; it was all rucked up over her belly, and the top of her white tights was there too. Her arms were folded across her chest.

What the FUCK are you playing at?

She unfolded her arms, stretched them out sideways, then said, You can't go getting a girl all worked up and then just leave her to stew in her own juices.

She put her hands on her hips and pushed them out towards him. He was breathing heavily, he bent over her, both arms around her back, pulled her towards him. He ran his mouth over her breasts, down to her navel, up again onto the breasts; one nipple he took in his mouth, moved his head round and round, trailed with his tongue across to the other one, licked. She was leaning back, she was holding his head in her hands.

Your nipples, he said, They're like raisins.

Don't talk. She pressed his head against her.

It's just . . . I love you.

Don't talk shite, she said.

Quality Control

It was nine o'clock on a Monday morning and Gary Innes was banging on the door of a lock-up garage in North Leith. He stopped knocking after a while and took something out of his back pocket, a letter; he unfolded it and gazed at it for a few moments, then checked his watch and looked again at the notice pinned to the lock-up door. It was a rectangle torn from a corrugated cardboard box, and there was writing on it in red biro: SCOTBOARD SKATEBOARDS.

Gary Innes folded up the letter again and stuck it back in his jeans. He looked around: there was no sign of life anywhere, except for the seagulls circling the flour mill, and a baby crying somewhere in the high-flats that towered overhead. He took a step back from the door as if about to turn and walk away, hesitated, then stepped forward again, raised his right arm and thumped on the door with the end of his fist. This time the door slid open immediately and an elderly woman in a sari was looking out at him.

Eh, hello, he said after a moment, I was beginning to think there was nobody at home there!

The woman shifted to look past him, scanned the empty

parking spaces for a few seconds, then moved back inwards and slid the door to slightly.

My name's Gary Innes, he said quickly, I'm supposed to be starting work here like. Quality controller. See, I got sent by the job centre.

He took the letter out once more, unfolded it, and held it forward for the woman to look at; she flinched and closed the door till there was a gap of only a few inches.

Look, said Gary Innes, Is there a Mr Ghopal here at all? That's the name I was tellt, anyway.

There was silence for a moment, and then the woman nodded her head once, made a pushing motion in the air in front of Gary Innes with the flat of her palm, and, after he had stepped back a pace, she slid the door completely shut.

Almost immediately there was the sound of voices raised inside the lock-up, and the door slid wide open once again.

Gary, Gary: Mr Innes! Come in sir, come right in, and good-morning to you. A middle-aged man in a light-grey suit was standing in the doorway; in his right hand he held a clipboard with a sheaf of various papers attached to it, and in his left was a portable phone.

It's about the job, said Gary Innes. This is the address they gave me, but they said it was a factory, ken? So I wasn't sure if I had the right place.

You have, you have, Mr Innes, said the man. We're starting small, but business is good, virtually booming: soon perhaps we will move to a bigger premises, but for now we are really just a small family concern. But come in, come in, let me show you.

He stepped aside and waved the clipboard towards the innards of the lock-up. Gary Innes walked in, and immediately the door was closed shut behind him.

Are you Mr Ghopal, by the way?

None other, said Mr Ghopal, striding towards the back of the lock-up, Absolutely none other. Now if you would follow me through here . . . Mr Ghopal drew aside a curtain and motioned for Gary Innes to enter the dimly lit area beyond. Here, sitting around a long trestle table, were half a dozen women of various ages, including the one that had originally come to the garage door. None of them looked up as Gary Innes and Mr Ghopal entered the workshop area, they were all working quickly assembling skateboards: every few seconds one of the women would turn and lean back to pick a board from one of the large cases which were scattered about the floor, then they would take two sets of wheels from another box and screw these onto the board; finally, from a pile in the middle of the table, they took a few multi-coloured paper stickers, peeled off the backing, and stuck a couple of them onto the top of the board and another one on the bottom. These stickers said things like: SURF-BUSTER, MEGA-RIDE-MASTER, and KILLER-BOARD.

When the ladies have finished the assembly process on a reasonable number of skateboards, said Mr Ghopal, One of them stops assembling and starts packing. Usually we put two dozen in a carton and then we send them out to the shops, where they sell for only two pounds fifty, which is a very competitive price. So business is good. But it could be better business even if I could have someone packing full-time, and therefore none of the ladies would have to stop assembling at all, you see? You!

But I was told quality controller, said Gary Innes, I was to get some kind of training in that line, ken?

Absolutely, Mr Innes, absolutely, said Mr Ghopal, I was just coming to that part of the job description. Come with me please.

Gary Innes followed Mr Ghopal down to the far end of the lock-up, where the light from the bulb over the trestle table hardly reached. In one corner was a stack of skateboards, nearly as high as the ceiling, and in the other corner was a pile of large cardboard boxes, folded flat. In between these two piles there was an area of concrete floor, empty apart from two bricks lying in the middle of it.

Your job is this, said Mr Ghopal. You open up a carton, folding the flaps in at the bottom for sturdiness, then you fill the box up with twenty-four skateboards and fold the flaps over on top.

But . . .

But you are to be trained as a quality controller, exactly Mr Innes, that is what we are getting paid by the MSC gentlemen to employ you as, and that is what you shall do. Now, after you take the boards from that pile, but before you place them in the boxes, I want you to balance each board on those two bricks there, one brick at each end so that the wheels are slightly off the floor, you see? Now you jump up, stand on the board on the bricks: if nothing happens then fine, you put the board in the box; if by any chance you come across one or two that crack or even break, then put them to one side, and we'll have the ladies take off the wheels again for re-use, okay?

Eh, aye, I suppose so. Gary Innes rubbed his forehead. That's it, is it?

Meanwhile Mr Innes, meanwhile. In the future, who knows what? But for now we are just a cottage industry, okay, strictly hand-built. He looked at his watch. Anyway, now I must leave you: I have some calls to make, and this thing doesn't work in here, with those high-rises above us and all you know. So goodbye! I will be seeing you again before the lunch break, and we can see how you are getting on then . . .

Mr Ghopal walked away, passed the ladies at the table, turned and waved as he came to the curtain, then disappeared behind it. A few seconds later there was the sound of the door sliding open and then shut again.

Quality Control

Gary Innes took a bright blue skateboard down off the pile, balanced it on top of the two bricks, and stepped up onto it, right foot first, then left. There was a splintering noise, and the board broke in two under him. He looked across at the women, but none of them raised her head to glance in his direction. Indian pop music was now playing quietly from a radio somewhere. He shrugged, picked up the pieces of the broken board, and threw them away to one side. The next skateboard he took down off the pile was fluorescent green; he placed it carefully on top of the two bricks, checked it wasn't off-balance or wobbling at all, then stepped up onto it, first one foot, then both. There was a sharp crack, then a slow splintering noise . . .

Oh shite, said Gary Innes.

Two and a bit hours later, there was the sound of the front door being opened, and then Mr Ghopal appeared through the curtain. He said a few words to the women, one or two of them nodding and smiling in reply, the others not looking up from their work, and then he walked down to the dark end where Gary Innes was taking another skateboard off the pile, which was about half as high as when Mr Ghopal left. As Mr Ghopal approached, Gary Innes placed the board on the bricks, stepped onto it, and the board broke in two.

Damn and blast! said Mr Ghopal. A bloody dud!

Gary Innes said nothing, but picked up the pieces and threw them away to the far side, on top of a heap of about fifty broken boards.

Oh my God, what have you done? shouted Mr Ghopal.

Aye, there's been quite a few failures, said Gary Innes.

Quite a few! said Mr Ghopal. How many cartons have you filled with good ones exactly?

Four, said Gary Innes.

Ah, so you've packed four boxes have you? said Mr Ghopal, slightly less loudly.

Eh, no, said Gary Innes, I've packed the four good boards into that box there. All the rest, eh, failed quality control.

Mr Ghopal stared at Gary Innes for a few seconds, turned his back on him, and marched up past the women to the far end of the workshop. There, he faced the wall, gave several loud shouts, then stood silent for some moments. Finally he turned, walked back down to where Gary Innes was standing, and spoke in a very low voice.

You're fired, said Mr Ghopal.

He pointed towards the gap in the curtain, but Gary Innes was already moving. It was eleven-thirty on a Monday morning and Gary Innes was walking out of a lock-up garage in North Leith.

Hours of Darkness

He came striding out of the north just as darkness was falling. Away to his right dark fields stretched out, black furrows creased across the red earth, boulders tumbled in by the dykesides, gangs of crows and gulls picking over the broken ground. A step to his left the cliffs plunged down to rocky coves scattered with cracked slabs split from the cliff-face, and already deep in shadow. From time to time there was the sound of a tractor inland, and always the blattering of the sea below, beating on the cliff-foot, raking through the pebblebanks.

He walked on. The grass on the heuch-head was short and had a spring to it, and his boots made no sound as they fell. It was good there was no vegetation to kick through or trip over, but still he had to watch out for sudden incuttings of the cliff and tummocks of bracken or gorseroot that could catch his feet.

A few yards ahead an empty fertiliser bag lay across his path, weighted down by a puddle of water and black ooze. He slowed down and stepped forward carefully, then raised the landward edge of the bag with the toe of his boot. The puddle ran away into the grass, leaving a circle of sooty particles on the weathered plastic, and immediately the bag began to stir in the faint uprise off the cliff. He lifted his boot another few inches and the bag leant up into the air then slid off his foot towards the cliff-edge; for a second it rested there, then slipped out into nothingness, hung momentarily, then folded in on itself and fell quickly towards the sea. It was lost in the darkness long before it reached the bottom.

The ground was rising again in front of him, steadily but quite steeply, and his breathing was getting heavier; he hooked his thumbs into the shoulderstraps of his backpack and kept up the pace. The sun was well down behind the hills in the west. Skeins of high cloud were running in from the same direction, their bellies rodden, carrying over the hills and moving quickly down the length of the howe and towards the sea. If they kept coming and spread and thickened, and if low cover followed, some of the day's heat might be retained. Otherwise it was set for a chilly night out. But if the cloud did come, the last of the light would go quickly. He had to ignore the pain in his feet and keep moving while he could still see: he had to get off the cliff-top before it was total darkness.

After a time, the cliff swung up and out into a headland with some kind of cairn or triangulation point on top. He avoided the steep climb and walked on in the lee of the dykes and fences that marked the end of the farmlands, eyes on the ground in front of him. Sudden loud birdnoise made him raise his head and scan the nearest park. Two hoodies had turned on a gull and were jabbing for its eyes with their beaks, lifting their broad dark wings and louping around as they did so, blocking the gull from taking off. As he watched, the gull seemed to give up the struggle, stopped flapping and mewling, and cowked a stream of stuff out of its open maw. One of the hoodies immediately went for the spewings, caught them up in its black neb and swallowed with jerking movements of its swack feathered neck. The other crow seemed not to have seen what the gull had done, and continued attacking it, stabbing with its thick parted beak, beating its wings, screaming and cawing loudly.

He watched for a few seconds, then lifted his hands clear of the straps and brought them together in a sharp clap, at the same time pursing his lips and whistling a piercing high note. The gull whipped its head round, and as it looked at him the hoodie struck it hard on the side of the skull just behind the eye. The gull staggered sideways, then lifted a wing and seemed about to steady itself, when the crow struck again and the white bird was tipped over a dreel into the deep furrow that separated two ploughed rigs in the park. Immediately, both crows were onto it.

A few minutes later he was going downhill towards the lights of the village. There weren't many lights, only half a dozen streetlamps amongst the buildings down near the water and a few more zigzagging up the steep hill at the head of the bay. Under each of the hillside lights a small piece of narrow road was visible, tacking in angles up the slope, climbing steeply. He walked on, keeping his eyes on his feet most of the time, though the path was now fairly well trodden and wide, and the drop from the cliff-top to the dark water below was lessening all the time. He paused, looked ahead, then went on down the long steady descent at an even pace, till the path dropped away sharply in front of him in a slide of mud and rocks that tumbled down to a small pebble beach. At the far end of the beach was a jetty, with a broad open area of flat ground at the head of it, then the village. He paused again and looked across to the lights. The strange thing was how few house-lights there were: only three or four lighted windows could be made out amongst the black shapes of the houses; most of the village was in darkness.

As he stood at the pathfoot, the sound of a fast-moving car rose over the sifting of the waves, then died down, then got louder again. The car slowed, changed to a lower gear; now his eye was drawn to the road at the bayhead by headlights at the top of the hill. The lights suddenly dived, and the car changed gear again and started down the brae, still travelling fast. After a few seconds, there was a screeling of tyres, and the lights swung round at a sharp angle and were pointing towards the far side of the bay. A couple of seconds later and the car switchbacked again, the lights catching his eyes. He looked down, studied the slide in front of him, then scrambled quickly downwards across the scree and started walking along the beach.

The sound of the car's motor was hidden by his boots crinching through the mowrie, but half-way along the beach three blasts on a carhorn sounded out, and shortly afterwards the headlights emerged from the seaward side of the village, wove across the open ground, then disappeared. He carried on walking.

The far end of the beach was marked by a grassy rise. He walked up and over this, and found himself at the start of the village. One straight street led away in front of him, low houses with small windows lined along each side, shacked up against each other, their doors opening right onto the roadway. He headed down the middle of the street, his breathing evening out after the trachle across the beach. There were no cars about, not even parked, and at this end of the village there were no streetlamps at all; it was almost pitch-dark here, down in the hollow of the bay. Fifty yards ahead, though, the road seemed to open out, and there were lights on there.

It was the village square. Directly opposite the street he'd come along was a small hotel, windows beaming out yellow light; a few cars and a lorry were standing in the middle of the square, and there was a post-box set into a white-harled wall. An opening on the left headed towards the jetty and the sea, and one on the right was the road that led to the hillclimb at the bayhead. There were a couple more modern-looking houses up in that direction with lights on, or the telly flickering through uncurtained windows. But still there was no one to be seen.

He crossed the square and went into the porch of the hotel, scrubbed his boots on a mat there, and unslung his pack. There were burrs of gorse and grass-ears stuck to the shanks of his breeks, and patches of reddish mud dried on his knees; he bent down and brushed at the mud, knocked the worst of the burrs off, then straightened up, wiped his hands under the arms of his jersey, and opened the door marked BAR.

He stepped in. There was a slight pause in the conversation, but it didn't stop: one guy, at the end of the bar, was telling a funny story, and two others were laughing at it and adding comments of their own. The three of them had glanced over as the walker entered, but turned back to their drinks and their yarn almost immediately. In two steps he was leaning on the bar. There was no one behind it. A door at one end led to some kind of unlit backshop, but nobody came through it. He moved along the bar and parked himself on a high stool there, letting his pack drop to the floor by the bar footrail. He eased his shoulders slowly up, back, down, and forward to rest again; he circled his head round, loosening his neck; he stretched his arms up in the air, arching his back at the same time. Then he sat still: upright on the stool, hands flat on the edge of the bar, feet twitching occasionally in their heavy boots as they rested on the footrail.

The storyteller was talking louder, getting to the end of his tale. Another thing about New Zealand, he said, See what this guy tells me? He says the burns are stappit full of salmon – fairly hoaching with the buggers! – and you can hardly get moved through the country for the grouse and, eh, kiwis aneath your feet!

So you can just reach out and pick them like tatties, said one of the listeners.

The storyteller ignored him, except for forcing a wider grin and raising his voice. And see what this boy says? he went on. See all these beasties? Well you can just go out with your gun and shoot as much as you like. No gamie bastards or nothing! Anything you see, the old twelve-bore, bang bang, you don't need nobugger's permission. It's a hell of a place New Zealand, he said, Fairly puts Scotland in the shade. Christ aye, I said to him. Permission? You need permission to pish on a dyke in Scotland!

The storyteller laughed, and half a second later the others joined in. One of them repeated the punchline, shaking his head. After a few moments' laughter, the storyteller leant forward on his elbows, still chuckling to himself, and said loudly down the length of the bar, Are you needing a drink son?

Eh, aye, a pint, said the walker. I'm needing a pint.

Ha! The storyteller laughed again. He had a fat neck and face, and when he laughed his jowly cheeks vibrated. Hold on a minutie, he said, then slid backwards off his stool, walked over to a door marked PRIVATE at the far end of the room, and went out. There was the sound of heavy footsteps treading up a flight of stairs.

One of the storyteller's friends cleared his throat. Aye man, he said, and nodded down the bar. He had a baseball cap on, and the peak of the cap cast a band of shadow across his eyes.

Eh, hello . . .

The other man nodded too, then looked away, shaking his head. Permission to pish, he said quietly. What a load of shite!

Christ I ken, said the one in the cap. No one tells me when to pish or not! He's in a world of his own, that bugger.

The other one pulled a fag out of a pack lying in front of him on the bar. He nipped one end of it between the nails of his thumb and forefinger, ripped the filter off and flicked it to the floor. He lit up, smoked hard for half a minute with his head thrown back, then lowered his gaze, looked down the length of the bar and said, You ever been to New Zealand son?

The walker looked up. Me? No, I've never been anywhere.

The smoker inhaled, narrowed his eyes, and exhaled. You must've been somewhere, he said. I mean you're not from round here, are you?

Not exactly, said the walker, But not far away. Not New Zealand anyway!

The smoker rested his fag on the edge of the whisky ashtray, stared at it for a second, then snatched it up and pointed down the length of the bar with it, pincing it like a dart. I'll tell you something for nothing, he said loudly. Fat Boy's never been there either!

He's a lying bastard, the one in the cap said.

Eh . . . but surely he never said he'd been himself? Was it not some guy he'd met who was saying all that stuff?

The smoker jabbed the air with his fag and snorted, Ach, that's a load of shite as well. Who would talk to him?

He's a lying bastard. He doesn't ken fucking anybody.

Fat arse and a big mouth, that's him. He kens fuck all about New Zealand, but anything to run this place down . . . Christ! The smoker leant to one side for a moment and spat on the floor. He straightened up. Not an ounce of patrioticness in his whole fat fucking body! he said.

A pause.

It's nothing to do with me, said the walker.

It might be, the one in the cap said quickly. Just don't believe everything he tells you, that's all.

There was the sound of footsteps descending the private stair.

That'll be Fat Boy now, said the smoker. Watch this: ten to one he spouts some shite about shagging the barmaid up in her room . . .

The door opened and the storyteller walked in. He clapped his hands together. Now then, he said. He stepped round the back of his two friends and, lifting the hatch, squeezed in behind the bar. The lady of the house is busy at the moment, he said, and, half-turning to his friends, added, Getting her knickers on!

The two of them laughed, not meeting his eye, then the smoker lifted his head, eyebrows raised, and said, See?

See what? said the storyteller, looking round at his friends, frowning, then quickly back.

The walker shrugged.

I was just telling the boy that Anne would likely be busy, said the smoker.

She's aye busy when you're needing a fucking drink, said the one in the cap.

Oh aye. The storyteller laughed, a frown still on his face. Is that right? he said suddenly, leaning over the bar.

Eh . . . aye, that's what we were talking about, said the walker, looking into the frowning jowly face.

The storyteller drew himself up, laughing quietly. It's just I wouldn't like to think you were talking about me behind my back.

The one in the cap whispered something to the smoker.

The storyteller whipped his head round. What was that?

The two of them stared at him. Nobody moved. Eventually the one in the cap let out a long loud sigh and said, Nothing, nothing. Fuck all.

The storyteller stared at him.

The walker coughed, turned it into a clearing of the throat.

Christ, will you look at that. The smoker pointed down the bar. The laddie's parching for a drink.

That's just what I was fucking saying: empty glasses man! The one in the cap lifted his empty pint tumbler and shook it in the direction of the man behind the bar. Are you going to serve us or what, eh?

The storyteller clapped his hands together again, unwrinkled his forehead and said, Aye aye, I'll pull them the now till Anne gets down, no bother. But I'll get our visitor first, okay lads? Hospifuckingtality, ken? He turned away from his friends. Now, what'll it be pal?

Well, I was thinking actually . . .

The fat man had scooped a glass up from under the bar-top and was tossing it up in the air, catching it again as it spun down past his chest. He grinned. What were you thinking?

I was thinking time was getting on, ken, and I was actually needing to get going fairly soon. The walker coughed again, scanned the back of the bar. So maybe I'll just have a bit of grub, and then head off. Whatever you've got . . .

The storyteller placed the glass down on the bar and looked along at his friends. The smoker blew out a cloud of smoke, and the other one pushed his cap to the back of his head, twitching his eyebrows and blinking.

So, eh, have you got any food? I mean do you ken if there is any? A pie maybe? Or a bridie?

Silence.

I was looking around for one of those heated cabinets with the grub in it, the walker went on, Or a toastie machine or something. I'm wasting away here!

The storyteller had sat down on a seat behind the bar. He was shaking his head, cheeks puffed out and wobbling. Then he said, No, you're out of luck. There's nothing. They don't do food at this time of year.

What, nothing at all? Are you sure?

The storyteller shook his head again, sighed, and looked down at his feet.

Here, said the smoker from the end of the bar, There is pickled eggs . . .

The storyteller looked up, eyes half-closed, and gazed into space for a moment. Aye, he said slowly, Pickled eggs . . . He got to his feet and went ben the backshop.

And nuts! called the one in the cap, There's crisps and nuts as well! He laughed, and the smoker joined in. Christ aye, he continued, There's no need to go hungry in this day and age.

The storyteller stuck his head through from the backshop, grinning. Success on a plate! he said, and held out a big glass jar with half a dozen eggs sloshing about in a few inches of cloudy vinegar. So, how many'll you have son?

I think, eh, two; I reckon I'd manage two. Well, how much are they?

They're twenty-five pence, said the smoker.

Aye, that's about it. So fifty in total, eh? The storyteller slid the jar across the bar-top. I'll tell you what: choose your own. How's that for service? Whichever ones you like.

Right. Ehm. Have you got a fork or a spoon or something?

Oh . . . The storyteller scratched his cheek. Hold on a minute. He disappeared into the backshop but came back through again straight away. There might be something through there, he said, But it's too dark to see: fucking light's gone.

There could be anything through there, said the one in the cap. I mean we've only your word that Anne's upstairs.

The storyteller frowned. What are you getting at?

Ah well, said the smoker, half-smiling and winking at the walker, Maybe you're keeping her tied to a bed of beer-kegs through the back and giving her a sly poke every time you nip through there.

Aye man, we all ken how she's daft for you: you've tellt us often enough!

The two friends laughed loudly. The storyteller took a step towards them, then stopped, rubbing the palms of his hands up and down the flanks of his thighs. His big cheeks were blotched with red. Ha! Pair of jokers! he said, forcing a laugh, then turned back to the walker, clapped his hands and cried, A fork!

Well I need something, said the walker, not looking down the bar. I mean . . . He lifted the jar up to eye level and looked at the eggs bobbling about in the vinegar.

Ah-ha! said the storyteller, Bright idea! He turned his back and started rummaging through some stuff on the shelf under the gantry: matches, fags, dart-flights and other pub gear. After a few moments he turned round. Ah-ha! he said again. He unscrewed the top from a small plastic tube he'd picked up, held it six inches above the bar-top, and shook. Several dozen cocktail sticks tumbled out and fell in a pile on the bar. That'll do you pal, eh? he said, beaming.

Aye. Great. The walker pulled one of the sticks out of the heap, examined it for a second, then took the lid off the jar, dived his hand in and speared one of the eggs. Vinegar ran down the back of his hand and up his sleeve as he lifted out the egg. He let it drip for a moment, then stuck the whole thing into his mouth, pursing his lips around the cocktail stick as he pulled it out. He chewed. Then he picked out another egg and ate it in the same way. This time it took longer to chew the mouthful. Eventually he wiped the back of his dry hand across his lips, reached into his pocket, and came out with a handful of coins. Fifty pence you said?

The storyteller was screwing the lid back on the egg jar. Ach forget it, he said. The bastards are out of date anyway.

Outside, it was even darker than before. As he stepped from the porch, a streetlamp on the far side of the square flickered and went off. He swung the rucksack up onto his back and walked out.

There was still no one about and no cars moving, so he walked slowly across the roadway into the middle of the square then stopped and looked up at the surrounding buildings. A lot of the walls seemed to have been harled recently, or at least freshly painted, and the roofs of the buildings had bright red pantiles in snug rows, none missing or cracked, no moss growth, no soot and water stains. But the buildings weren't modern, they were old, really old-looking, with small narrow windows and low doors, and all of the angles seeming not quite straight. And the corners of everything – windows, doorways, steps, gables – were rounded, like they'd been worn down by years and years of salt wind off the sea, or maybe rounded up by years and years of painting and patching. But all the buildings were empty: no lights on inside, no curtains in the windows, no names on the doors . . .

In the middle of the seaward side of the square was a tall thin tower with a pointed roof and a clockface three-quarters of the way up; there was only one hand on the clock, and it was hanging straight down, as if it was about to fall off and spear down any minute. On each side of the tower was a small one-storey building with bars on the windows and fresh white harling on the walls. The two buildings leant into the base of the tower as if they were buttressing it up, or maybe as if they needed to lean on it for support. Also joined to the tower was a set of stairs that stuck straight out into the square and led up to a small round-topped door let into the wall at first-floor level. Above the door was a notice of some kind, a plaque maybe, stuck onto or carved into the wall: there was writing on it, and a group of symbols.

He crossed over towards the tower and started to climb the steps. They were very worn in the middle, trodden down to half their original height, and he stumbled over one of them in the dark; the sound of his boot scuffing on the worn stone then thudding on the step below echoed round the square for a second, then quickly faded away and was covered by the noise of the moving sea drifting up the narrow street from the shore. He gritted his teeth, and carefully carried on up.

The round-topped door looked old and thick; black iron diamonds studded into the dark wood. He stood on the top step and looked at the door for a second, then reached out and put his hand through a ring of iron that stuck out of the door at waist height. He moved his hand, first one way then the other, feeling for give, then grasped the ring with both hands and twisted it clockwise. From the other side of the door came a rattling, grating noise. He put his shoulder against the door and shoved. Nothing happened. He twisted at the handle again, first clockwise, then the other way, all the time shoving at the door with the whole of the side of his body. There was a slow rasping sound, two pieces of rusty metal dragging against each other, but the door didn't budge; and now the iron studs were pressing into the flesh on his shoulder and arm and hip, digging through his clothes and pressing sharp edges into his body. He stopped shoving, leant away from the door, breathing heavily, then took a step backwards onto the next stair down. Shit, he said. He was getting his breath back now. After a few seconds more, he lifted his head and gazed at the carving on the wall above the door.

The stone panel was worn and crumbling, but he could make out a coat of arms there: three swans sailing along in a triangular formation with a big five-legged star in the middle. On a separate upper panel of the carving was an inscription. This was worn too, like the stone was slowly flowing in and filling the incised letters, and he had to stare for a long time, moving his head to catch the light from the streetlamps around the square. Eventually, he worked out what it said:

THIS FABRIC WAS BUILT
BY EARL JAMES BRAIDON
AND TOWN, FOR CRIBBING
OF VICE AND SERVICE
TO CROWN: 1593 A.D.

He stared at the carving for a while, then said aloud to himself, For cribbing of vice. Town and crown. He frowned. Cribbing . . .

A crash, a loud crash behind him, and angry shouting following: instantly he was crouching down and hugging in to the shadow of the wall up the stairside. More loud bursts of shouting across the square. He slowly shuffled round on his hunkers till he was facing out the way. In front of the hotel, some kind of scuffle was going on. The fat storyteller was standing in the road, swaying, looking back at the door into the hotel porch, which was being blocked by his friends. Bright lights had been switched on inside the porch, and the two of them were cut out in sharp black silhouette as they stood there, motionless, while the storyteller stottered in front of them, shouting in short angry blurts and shaking his fists at them in between. The storyteller shouted again, waving a hand towards the upper storey of the hotel, where one window was lit. One of the men on the steps, the one in the cap, said something in reply, jerking his thumb at his chest as he spoke, then the fat man made a run up the steps, dived between the two of them and lunged at the hotel door. In an instant the others had grabbed the sleeve of his jacket and his hair, and were pulling him away from the door back level with themselves. Then the one in the cap shoved him in the chest and the smoker struck the side of his face, and the fat man tumbled backwards down the short flight of steps and fell onto his back on the roadway. He lay still. For a few seconds his friends looked down at him, then one of them turned and went in the hotel door. The other followed. The fat man lay on the road.

The stone of the tower steps was cold, and now there was a dampness as well, seeping through to his skin. Slowly the walker got to his feet, looking all the time at the body lying on the road across the square. It wasn't moving at all. Oh shit, he said again. Poor bastard.

Then the fat man moved. He raised his left arm into the air directly above him, then his right, held them there for a second wiggling his fingers, then brought both hands down behind his head. He started to shout again, lying in the road, head pillowed from the cobbles by his hands. I'm . . . not . . . worried, he shouted. Ha! Ha! Ha! He fell silent.

Suddenly the fat man jumped to his feet and started walking quickly towards the tower steps, shouting as he came, FUCK YOU! I'LL FUCKING KILL YOU! His voice was almost screeching. It echoed round the square. The walker watched, backed against the studded door, as the fat man strode towards the tower. YOU'RE FUCKING DEAD! FUCK HER! YOU'RE ALL WASTED, YOU FUCKERS! Ten yards from the foot of the stairs he stumbled, came on more slowly for a few steps, then stopped altogether. For a moment he just stood there, then ground his head round over his shoulder to look back the way he'd come. He looked to the front again. He shook his head. He seemed to be chuckling to himself. You stupid bastard, he said in a quiet voice, then chuckled some more. It's a joke! It doesn't worry me, he said, then turned on the spot and walked quickly off across the square, passing the hotel without a glance, staring straight ahead, walking swiftly across the square and disappearing up the road that led to the hillclimb. In half a minute the echoes of his footsteps had faded away completely.

The light in the hotel porch went off. A few seconds later the light in the upstairs room went off too. There were no other lit windows in the square, and there was no one going about: from the top of the tower stairs the square looked big and empty, its corners lit by streetlamps but the buildings inbetween dark and the central area dark too. The walker went down the steps, turned left then left again into the narrow street that led to the sea.

He was walking quickly, keen to get away from the square, and he headed straight down the middle of the road, ignoring the narrow pavements in by the low windows and doors of the houses. But there was something about those windows . . . He steered in to the side of the road for a minute, walking in the gutter, staring at the housefronts as he passed. He looked to the front again, frowning, keeping moving. Then he stopped. He stepped sideways onto the pavement, then half-turned and stood gazing at the nearest window. After a moment he shook his head, bent forward from the waist and gazed at the window from a foot away. Suddenly he straightened up, laughed, and said, For God's sake! He reached out and knocked on the window-pane with his knuckles: there was a dull wooden thud. He laughed again, and slowly turned to look up and down the shadowy street. It was clear now, obvious once you knew. None of the windows really were windows: they were all boarded up. Instead of frames and glass in the window-holes, black-painted boards had been slotted it, then thin white lines marked on, one down the middle and two crossways, so now – on a gloomy dark night, from the corner of an eye, or with a straight look even till you knew – they really looked like real old windows. He laughed. It was typical, typical clever stupidity: service to crown!

He started walking again, back in the roadway, striding along. He was heading for the darkness ahead, beyond the endhouses, where the sea was moving against the shore.

*

At first it seemed there was nothing but darkness in front of him. He stopped. After a few moments he was starting to make things out: some of the light from the village streetlamps carried this far, and several tall thin objects in the foreground were faintly lit by it, less dark than the total darkness between them. There were no stars, no moon; the cloud had come over fast and was lying very low: his footsteps had been dull as he walked the length of the street towards the shore, deadened before they could echo back off the freshly harled walls and the boarded windows. Now he was walking on grass, short grass over flat even ground: a kind of links between the houses and the sea. The sound of the sea was deadened too: there was no crashing of breakers or rattling of battered pebble shoals, just the thud of lumps of water landing on wet sand and stone, weights of water heaving up then thumping down on the sodden shore.

He walked forward slowly through the damp, heavy air. After a couple of steps a pole loomed up directly in front of him, tufts of reedy grass around its base, its top stretching up into the darkness further than he could see. He stretched an arm out and moved towards it, a step, then another step. His thumb hit wet wood and he grasped it, the pole, half-circled it with his fingers. His grip slipping on the greasy wood, he swung his weight half round the pole and looked back the way he'd just come. The village seemed brightly lit now, though there were still only the few streetlamps in the square and a scattering of others through the village, mostly towards the hill end. But compared to what his eyes had got used to, the pitch-darkness where he was heading, the village looked very well lit.

He completed his circle about the pole then let his fingers slide from round it and walked on into the dark. It was really deep black now, he couldn't see a thing: he shouldn't've let himself look back at the village lights. But he kept slowly on anyway, blinking his eyes to ease the dazzlement. The sea was dead ahead, still thudding on the wet beach, the sound dulled by the damp air and the clouds overhead, and he was heading straight for it. He couldn't go on much further, but he couldn't stop either: the links were too open, the poles gave no shelter. Here he was nowhere. He kept on moving.

Soon he could make out poles off to both sides and up ahead as well: he was right in the middle of them. One appeared right in front of him; he reached out an arm and pulled himself towards it, then leant there, both arms round the pole and back to touch the sides of his body, listening. His breathing was loud. He hadn't been moving fast, but something about walking through darkness, and the pain from his feet as well maybe, made his lungs feel heavy and his breathing hard. He waited till it quietened, then listened again.

Voices. He heard voices. Talking. Somewhere in the darkness there were voices talking, two or three voices. Off to the right maybe. Ahead and to the right. It was hard to tell with the thuds of the sea and the sounds dulled and flattened by the hanging damp. He let go of the pole and set off for the next one on the right. He paused when he reached it and listened some more. Now the voices were definitely closer, still to the right and still ahead, but closer too. He stared into the dark then started off towards the next pole ahead, crossed from there up a slight rise to one on the right, then one more to the right, then stopped.

From down in the ground twenty yards ahead bright flickering lights shone upwards, red lights and yellow: a fire, faint tails of flame rising up from the ground, flitters of pale light crossing the turf in front of him and fading away into black. The voices were coming from down in the ground too. There was talking and laughter, and some of the talking was female, at least one woman's voice, no, two female voices and one male as well, all youngish sounding. He could hear them clearly now. And now he could smell it too, a reek of damp smoke, burnt woodsmoke in the wet heavy air, salt and ash on his tongue as he drew breath.

There was a pause in the talk, then a muffled thump and an immediate burst of crackling and fizzing: something had been chucked on the fire. After a few moments the voices started again; they floated up and over the links with the smoke and the faint firelight, up out of the ground, up from under the level of the links. It was a harbour. Twenty yards in front of him the links ended in a drop edged with stone, and the edge reached away round to the right, holding the earth and grass from crumbling and washing into the anchorage; and out on the left the edge became a wall, a jetty wall stretching out over the black water, the waves dunting against its base. And down on the bed of the harbour the fire was burning, in the crook of the jetty arm.

He dropped to a crouch and moved forward slowly, keeping his face to the ground. Ten yards on he got down on all fours and raised his eyes to look around. Now he could see the stretch of links beyond the landward edge of the harbour; a car was parked there, scrapes in the paint and an unmatching door showing up in the light from the fire. But the folk who had parked it were still out of sight, hidden down inside the harbour, burning their fire and laughing. The grass was dewy on his hands, and wetness was soaking his breeks. He couldn't stay stuck here forever. He moved, crawling on slowly towards the edge, keeping low to the ground but knees bent, ready to turn and run into the dark if he had to. Three yards from the edge he could see it all. The harbour was filled in, or silted up, aye that was it: a high bar of sand closed off the mouth, and from there to the edge where he was crouching the sand sloped down steadily, strewn with odd bits of driftweed and rubbish, a single long pool of dark water at the foot of the seaward wall. In the centre of the sand sat two women and a man, all about his own age; they were gathered round a wide low bonfire, a couple of bags beside them, a scatter of odd pieces of wood drying by the edges of the fire. As he watched, one of the women passed a bottle of clear stuff to the other woman, who took it, smiling, then drank; then, lowering the bottle from her mouth, she wiped her lips and said something, rolling her eyes. The man sitting beside her gave her a shove, and the other woman laughed, shaking her head.

The walker was cold from the wet grass now, and the fire looked fine and warm. And if they had drink they'd maybe have food as well. He slowly stood up and took a couple of steps forward. Hello there! he called out.

The three faces turned towards him, red in the flamelight of the fire. The bottle had disappeared.

Who goes there, friend or foe? shouted the woman he'd seen drinking.

I was just passing and I saw your fire. He shrugged, opening his hands wide towards them.

The three of them looked at each other across the fire for a moment, then the other woman called, Come on down, there's a rare heat off this thing, plenty to go round!

He took another pace forward; his toes were at the edge of the drop. How do I get down? he said.

There's some steps just over there, said the second woman, and lifted her arm to point backwards into the darkness behind her.

Right . . . He walked in the direction she'd indicated. Half-way round the landward edge he found a ladder-top, clambered round, and started down it into the harbour. The ladder felt like it was falling to pieces as he climbed down, coming away from the wall with the weight of him; a couple of rungs from the bottom he stepped backwards and jumped down onto the sand.

He turned and walked towards the fire, bowing his head to examine the palms of his hands in its light as he approached. Flakes of red metal were sticking to his skin, and brown powdery stuff lined along the creases across his palms and in his finger-joints. He stopped a few feet away from the fire, nodded at the three of them sitting there, and held out his hands to them. Look at this, he said. That ladder's rusted away to nothing: I'll never get up it again.

The woman on his right laughed. You shouldn't've come down that old thing. God! I said the steps; there's proper steps over there at the end, past the ladder: solid stone jobs!

Oh. I didn't see those. It was too dark. I just saw the one way down.

Never mind that now, she said. Come on and have a seat, that's the main thing.

He took his pack off and dropped it behind him, then nudged a couple of stones away with the toe of his boot and sat down on the sand, his feet close to the fire's edge. On his left was the man and one of the women, sitting close together; on his right was the other woman, the one who'd pointed out the steps. Her hair was hanging long over her face, and now she pushed it back behind her ears, half each side, and looked across at him.

Well, she said, It's not often we get anybody dropping in on us here, is it?

The other woman looked out into the darkness. Mind you, we could fairly do with some new company, she said. The man beside her sighed.

I wasn't expecting to find anyone here, said the walker. He started to rub his hands in front of the fire. Hih, I thought I was the only human life for miles around.

The other man smiled. Ach, you are, he said. Me and Claire are aliens and Melanie here is a hologram. He twirled his hand at the woman next to him. I mean to say, how else could you get such perfect beauty in female form?

Melanie groaned, but turned back towards the fire, half-smiling Aye, not that you're drunk or anything Ray!

I am not drunk. Happy maybe. You can call me happy, that's fair criticism, but not drunk. No way.

Okay, not drunk then: bleezing.

Ray was about to say something back, but Claire broke in. Och, shut up you two, shut your cakeholes! She laughed. Here, mind when you used to say that, when you were a bairn? Cakehole! Shut your cakehole Mel!

My God, you're blootered as well! cried the other woman, but then she joined in laughing with Claire.

During the laughter, Ray leant back behind Melanie and pulled forward a shoulder-bag from a few feet beyond the firelight. He lifted it onto the sand in front of him and unzipped it, then looked up, grinning. He clapped his hands, then said in a fake slimy voice, Well ladies, shall we continue?

Aye, said Claire.

What were you doing? asked the walker.

Ray pulled out a half-empty bottle of vodka.

Nothing, said Melanie, Nothing at all. It's just the way he says it makes it sound interesting.

Ray had taken a drink from the bottle, and handed it to Claire, who was now upending it. Next, Ray took a bottle of diluting orange out of the bag, unscrewed the top, and took a gulp. The vodka was passed to the walker. Ta, he said. Voddy for the body. He took a short scoosh then passed the bottle on to Melanie.

She took the bottle, gazed at it for a moment, then said, Well, I hope he's not bloody HIV.

Claire lowered the orange bottle into her lap. You can't catch it off saliva, she said.

Still . . . Melanie looked at the walker out of the side of her eye, wiping the top of the bottle with her sleeve at the same time.

Silence.

Here, Claire, said Ray. See if you can't catch it off saliva? Does that mean you won't mind if I spit on you?

Everybody laughed again, and Melanie took a drink of vodka.

The walker cleared his throat. Listen, he said. It's good of you to be handing round the bevvy and that, but what I'm really needing is some grub. I'm not on the scrounge; I'm just asking if there's anywhere around here I can get a feed.

The three of them looked at each other. After a second Claire said, There's nowhere around here. That's the thing about this place: there's nowhere for a couple of miles, nothing.

Unless you tried the Arms, said Ray. See what Big Anne could rustle up for you.

Aye, you could try there, said Melanie, Up in the square . . .

The walker shook his head. I've been there already.

No go? said Claire.

A pickled egg and a packet of nuts . . . The others laughed. The walker pulled a blue bag of peanuts out of his pack side-pocket. Ah well, he said, and tore a corner of the bag off with his teeth. He held the nuts out towards Melanie and Ray, but Melanie shook her head and Ray was drinking from the vodka. He offered them to Claire, and she reached over and held her palm out in front of him. He put the bag in it.

No, no, she said. Just pour us out a few, I'm just needing a taste.

The walker hesitated, then tipped the bag up and emptied a heap of nuts into her hand.

Enough! She sat back and started to chuck them into her mouth one by one. She chewed slowly, gazing into the heart of the fire.

The walker put his head back and poured in a big mouthful of nuts. After a few seconds' chomping he accepted the vodka bottle from Melanie, gulped down the nut-mush, then took in a mouthful of drink, swilled it round his teeth and swallowed. He carefully wiped some particles of peanut from around the neck of the bottle then passed it on to Claire.

I must admit, he said, I kind of screwed up as far as the food was concerned, I should've planned it better. Hih. Well, I thought I had planned it, but it turns out my plans have gone off agley, as they say.

How, what happened like? said Ray.

Well, just that I thought I'd be able to get some grub here. I was remembering that Haven o' Braidon was a fair size of a place, the kind of place that would have a pub and a chippie and a Spar shoppie even.

Dear oh dear! Ray chuckled.

You picked the wrong place to look for bed and board, said Claire.

The Haven's nothing but a big black hole in a cliff, said Melanie. There's nothing here. It's a shitehole. I tell you, I'm just going to piss off from here completely, go to London or Glasgow or somewhere. This place is fucking rubbish!

Ray stood up, stepping apart from Melanie. He began to say something, then shut his mouth and looked away. There's a petrol station up over the brae at the junction with the big road, he said at last. They've got a microwave that heats up burgers and that. He lifted his left leg and waggled his foot; sand shook out from the turn-ups of his jeans.

Ach, they'll be closed years ago, said Claire. It must be nearly midnight.

Ray shrugged. Ah well, he said, and turned away into the

darkness. I'm off to get some more wood for the fire. Anybody coming?

Nobody spoke.

Ah well, suit yourself. Don't finish the vodka before I get back. He walked away into the dark. After a moment there was the sound of him walking up some stone stairs, then his footsteps on grass, then silence.

Right, said Melanie, Let's finish the vodka before he gets back.

Claire looked across at her. Was that not a bit of a hint from Ray the Rave there?

Melanie snorted. He can hint all he likes, I'm biding here. She shook her head. I'll tell you pal: he's a long, streaky bastard. I hope he falls over a fucking cliff.

Och Mel! Claire turned to the walker. She loves him really, she said.

The walker raised his eyebrows. Is that what you call it?

Melanie picked up a bit of stick and started poking about the edge of the fire with it. Let's talk about something else, she said. On second thoughts, let's not talk about anything. Who's got the voddy?

They sat without speaking for a couple of minutes as the bottle was passed round and the last inch of vodka split between the three of them. Melanie took a swallow of the diluting orange and gave the bottle to the walker, who handed it straight on. Claire took a sup, then screwed the top back tight and wedged the bottle into the sand beside her. She pushed her hair back behind her ears again and turned to the walker.

Tell you this, she said, I reckon you'll need to get yourself a new map. I mean, if the one you've got now has Haven o' Braidon down as anything more than a rickle of stones and half a dozen inbred alkies, well, it's useless. Worse than useless!

Hih. The walker chuckled, then looked up at her. Do you want to see my map?

Aye, come on, said Claire, leaning forward. Show us where you've come and stuff.

The walker nodded. He reached down to his feet, stretching his back slowly, and untied the laces on his boots. He yarked the laces on the left one out of their holes down to past his ankle, gave the tongue a pull, then shoogled at the boot, gradually working it down over his heel and off his foot.

Melanie looked up from the bit of the fire she was poking at. I thought you were going to show us your map, she said, Not the holes in your socks.

He didn't reply, but took off the right boot in the same slow way, grimacing.

What's the matter? said Claire. Blisters?

He shook his head, eyes closed, and started to peel off his right sock, rolling it down the ankle, lifting it over the heel, and leaving it bunched up around his toes.

Claire and Melanie looked down at his foot. He was holding it up off the sand, balancing on the bones of his backside. He peeled down the other sock. Both feet were in a similar condition: there were only a few bits of pale, clean skin visible; most of it was covered with reddish stuff, blood, rubbed into the pores and creases, matting the hairs. Some parts were in a hell of a state: all around the right heel were patches of red-raw flesh, and the soles of both feet were worn away too, big flaps of white whorled skin hanging off like strips of cloth. Claire drew a breath in through her clenched teeth, and held it.

Don't worry, said the walker. They're not sore at all. They're kind of numb. It's not a problem, not as bad as it looks, anyhow: half that bleed is probably dye out of my fucking cheapo boots! He held up a finger. Wait . . .   A wad of paper had fallen out of his left sock as he pulled it down; he picked it up off the sand. Another one the same was hanging down from the base of his right heel, stuck on with a mess of dried blood; he took hold of the paper by one corner and tugged at it gently a few times, then gave a sharp jerk and pulled it clean off. A shaky noise like a laugh came out of his mouth.

Christ, your feet are in a hell of a state . . .

You don't say, Melanie! Claire was frowning. Maybe we should wash them or something. Here, we could seal up the wounds with alcohol like they do in the films: pour some of the vodka over them.

Could we what! said Melanie. Anyway, it's finished, unless the rich kid's splashed out and got another bottle planked somewhere.

Forget it, said the walker. They're fine. Look at this though. He moved round into a kneeling position, then started to unfold on the sand in front of him the wads of paper he'd taken from inside his socks. The one from the left sock unfolded easily, it started to come apart along the creases as he laid it out; the other one he had to pick at with his fingernails to get started: the leaves were matted together with dried blood and hard to separate. Eventually he spread that piece out on the sand too and lined it up with the other half. The two parts made up a map of Scotland. It was hard to make it out at first, as the paper was covered in a grid of thick white lines where the map had been folded and the print worn away; where the lines of the grid intersected, there were holes worn right through the paper. There were also stains of sweat and dye all over, and on the north half of the map, which had been under his right foot, there were large patches of blood, dried-in browden red and yellow, even dark brown where there were thick gatherings in the folds of the paper. One of these brown crusts lay right over the north-east coast from Aberdeen to Montrose, covering all the bays and cliffs and villages down the coastline, and spreading out into the blue of the sea.

Now you know how I went wrong, said the walker, kneeling and looking over the tattered map. I just had to go on what I could remember before it got knackered: this morning, up at Muchalls, before I put it in my boots.

The others looked from his feet to the map and back again. Claire pointed at the side of his heel. Look, she said, There's a whole bit of it printed onto your skin: there's Inverness and the Black Isle!

I ken I'm thick, said Melanie, But was it not a pretty daft place to keep your map in the first place?

Aye, no doubt. He shrugged. But I needed some padding, see? My feet were just getting blistered to fuck, these socks are that skinny.

They're worn away to nothing, said Claire. You should take better care of yourself . . .

Melanie was away to add something but stopped, cupped a hand up round her ear, and peered out beyond the fire.

What is it? said Claire.

Shh . . . Melanie listened some more, then said, It's just, I thought I heard something, somebody creeping about out there . . .

The three of them sat in silence, turning their heads out to the darkness. Suddenly there was a loud rattle of kicked rocks. Quickly, the walker folded up the torn pieces of map and shoved them into his jacket pocket.

At that moment footsteps came down the stone steps and across the sandy bed of the harbour, and Ray walked into the firelight, carrying an old fishbox piled up with an assortment of driftwood. He dropped the box at the far side of the fire then started to unload it, throwing the branches and plank-ends and lumps of wood onto the sand. Melanie and Claire spread them out in a single layer all around the fire, and at once the walker could see trickles of steam rising up from the wet wood in the firelight. When Ray had emptied the box, he stood up again and crashed his foot down on the corners of it, wrenching off the side panels; then he lifted the bottom of the box and broke it over his knee, cracking it into three slats. He flung all the pieces down at the edge of the fire, then walked round and flopped down in the sand by Melanie.

The worker returns! he cried, slapping his hand on Melanie's thigh. Right, where's the . . . Fuck's sake! He stopped, staring at the walker. What are those things on the ends of your legs?

Eh, plates of meat?

Christ, that's terrible: cover them up quick, before I spew!

The walker laughed. I was just going to, he said. It's getting a bit warm down here: the heat from the fire'll be giving me chilblains. He started to pull on his socks, then leant further forward and slowly fitted his feet into the boots.

Ray was shaking his head. How the hell did they get into that state?

Och, just wear and tear. I've been walking.

Christ, I can see you've been walking, but where from? Timbuktu?

Close, said Melanie, Muchalls.

Claire looked away as the walker laced up his boots. You're mad, she said. You should leave them out for a bit, relax them . . .

Nah, they'll swell right up if I leave my boots off. Hih, cribbing, that's what they need, good tight cribbing. Ha! But talking of relaxing, my, eh, bladder could do with a bit of a relax: where do you go when you're needing a pish around here?

Just go up and over the harbour wall, said Claire, placing a big bit of driftwood on the fire.

There's seaweed for bog-roll, said Ray.

Right. Thanks. He got slowly to his feet, checked his inside pocket, and walked off towards the steps that Ray had used earlier. Behind him he could hear Melanie asking Ray if there was any more drink, and rummaging in the bag, and just as he was reaching the foot of the steps, Ray shouted, Hey, watch out for the famous leaping lobsters of Braidon Bay! I hope you've got some protection! Then there was laughter, and when it stopped Claire called, If you're not back in an hour we'll send out the coastguards!

He carried on up the steps, crossed the top of the harbour wall, and went down some more steps on the far side, down out of the last of the light from the fire.

He was squatting with his trousers round his ankles when he heard someone coming down the steps behind him. He didn't look up, but slowly withdrew the needle from his thigh, releasing the lump of flesh he'd pinched up with the other hand, then slapping his leg there a couple of times.

Is that you? It was Claire.

Eh, aye, I'm over here. He put the syringe away in its clear plastic case and laid it behind a rock off to one side, then rose, yanked up his breeks, and turned to look at Claire standing half-way down the steps.

Where are you? she said.

He stepped sideways out of the dense shadow of the harbour wall. Ta-ra!

Christ, there you are, I didn't see you! She came down another step. Maybe just as well, eh?

Hih, aye, maybe just as well . . . He bent his head to do up the buckle on his belt.

She stepped down onto the pebbles and came towards him. I wasn't trying to catch you out or anything, she said. I just had the feeling that Mel and him wanted me to piss off for a bit. So I thought I'd come and see if you'd finished, eh . . .

. . . pissing off?

She laughed. Aye, I suppose so.

I'm finished all right, aye. I just have to . . . Hold on a minute; could you . . . He waved a hand towards the end of the beach and she nodded and turned to look off along there. He knelt into the shadow of the harbour wall and felt around at the back of the rock he'd been squatting beside.

Have you lost something?

No, no, he said. I'm just . . . His fingers touched the smooth plastic. Got it!

What is it? said Claire, turning and looking at him as he stepped out of the shadow and examined the case in the moonlight for a second.

He glanced up, found her staring. Nothing, he said, at the same instant slipping it back inside his jacket pocket.

No, hold on, she said. What was that?

Honestly, nothing. It's just . . . I should be more careful.

Shit, she said, and took a pace backwards, then another one, till she reached the foot of the steps.

Sorry, he said. It's nothing, nothing at all.

That's not what I'd call it, she said, and backed up the steps, her hands feeling for the wall as she went, her eyes fixed the whole time on the walker.

Listen, he said, It's nothing, really.

She stopped, stared at him for a few seconds, then said, Is that all you can say, bloody *nothing*?

He opened his mouth, then shut it again and shrugged. What's the point? He stared into the darkness beyond her for a second, then shifted his gaze back to her and said, I know that look on your face: you've made up your mind. What can I say that'll matter?

Anything! Say anything! I mean that was a needle there, wasn't it? What is it, the works you call it? And after Mel talking about AIDS and that. Jesus, say anything!

He paused, looked down at the ground and kicked a pebble with the toe of his boot. I'm diabetic, he said at last.

Claire looked at him, then sat down suddenly on the steps. She rubbed both hands into her forehead, then looked up. What did you say?

Ehm . . . I'm diabetic. It was a needle, but for insulin, that's all. He patted his jacket over the pocket. I have to stick a dose of this into me a couple of times a day, or else I get a reaction, ken: I flake out.

Shit. She leant back against the stair, throwing her head back and resting on her elbows. Sorry, she said. She raised her head to look at him again. I'm really sorry.

You don't have to feel sorry for me, he said, sticking his hands into his jeans' pockets. It's nothing. I wish I'd never mentioned it.

No, no: I'm sorry for jumping to the wrong conclusion there. I was worried, that's all. I mean I don't know who you are or anything . . .

He was silent.

I don't. I don't know anything about you, what you're doing here . . .

So you just thought the worst thing possible straight away. He shook his head, looked down again. Folk are always doing that.

She gazed at him for a moment, then jumped to her feet and started to come down towards him again, her eyes on the shadowy steps. At the bottom she put her hand on his shoulder and rested it there for a second before pressing down on it as she jumped off and onto the beach beside him. I should've known better as well, she said. There was a girl in my class at primary school was a diabetic – Tracey Coutts – and she was really bad for it: she kept running out at playtimes and buying all this chocolate and Love Hearts and stuff, and then she'd scoff the lot and go into this kind of fit . . . what do you call it?

A hypo. He coughed.

Aye, hypo, that's it. She'd eat all these sweeties and then start shaking all over and kind of faint, take one of these hypos.

He cleared his throat and seemed about to say something, but turned instead and walked away from the lee of the harbour wall, through the greasy black rocks there and onto the mowrie beach. Claire followed after him, and fell into step at his side. Aye, he said after they'd walked for a while, Your diet's very important. It's a balancing act: you have to keep the sugar at a certain level in your blood, or else – doosh! – black-out.

It must be a worry having that hanging over you, the thought you could just black out at any minute.

Ach, I don't think about it anymore. You just have to concentrate on the regular food and the regular jags, and put the hypos out of your mind. I don't worry about hypos at all anymore. They don't worry me. It's always there, but I don't worry about it. I just don't. Anyway: blah blah blah. It doesn't worry me.

They walked on in silence. After a few moments Claire started humming something under her breath. Then she came to a halt and crouched down. It's amazing how your eyes get used to the dark, she said. When you come away from the fire it seems like it's pitch-black out here, but after a wee while you start to make things out.

He looked down at her. What can you see?

I was just wandering along in a dwam there when I noticed this patch of stones, a really good lot of skimmers. Look!

He poked the toe of his boot into the patch of flat slatey stones. That's the good thing about walking, he said, You notice a lot of things you'd never see in a car or on a bike.

Aye, like you notice your feet are bleeding to death! She picked up a couple of the skimmers and weighed them in her hand. Come on, let's have a go. I bet I can beat you, I can do seven!

Never.

Aye, look. She balanced herself, half-kneeling, then drew her arm back slowly and flung it forward, sending a stone spinning out over the water. One, two, three, four . . . ach!

What?

Four: not bad for starters.

That was never four.

Aye it was! Look, I'll beat that this time. She waited for a lull in the waves then skimmed another stone out across the water. One, two, three, four, five . . . Five!

Come on, how can you say five? I only saw one; it's too dark to see after that.

Ah-ha!

Ah-ha what? Don't ah-ha me with your fives! It probably sunk straight after the first bounce.

No, I could hear it. There were definitely five splashes.

He laughed. You're a joke! Here, let me have a go. He felt around amongst the pebbles at his feet, then half-straightened up and spun one out over the waves. One, two, three, four, five, six . . . I got six!

That's nothing! She shook her head, her hair swinging. I can do seven, any day.

Oh aye, seven? Just listen to this then. One, two three, five, eight, seventeen, twenty-three . . . Twenty-three! A new world record!

She hooted with laughter, he carried on shouting about his twenty-three skims, hobbling a dance at the edge of the water. Eventually he stopped still and laughed too, then paused to shout, It's probably in Norway by now: hello vikings! He laughed again.

Claire grabbed him by the arm and dragged him after her, up the narrow sloping pebbly beach to where it ended in a small bank of sand with a mat of grass rooted in along the top of it. Hup! she said, and pulled herself up on top of the bank. She turned to sit with her legs dangling over the edge, then held her hand out and hauled him up alongside her.

For several minutes the two of them sat quite close together, not speaking, just getting their breath back, occasionally letting go a laugh or two, and looking out over the dark sea. The cloud cover had started to break up some time before, and now there were long rips appearing right across the sky, and through the holes in the cloud a few stars were visible; every so often, as the tears shifted and widened momentarily, ragged sheeds of moon would appear, high overhead, and the tops of the waves diving in the sea would be picked out for a second, curves of white silver appearing then crumbling into black, rising again and falling again, silver into black.

There was a faint sound away over to the left, and both of them turned and gazed at the dark harbour walls with the glimmer of the fire glowing inside. They listened, but there was no more sound from there, only the waves raking through the stony shingle on the beach in front of them.

Then he said, I've got another packet of peanuts in my bag back at the fire.

Do you want to go and get them?

Well . . .

It's just the main reason I came after you was to leave the two of them by themselves for a while. Let them patch things up a bit.

What, are they fighting?

She turned to him, pushing her hair back and arching her eyebrows. Could you not tell?

Ach, I'm out of practice at that kind of game. But I suppose I did think Melanie was being hell of a sarky all the time.

Oh aye, taking the male side immediately!

What? No, I just . . .

Tch, I'm only kidding. Mel does come across as awful bitter sometimes. She's fed up with this place you see. But Ray's quite happy: he's got a job. She looked down. Old arguments . . .

I suppose I don't like the place I live either.

Where's that? South somewhere?

Eh. He frowned. I can't remember. I've been walking too long.

She laughed. Can you not remember your name either? You went out of your way not to tell it earlier on.

Did I? Hih! He swung his legs round onto the grass and jumped up. Talking of going out of our way, he said, Let's walk a bit more: my toes are throbbing away dangling in space there.

Claire got to her feet and started after him. We could easily go back for your nuts if there's any danger of you taking a hypo thing. Cause look: I'm really sorry about back there. Am I forgiven?

Nah, he said after a moment. I'm fine. Anyway, I've got these glucose tablets in my pocket; if I start to feel woozy at all, I'll just have a couple of those: pure energy! I feel fine now though, like I could walk forever: all the way! He started singing, Keep right on to the end of the road . . .

She laughed.

They walked along the grassy links till they got so narrow – a rising heuch on one side and a rocky part of the beach on the other – that they had to stop. They stood there for a few seconds, then Claire pointed to a patch of clear sand over beyond the rocks, just where the cliff swung out towards the sea, high and craggy, the southern edge of the bay. They clambered down and started picking their way through the sharp rocks and black pools towards the light circle of shingle.

He paused and looked up at the cliff looming in front of them. What's on the other side of that? he said.

She stopped just behind him. Doolie. Where we live.

Is that the same as Inverdoolie on the map?

Aye, but everybody just calls it Doolie; saves wasting time on the place.

They headed on towards the patch of sand again. So is this what you Doolie folk do? he said. Drive out to your local beauty black spot and sit up all night getting rat-arsed?

You can talk! Walking about net-greens in the dark? Jumping out on folk just minding their own business? Is that what you do?

He laughed. Well, it's hard to meet folk these days. Jumping out on them's my last resort: it's all I'm left with.

Here we are. She stepped high over the last of the rocks and onto the sloping circle of sand beyond. It wasn't as big as it had looked from up at the end of the links. She turned and gave him a hand as he stumbled over the rocks after her. There are friendly folk about, it just depends how you look for them. She smiled at him as he stepped onto the shingle beside her.

Ach, I reckon I've given up looking. Too many knockbacks. Just keep on walking, that's my philosophy.

Christ, talk about Mel being bitter!

I'm not bitter. Cause it doesn't worry me. I like being by myself. Just walking on, I like it. On and on.

She looked at him. Oh aye?

Aye.

I don't believe you.

It's true. I'm used to it. I like it.

She laughed and took a step towards him. Well, if you like walking so much, come on, let's go on further!

There isn't any further, is there? Unless we go round the head?

Ah-ha, just look over there though. She stood beside him and pointed to the foot of the cliff twenty yards ahead, close to where the waves were raking the shore. Do you see them? she whispered.

See what?

Look.

He looked. The cliff was dark and split up and down with cracks and shadows of rocklums, and ledges and shelves cut sideways shadows, deep against the dark rock too. But down at the base, where the cliff joined the shore, was a solid black band, a long low slot in the rock, totally dark in the faint star and moon light.

What is it? he said.

Come and see. She crossed the sand to the point nearest the cliff-foot, then paused. He stopped just behind her. Ahead were piles of black shattered crag-stone and pools of glinting water. Watch this, she said, then picked up a pebble and tossed it under-arm into the black hole in the cliff. There was a sharp crack, then a rattling noise, then the echoes of the crack and rattle, a fainter series of echoing patters, then silence.

Christ, he said after a second, It's a cave.

Aye! Brilliant, eh? Well actually it's three caves, it kind of widens out and splits once you get in the entrance there. I used to come here with my folks when I was a kid. Picnics on the beach, ken? I haven't been up this end of the bay for years though.

It looks a bit spooky. Does the water not come up into it?

She looked out to sea. The tide won't be turning for a couple of hours yet. Come on, we should have a look inside. Well, we won't *see* much, but we can feel our way in: you'll get the atmosphere of the place anyway.

For a few seconds he didn't reply, then he said quietly, Claire, will you hold my hand?

What? In there? Scared of the dark are you? She laughed. Aye, sure, come on.

She stepped out of the circle of sand, setting one foot down on a flat boulder and looking ahead for the clearest route to the cave-mouth. Suddenly he reached out and grabbed her elbow, pulled her back off the boulder and towards him. He said something under his breath: Now, now, now . . . She half-lost her balance and fell against him, pushing her free hand against his chest to keep herself upright. He was still holding her other arm tightly.

What are you doing? she said.

You know fine well what I'm doing, he said in a hoarse voice. He took hold of her free arm, and held her still while he lowered his head and half-turned it to press his mouth to hers.

She jerked her face away, his breath hot on it, and tried to shake her shoulders free of his grip. You've got the wrong idea, she said. Let go of me, now.

No, no, it's the right idea. He moved one of his arms round her back and bent to kiss her again. Please, Claire, please. I just want to . . . a kiss in the dark. No one'll see. Please?

No! Let me go!

Claire! He was raising his voice now, and breathing loudly too. His boots were kicking up sand as he struggled to keep hold of her. Come on! Claire, into the cave, come on! Please . . . He pulled her against his body. COME ON!

Suddenly he staggered off to one side, yowling with pain, still holding onto her arms. She flung a glance down and now brought the ridged heel of her monkey-boot down on his other foot. He yelled again, and she twisted and dug down onto his toes and the top of his foot, shaking him off her shoulders at the same time. He started to fall over backwards, and let go of her, throwing his arms out behind him to break his fall. He yelped loudly as he landed amongst the jaggy rocks, one arm twisted behind his back.

Quickly, Claire stepped backwards across the circle of sand.

Fuck you, she said in a steady voice, and he heard the sound of her spitting, then her turning and moving off through the rocks, sliding on pockets of pebbles, splashing in hidden pools, heading straight for the narrow tang of the links.

He closed his eyes and lay back. He hadn't felt her spit hit him, but his back and left arm were already soaking, drookit in the cold water of the rockpool he'd fallen across.

He was sitting in the middle of the circle of sand, looking out over the sea. A small yellowish light had appeared from behind the headland and was moving slowly northwards across the dark water. He followed it with his eyes for a long while, shivering from time to time: the whole back of his jacket and large parts of his breeks were soaked through, and it was cold sitting about, away from the fire. He shivered again. Suddenly he frowned, put a hand up to his forehead, and felt it damp with sweat, chill sweat. He held the hand out in front of him and gazed at it for a second, rubbing his fingertips together, then shook his head a couple of times and looked at his hand again. He wiggled his fingers about in front of his eyes in the half-dark.

He got to his feet, staggering slightly as he rose, and thrust his hands into his jacket pockets. His left hand came out empty, the right one clutching a wad of tattered, bloody paper: his map. He looked around the sloping circle of sand; it was churned up with footprints all over, but there was no sign of his glucose tablets. He checked his inside pocket: nothing. He fell to his knees and scrabbled about in the sand where he'd been sitting the past while, howking up damp handfuls and flinging them away to each side. After a minute he stopped, leaning on all fours over the foot-deep hole he'd dug, breathing hard. The bottom of the hole started to fill with water, sucking sand in from round the edges, collapsing the walls he'd scooped out. He got slowly to his feet, wiped the sweat off his forehead, and started to search carefully amongst the rocks that surrounded the patch of shingle.

Almost immediately he found what he was looking for. In the middle of the shallow pool he'd half-fallen into earlier on, lay the yellow and red wrapped tube of glucose tablets. He shoved his sleeve up to the elbow, stuck his hand in the cold stingy water and pulled out the wrapper and its contents. It squelched in his fingers. Kneeling at the side of the pool, he peeled open the paper tube; a dribble of grey mush ran out over his hand and down onto the sand. He clapped the hand to his mouth and licked the stuff off his skin, working his mouth on the traces of grainy slush and trying to swallow. Straight away he was retching, down on his knees, his hands flung out to steady him against the nearest rocks. He retched, relaxed for a moment, then retched again. He lifted his right hand to wipe sweat from his brow and found he was still clutching the remains of the map.

He sat back on his heels and gazed at the folded wodges of paper in his fingers. His hand was shaking. He started to unfold one of the pieces, but the leaves were welded together with dried blood starting to soften and run after the dooking; he flung that half of the map away, and it skited onto the dark water of the pool in front of him, rested on the surface for a moment, then zigzagged to the bottom, disappearing in the drumlie depths.

He was concentrating on the other piece of map. He was trying to get his fingers in between the folds of the paper, but the paper wasn't keeping still, and there wasn't enough light to see properly. His fingers were trembling too, fumbling over the damp edges of the map, rough now with stuck grains of sand from the times he was dropping it.

He was feeling tired out with the effort. He paused to rest and looked up. The sea was moving in front of him, but it was all very dark now, and hard to make out where the sea ended and the shore began. He remembered he'd been watching the light of a ship a moment before, and he scanned the black face of the water for it, but it was nowhere in sight. It must have gone down over the horizon.

He had something in his hands. It was a wad of paper. He looked at it briefly, then laughed to himself and tore it in half and in half again. He tried to tear it a third time but his fingers couldn't hold all the pieces, he was too tired. Fragments of white paper tumbled down onto the sand. He watched them fall, then swung his arm out and flung the remaining pieces towards the sea. They flittered towards the rocks in front of him, some of them floating down onto the dark water of the pool; he watched them resting there, white sprinkled on the black, trembling, floating and soaking through, and sinking slowly into nothingness.

There was a roaring noise. It was the sea.

He was walking. So tired now, he had to have a lie down. He made his way across a field of jagged rocks, slipping often, dunting his boots and banging his shanks. His eyes were beginning to close over.

The night was very dark now. It wasn't the night, it was the cliff glooming above him.

There was a roaring noise. It was his head.

He walked on into the cave mouth.

He walked on.

Three Nasty Stories

Two Young Fuckers

There's these two young fuckers and they've been in this pub on the western side of Edinburgh which is meant to serve the best beer in the world, not just the country or the city for fuck's sake but the whole fucking bastard world as if that was possible to know, and anyway as they come out the door one turns to the other and he says, Ken this, the funny thing is, near every time I've been in there I've been sick right after, aye, not actually puked up like, but felt a bit queasy, ken. And the other one looks at him without turning his head, pretending to pretend he's not looking or some funny fucking game, and he says, Well mind and not puke on me if you're going to start any of that capers the now, me with my suit on and all. Settle, settle, says the first fucker, I'm A-1 at the moment man, in fact I could've done with a few more maybe, I mean to say coming all this way and then only having the two. Ah but you see, forward planning, says the other one, This is the kind of party where the cunts'll've laid on drink and that, and we should get there before a certain time before the bastards finish the fucking stuff. Anyway, listen, there'll be a paki open here somewhere and we'll get a wee carry-out to keep us going like.

So they carry on down the road, or down the fucking pavement actually to tell the truth, and the one in the suit, the one that knows about the party, well he asks his mate how much dosh he has, and the mate says, Fuck all, and the one in the suit says, Jesus Christ for fuck's sake, and rakes in his pocket, and counts how much he has, although probably he already has a pretty exact fucking idea knowing this kind of in-charge cunt. And he counts out what he's got and he's got: four pound notes, one fifty-pence bit, four tens, a five, eight twos and ten fucking one bastard pences, okay? Which makes a total of five beautiful pounds and twenty-one miserable pence, probably. And as they're walking along the one not in the suit – for fuck's sake, call him the thick one – the *thick one* is asking the one in the suit, So where exactly is this party anyway? And the one in the suit says, Well it's at the flat of this fucking goth fucking dame I was talking to in the Cellar Bar this morning; she's twenty-one and her name's Blackbat or something, I don't ken, Fruitbat maybe, of all the shite. Anyway, you ken that tall cunt with the red hair that drinks in there? Well, it turns out he plays the drums or something, and I reckon this dame must've gone home with him for a musical shag the night before after his gig. Which is the way these cunts talk by the way, fucking stupid cunts. Anyway she was half-pished cause it was her birthday and that, ken, that's what she was saying at least, and she was saying about a party at her place the night, and telling everybody – though maybe that was only an excuse to get the drummer bugger round for some more thumpy sex of course – telling everybody about this party, and she had to shout the address about ten times before the deaf cunt got it into his skull, and that's when I heard it like. Oh, so she didn't actually ask you then? Nah, but what the fuck, she won't mind that she didn't when we turn up, right?

The one without the suit, sorry, the thick one, is looking a bit worried – maybe he's wondering how the besuited bugger knows there's going to be booze on the go – so it's him, the thick one, who says, There's a paki open, and cuts across the street, and shouts back, Come on and we'll get a couple of cans or something, and him that goes into the shop first, although and despite the fact that he's not the one with the fucking cash, which is a bit of a breach of drinkers' fucking etiquette you'll agree. But there you go. The guy behind the counter watches them from the minute they walk in the door, but they just ignore him, they just make straight for the shelves by the side of the till where the booze is, and they scan the selection. Look, you can get bitter for thirty-two a tin, says the thick one. Bitter? says the one in the suit, For fuck's sake man, call yourself Scottish! Well . . . No no no no, says the one in the suit, and he starts looking up at the high fucking shelves where the spirits and fortified wines are, and then he goes, Ah-ha! and reaches up and takes down a bottle. And his mate looks up and sees an orange cardboard star saying WHISKY '4.99', and he looks down and he sees the one in the suit holding a bottle with Prince Charlie's Barley Bree on the label. The one with the suit turns to the counter and plonks down the bottle and the shop mannie watches him as he howks round in his pocket and brings out the dosh, and as he lays it out onto the counter: four singles, the fifty, the four tens – then he picks up one of the tens and puts down the ten ones instead – and then he puts three of the twos back in his pocket and clacks the other five fuckers down, and finally he lifts one of the pennies and puts that back in his pocket too. Then he looks up at the guy behind the counter and sort of smiles at him, but he just scrapes the money off into his hand and counts it all into his till. The one in the suit goes to lift the bottle, but the one behind the counter grabs it before he can, whips out a sheet of purple paper from below the counter somewhere and rolls the fucker up with a little twiddle on top that he doesn't seem to know how to deal with. And then he lets the one in the suit lift the bottle, and him and his mate walk out.

Dirty bugger, says the thick one. Tricky cunt, says the one in the suit. He rips off the paper and chucks it into the gutter, unscrews the top off, chucks that too, then shouts out, Here's to us, who's like us, no cunt! And up-ends the bottle into his fucking gob and takes a good long scoosh. Jesus fucking pishwater! he says, and holds the bottle away at arm's length towards his mate. Have you ever drunk battery acid? The thick one grabs the bottle and takes a drink. Well now's your fucking chance. Here, hold on till I find the fucking top. The one in the suit goes back and looks around in the gutter beside where the purple paper is, fishes around in the puddles the minky bastard, and comes back with the top of the bottle, which he spits into, swills around a bit, and then flicks out at the pavement. He checks to see if it's clean, and sticks it into his top pocket. Still and all, says the thick one, Not bad for four fucking ninety-nine. I tell you, my fucking neighbourhood's going downhill faster than fucking Meadow-bank Thistle, you can't get a bottle of whisky for less than a fiver for love nor money, maybe even less than six! Six quid for some cunt's idea of a vat of fucking chemicals for Christ's sake, whisky my pish! See the bottle, says the one in the suit, and takes it, and wipes the top and takes a drink. Now listen, he says, I reckon if we cut along here and then through that fence we'll be down onto the fucking motorway and that'll take us right down to the fucking west end near enough, none of this fucking around with fucking Gorgie-Dalry. Ho! Let's go!

So the two stupid fucking half-drunk cunts head off down the street, which right enough ends in a fence which there's a hole in, which they go through, which puts them at the top of a wee embankment of weeds, which they go down in the half-dark, the one in the suit fixing the top on the whisky for the duration, which he takes off again at the bottom, which is basically the hard shoulder of the fucking motorway and a wee bit of long grass at the side of it, which he drops the top of the bottle into as he's taking it off as the thick one's staggering down the slope, which the one in the suit tells him to get the fuck back up out of the road while he has a look. But he can't find the top this time, so after a minute he takes a scoosh out of the bottle, or maybe a scoof, and sets off walking along the hard shoulder looking a bit fucking bad-tempered. The thick one stands up from where he's been sitting on the embankment and follows after and gradually catches up. And as he gets up even with the suit he steps out sideways and as he does a fucking car on the motorway shoots by at a hell of a fucking speed, blasting its horn, and it just misses him by hardly anything, it just fucking skiffs his arm almost and then it's away down the road and out of sight. Fuck off! the two of them shout at exactly the same time, and they start laughing. Here you dead bastard, says the one in the suit, Have some of this before you actually get hit you cunt, and he gives him the bottle, which must be getting on for half-empty by this stage of the fucking proceedings.

The thing is for fuck's sake, they keep on going down the side of the motorway, and they're trudging on for hours, and it's more or less completely fucking dark by now, and they're still alive, and the bottle is near enough empty. One time the smart guy stops for a pish, and the other one holds the bottle while he does it, but he can't stand steady enough, and he urinates all over his shoes and the bottom half of his suit trousers, the drunken bastard, but the both of them just laugh and walk on again. About two minutes later the thick cunt stops and he says, Hold on a minute, I'm needing a fucking good old fucking slash as well, and it's down with the spaver and out with the dick, and the one in the suit says,

You could've fucking gone when we were back in the fucking bog for fuck's sake! and they both laugh and then the suit empties the last of the whisky down his throat. He waits till his mate's zipped up, and then he looks down the motorway and sees there's nothing coming and he says, Right, let's see a trial of fucking strength, let's see who can chuck Prince Charlie's fucking empties across the road the furthest. He takes hold of the bottle by the neck, swings it back behind his head, and then lets it fly, high up and quite far out. But it falls slightly short of the far side, in the fast lane, and smashes. Well I reckon that's the winner, says the thick one, and claps his mate on the back. Now where's this fucking party with all the fucking tarts at it? he says. Follow me, says the one in the suit.

They wander on down the motorway a bit further, the fuckers, and when they come to a bit where they have the choice of following a big curve away to the left or another big curve, away to the fucking right of course for fuck's sake, they take the one on the right and they curve round behind the back of some big offices and an expensive big fucker of a hotel and they come out onto a proper street, with pavements and that, a hundred yards up from the west end. And if you know the place you'll know the stupid bastards have spent a long while getting fuck all distance from Point A, but let that pass, on they go, on and fucking on blah blah blah till they're in a street with no shops, no pubs, no *nothing* except big fucking posh flats, pillars on each side of the door and that, big bay windows, quietness. And they're looking for number 58 and then they find it, not that that was particularly hard for fuck's sake. Just as well.

The whisky'll be in full flow through the veins and brains by this time, and the dense one takes a lean against the doorside pillar as the one in the suit takes a look at the names in the wee lighted rectangles beside the various bells. There's nobody here with a name anything like Batwoman, he says. That must've been her first name just. Shit. Okay, here we go. He presses the top button, and waits. Nothing happens. He presses again. Fuck all. He looks at the thicko as if it was his fault, and the thicko shrugs. The one in the suit turns back and presses the second-top bell, and then presses it again a moment after to make sure, then he presses it another time and as he's pressing it a voice comes over the intercom, an old woman's voice, saying, Who's there? Stop ringing now, who's there? The one in the suit bends down to the grille and says, Hello, is eh Batwoman there? Is that you? There's a pause, then the voice says, Stop ringing my bell this instant or I'm calling the police. What? Fair enough you old slag! shouts the suit into the intercom, And I'll call the fucking public cemy! He presses the third bell down – which by the way is the last one, which means these flats must be pretty fucking big if it only takes three of them to have a front this size, which makes the possibility of this being the kind of do where the booze is there in gallons more likely no doubt – and as soon as he's rung it a voice comes through the thing, Yeah? It's a man's voice this time, and he kind of drawls the word out like he's fucking stoned or American or some shite like that, and the thick one bends in over and says, Aye hello, is that the party like? Can we come in? Who is this? says the voice, and the one in the suit answers, Eh it was Batwoman who asked us, she invited us like, and we've got all this booze and that, see, so if you could just let us in and not leave us standing about like SPARE FUCKING PRICKS AT A WEDDING on your doorstep! And the voice says, There's no party here bud, and the intercom goes dead. The one in the suit sighs and presses the third bell again, and as soon as it's answered he says, Now come on pal and let us in, I mean . . . And the voice interrupts, Look I've told you, there's no party here, will you just shift your asses the hell away from here? Asses? shouts the smart one, Suck my fucking cock pal! And he punches the bell panel with his fist, and spits on it.

He turns to the thick one and says, Fuck! And the thicko says, Come on, let's away fucking home, fucking hairies are nothing but fucking trouble, give me a copy of *Escort* and a box of Kleenex any time. And the smart one in the suit says, The fucking bitch! I tell you, if she ever shows her face in the Cellar again I'll put my fucking boot in it, the cunt.

You Think I'm Thick but It's You that's the Cunt

It's you that shoves shit through the doors of paki families, you that fucks on the bus, that spits on the necks of old dears in the post-office queue, smokes like a lum in the health centre waiting-room, steals my food, kicks next-door's kids, smells, farts at the bar and says, Those blinking mice again, leans over while shitting and pukes in the bath, saves page-threes in the bog for wiping your arse and wanking, dosses down on my floor after a hard night's bevvying and comes over at four in the morning to nick my fucking blankets, rants on about how Princes Street'll be renamed William Wallace Avenue and Queen Street Robert Burns Boulevard and how the English'll be kicked out of course and while we're at it we might as well get rid of the darkies and the chinkies and the fucking Jews as well I mean for Christ's sake did you never hear of that cunt Hitler, has a cheesy cock, shows it: you.

Like yesterday in the Cellar when the gogo came over to put 50p of songs on the jukebox you tried to stick your finger up her arse. Through her fucking pants, you jabbed at her arse, her bending over to select her tunes, glittery golden knickers, and when she turns round and tells you to FUCK OFF you stick out your groin and rub it with your toastie, your cheese fucking toastie and your manky work jeans, then you shove it in your gob, the whole thing at once and the ends hanging out and you laughing like fuck with spit and juice running down your chin leaning your face into hers as she heads past you for the stage. It's not much wonder the lassie wasn't looking very happy as she was dancing. And that's all she was, a wee fucking lassie, probably seventeen or something doing this in her school dinner hour and that fucking reminds me, that is one thing I would like to be there to fucking see, that day, the day following the first of the month when once yet again you've failed to pay Sonia her maintenance and we're in the Cellar for a quiet stripper-time pint and fuck me, who's that cavorting on the wee stage? It's your Kelly, Sonia's Kelly, young Kelly your bairn. Say hello to your dad, I tell her as she goes by. She looks at you and you're saying, This is fucking out of order by the way, no daughter of mine . . . when the barman comes up, counts out three fivers, and sticks them down the front of her glittery golden bra.

Also: leaving aside drink: one-twenty for August's *Razzle*, twenty for a vanilla slice, thirty-five for bootlaces that time at the bus stop and then your fucking twenty-five fare as well, a tenner for Sonia a fucking tenner I tell you it's funny but not fucking FUNNY the way you're always owing her the day my giro arrives and never the days you get your pay, three-thirty or thereabouts for that chinkie we got delivered from the place in Granton, lemon chicken you had and prawn curry for me by Christ we must've been pished that time and especially cause like I said there was that place down Newhaven Road but you claimed you'd been there and it was shite so there was all that shenanigans with the Granton Lucky Star, them phoning back twenty minutes after we ordered to say, What was it you wanted again? and you saying, A yellow fuck, NO, lemon duck! and ten minutes later them phoning back again to say they'd fuck all duck and would chicken do? And you said, What's the difference, is it not all catmeat anyway? Jesus I'm surprised they came with it at all. I'd got a couple of bottles of sherry in that night as well I mind, but no: leaving drink out of it for now: I got you into Easter Road that time, against Aberdeen, well and truly shagged we were that fine day, three quid and three–nil, and in the Four-in-Hand after, but no: but there was sixty or something into that trivia machine and you were the one pressing the buttons and we lost that too, no you lost it, I never had a look in there.

Admit it cuntface, I never had a look in anywhere, it's always me who has to put my hand in my pocket when there's the slightest jingle coming from that region, BUT YOU'RE THE ONE WITH THE FUCKING JOB. But what's a few quid between pals? you'd say, Fuck all, you'd say. Aye, when it's me that's doing the betweening! But when you splash out like that TWO QUID for the taxi that time outside the Shrub when the rain was coming down like a urinal flush we never hear the fucking end of the fucking song-and-dance routine you get up to: you can't let a taxi go by without some wee snidey remark, and the number two pounds coming up creates great humour all fuck FUCK IT I was going to do a grand total but I've lost count so just FUCK forget it.

But roughly pal, mate friend mucker fellow-fenian drinking-partner bastard bosom-buddy chum cunt you cheating bastard you thieving fucker you the smart one the one with the suit the one with the job you cockeyed carrothaired spunktongued cunt, twenty-five quid I would say.

Lumps of shite in the lager: your tales of work stick in my fucking craw. I'll tell you: late every morning at the depot, two verbal warnings, half-pished from every dinnertime on, two written warnings, found unconscious behind a pile of pallets when you should've been crating up self-assembly bunk-beds, and AT LAST you get hauled up in front of Denver Dom the company personnel cunt . . . Before you say anything, you said, I'd just like to make apologies for my record, I realise it's pretty bad, especially lately, but in fact I think a lot of it's down to a certain drink problem I've had ever since, well, my father's funeral to be honest, you'll see there I had three days' leave to cover going up home for that just after New Year, and since then, well to be honest it was very sudden and I suppose my work's been suffering on account of drinking a lot ever since then, ken? The personnel twat looks you over. Hm yes, your record is exceptionally poor. Oh aye, I realise that, but I think I've got it under control now, the drink, I mean I realised I had to, I realise I mean I'm lucky to still be working here. How much have you been drinking would you say? Och a bottle a day I suppose. Of . . . ? Whisky, aye, at the worst. Actually I think you're lucky to still be standing, to still be living! Ha hm. Of course there's no question of such behaviour going uncensured, but I think given the circumstances of the root of the eh circumstances, your eh bereavement, and the fact that you are now taking the drinking in hand, I think I'll be able to recommend to the depot manager, em, two days' pay docked perhaps, and as long as you don't come up in front of me again . . . well. Och thank you sir, that's great, you said, and blethered on for another half-hour telling him about how you were a reformed character, and fuck me if the stupid necktied cunt didn't swallow the lot, take it all in, make wee approving notes in his folder as you mouthed off till the desk was piled high with manure and YOU'RE THERE TO THIS DAY! Remaining conscious till a decent hour each day must help, and you think I'm thick but that personnel prick, fuck's sake I'd've sacked you on the spot but then I ken you like he doesn't LUCKY BUGGER, and it also helps clocking in on time most mornings and it helps to do that if you can sleep on some poor mug's settee a hundred yards down the road from the gates instead of your own gaff away fucking miles away, away the other side of town, away fucking thirty pence on ANY red bus going down the Walk.

Before this place there was that room in a flat overlooking Leith baths, where the landlady found what day everybody's giro was due and arrived round to collect her rent on the heels of the

postie with a massive fucking alsatian in tow – or towing her on
the chain more like – and I had dreams of killing the bastarding
brute but could never afford a lump of steak to put the poison in.
From there I was going to move to one of the council hotline
houses in Niddrie or Wester Hailes or somewhere equally central
and stuffed with jobs: at least you could get straight in and your
rent paid as long as you didn't mind rats in the bath and fungus
damp in the bedroom and the kitchen taps not running if you'd
flushed the lavvy in the past half-hour. But you persuaded me not
to bother on account of I couldn't afford burglar alarms or pit
bulls or even venetian blinds for fuck's sake to keep out the crazy
fucking heroin junkies who were queuing up to break in and steal
my valuables, and when they saw I didn't have fuck all they'd jag a
few arteries on the broken window glass instead and give me
AIDS for not being a well-off bastard with spare cash and
consumer goods scattered around the shagpile. You were a cunt
to spout such shite and I was a prick to listen. So instead I scraped
in to that hostel down by the Shore which was handy for signing-
on but you could only stay there for three months at a time, so I
was out on my arse with a list of addresses of bedsits, B&Bs and
campsites, I'm not fucking joking. But I ended up in that
Buchanan Street place till they chucked us all out six months later
to gut the insides and blast the outsides and re-let them to rich
cunts at twice the price. In the room next to mine there was a girl
with a cat with paralysed back legs wrapped up in bandages that
she had to take off and wash the shite and piss out of every night
when she remembered: I wondered how she could ever forget
with this half-cat half-fish slithering about and stinking the whole
place out. And after that I moved in here, and after that you more
or less did too.

The cat in Buchanan Street liked me, and I got on fine with it.
You can put up with just about anything, but not for fucking ever.

When I first moved in the sound of it dragging itself up and down the hallway lino drove me mental, but at least it was someone to talk to. A friend. You cunt. It's time to be moving on. I'm thick and even I know that.

Three Nasty Stories

*After Not Eating for a Couple of Days I Got my Hands
on Some Liver*

Fucking bastards, fucking dirty bastards, you cunts, you fucking dirty cunted bastards. I am not down-hearted, no! I have half a pound of liver and two onions under the mattress, and soon I shall arise and slap the meat in the frying pan fucker, ripped lips of cow cunt slabbering blood through the grease. My blade was taken off me when I came here, but they couldn't take my teeth, the stupid fucking poor stupid buggers, I'll bite the onion tops off, vegetable nipples, I'll destroy them and skin them and chuck the bald bastard onions in: balls and bloody pissflaps in the pan. Let them sizzle, let them fry, let them frazzle and smoke, LET THE WHOLE LOT OF YOU BURN, let them char and crack and blacken: brittle flesh, give it to me then, in the gob, fuck!

I have my fork, I'll fork it, I'll turn it and skite them round, I'll prong and pierce it, fork it up in the air, inspect it beneath my nose: by Christ it's a tasty piece, a choice morsel and no mistake, and not a piss-tube bit of gristle in sight. Slice it you cunt, slice it fat cunt butcher man, move your creashy arse and lunk some great slab of the stuff from your chilled shelves, your cow morgue: you disgusting cunt, you shite-haired moch. Slice it, slice it, give me two fucking slices, two fat slices, yes yes, slice fuck yes. Maybe I should fuck it before I fry it.

And then the skirling of the meat, the heat of it melting through me, and me laughing too: yes you bastards, come on then you fucking cunts, I'll take the fucking lot of yous, you fucking yellow-arsed shit-shaggers! Fuck's sake, fifteen bottles of codeine cough syrup down the gullet, half a pound of liver and two bald onions, no contest. And fuck your hairy onions, fuck them to a pulp.

Now the streets are mine. I go down the stair and out, out into the clear air, clear and cold, but I breathe it in, I swallow the bugger, COME ON YOU CUNTING AIR, down my tubes and bags cold and clear then out it comes steaming and red: bloody misty clouds come out, they stagger out, they float, they sink, they split and spew, dark blood spits in the gutter in sputtery showers. And no one will be looking, as usual the bad fuckers will be hurrying past: get off my fucking street you bastards, off all my fucking streets! They're mine, these are my streets, these are my clouds of blood, this is my belly of liver: a pillar of liver burning away there, black hot liver up my arse stuffs me, rubs charred slice-ends down the slime inside my head, the brain-case you cunts, IT IS MINE, and you can all fuck off out of it, yous are barred.

They are smitten but they don't fucking realise it, they stride on past me, into the clouds of blood the cunts, they plunge, they lurch, they thrust along and away, away they go but there's blood in their hair, my hot liver breath in their lungs, they are well and truly fucked and smitten and plagued. You will live to regret this plunging past me, cunts, you'll live and then you'll die and then I'll have your livers!

I step out into the flow and follow the fuckers, they're faster than me, they hurry past, all I see is their backs. I turn and twist around as I'm walking, I jab my elbows out, I try to catch a few of them across the gub as they stride past on steady legs, so steady, so fucking left right left right up down up down rubadubdub softshoe-scuffle on the paving stones: STOP WANKING THE WORLD you cunts. I stand amazed, I see them, DON'T THINK I FUCKING DON'T FUCKHEADS, pouring out of doorways, spewing down steps, here they come, come, come again, keep on coming, the minky fucking millions hurtling by me: sleep in their eyes, sludge in their guts, snot in their mouths, shit in their heads. They'd scunner you the buggers, YOU SCUNNER ME YOU FUCKERS!

Probably I have been shouting, anyway my mouth is open: now I shut it once and for all. The reason is the fuckers keep rushing on by, and they don't even slow to go past me, they're like a million fucking little spunk-fish swimming up some cunt's guttering and drainage, panting panting, wiggling their little arses like maniacs, on and on and on and on for fuck's fuck's FUCK'S sake.

And that is it: I am too late, the message is x-hundred years useless, the world has long since come and come again, and every day a billion people are spunked onto the streets, and they swim off to fucking work and they've fuck-all idea where they're going the cunts, and THEY'RE ALL GOING TO DIE. Yes certain death to all sperm-fish, you'll be even more putrid and stinking than now you poor stupid buggers, because all the spunk dies, dies and rots and is washed away in the world's pish. All except one. All except me.

Fucking stupid bastards, fucking cunts hashing on to die, rushing like fuck, foot to the floor, swing those arms, into trains, into buses, hup hup hup, fucking hup your hanal harse. Hi-ho hi-ho, it's off to die we go: I can hear the sound of a million doomed cunts singing, some prick in a suit conducting. But they can't hear me, their lugs are stuffed with shite and anyway I'm saying nothing, it would be a waste of liver breath. Instead I walk unsteadily on, I go with the flow, the spunk masses know the way though they don't know they're all going to DIE at the last gasp and let me through for the final piercing, the final pronging: there's something about that fried grub I've guzzled, it's given me the fire and the blood and the spunk in my guts and brains, but it's more than that too, it's a message by fuck, fried food is the finish I bet my bottom arse.

And the flow is flowing to a stop now, flowing into the bus station and sticking to the platforms, clinging to the shelter walls, gathering round the stop signpoles. Soon the flow will be splitting up, spitting its dead-fish slime into commuter buses, and off they'll be hearsed to places of work, PLACES OF DEATH YOU STUPID FUCKERS. And now it is clear, I see it cold and clear: round about the station somewhere there's a fucking massive fried egg, and down the front of my pants there's a fucking massive steel fork: I must prong it and pierce it, the fucking sharp tines, the gold of the yolk, and it bursts and it spews, and it's yellow and wet, and it's thick and it drips and FUCK ME SIDEWAYS, WHERE IS THE FUCKING CUNT?

I am dancing in the roadway in front of the spunk-fish about to be carted off to work and die, but I've loosened my belt to have the fuck-fork at the ready so my breeks are about my knees and I'm dancing like a spastic spider, or maybe just like a spastic fucking and fitting at the one time. I shout at them, Do you know where you're going? Do any of you poor bastards know where you're all fucking going? Let me tell you, you're going to fucking die! You're dead meat! You already fucking stink and now you're going to die and fry and be gobbled and shat out by ME: you are offal, you are a pile of guts, you are black blood and foul liquor, your innards are festered to skittery bog-juice: DIE pricks, DIE cunts, DIE bastards, DIE workers. Listen: I don't want a fucking job, I don't want to fucking die, fuck your jobs, fuck your death, fuck you!

No cunt takes fuck all notice, no cunt looks or seems to listen. Are you deaf as well as fucking about to die? Listen! Listen you fucking dirty bastards! Or do I have to dance in front of you all fucking day?

Thistle Story

On my way to the pub one evening, I passed a public call-box. It was full of thistles.

I stopped and looked more closely. It was a perfectly normal phone-box on the outside, but the inside was stacked full of thistles, right to the roof. Some of the thistles near the ground looked crushed, but the ones at eye level were crisp and green, prickles glistening in the light of a nearby streetlamp. Some of them had wee tartan ribbons twisted round their stalks in bows.

I looked up and down the street: there was no one about. Who had put them in there? I had no idea.

Just then, the phone started to ring. I couldn't get in to answer it, because the box was full of thistles.

Lurch

I wakened to the sound of church bells ringing, a dog barking, and somebody playing the bagpipes. When the bells stopped I threw off my blanket, and as I was finishing dressing the dog shut up. I left my room, walked down the five flights of stairs, and went along the passageway and outside. The bagpipes had stopped.

I looked up and down the street. There were very few people about, but a lot of binbags, piled up on the edge of the pavement in front of each stair door. A bag at the bottom of the pile at my feet was split, and the contents were falling and seeping out into the gutter. Amongst the rubbish floating in the water there were dozens of tiny jigsaw pieces, some of them sticking together somehow in lumps of sodden cardboard, some of them drifting off individually in the direction of the nearest stank.

Excuse me . . .

A youngish person was trying to get a pushchair past, between me and the tenement.

Excuse *me*! I said. The rubbish on the pavement here, it's so narrow!

Aye, could you move then? she said, banging my ankles with the front of her buggy.

With certainty, I said, and pressed myself against the piled rubbish to let her by. But wait! I said, before she was completely past. One question: without the intervention of any hand or person, how long would it take this puzzle to jig itself together in the puddle into the proper picture? In your opinion. Totally by glance, I mean.

She looked at me, and down at the pieces amongst the spilled rubbish, and she said, Totally by *chance*, you mean.

I smacked my forehead with the palm of my hand: indeed, that was what I had meant, I think. I turned to say so, but she was already far down the street, pushing quickly. I didn't watch her for long – in fact I had very little time to spare – and almost immediately I was walking up the street in the opposite direction, every so often banging my head on the wall of the tenement-block I was passing.

This happened because of the unfortunate conjunction of two conditions I am afflicted by. The first is that, when walking anywhere in the vicinity of buildings, tall stone walls, or any other massive structures of more than a certain height, I find the course I am walking being constantly steered towards them: almost as if I am being attracted by some sort of gravity or magnetism to the stone, I am forced – there can be no other word for it – to walk closer and ever closer to the edifice in question. Even if I start off walking down the very outer edge of the pavement, where I'm banging wing-mirrors as I pass parked vehicles, within twenty yards or so I invariably find myself veering sideways, and before long I realise I am brushing the inside wall with the whole of that side of my body. To date, I haven't worked out an explanation for this phenomenon, but I have noticed that the problem is distinctly worse – that is the pull of the wall seems to operate stronger and more quickly – when it has been raining and the pavement is wet; this may be highly significant. The second problem I have is that I have a very bad limp – really it is more of a lurch than a limp – caused by the fact that my legs are of unequal length. Or, to be pedantic again, although both my legs would measure the same were a tape unrolled against each of them in turn, from hip over knee to sole of foot, one of them is in effect distinctly shorter, because it is badly bowed: it bends out the way, the knee in question actually joining thigh bone to shin bone at an angle of some thirty degrees. (This figure is nothing more than a guess, I admit, for I have not yet come across an instrument capable of making such a measurement with any useful degree of accuracy.) Some months ago a doctor gave me a prescription for a pair of built-up shoes – or rather a pair of shoes, *one* of which was fitted with an appropriately thickened sole – but so far I haven't had sufficient money to redeem his scrip. Luckily, the local co-op supermarket carries a small selection of medical footwear, and I was able to buy a pair of built-up slip-ons there at a very low price. It's true that the height of the thickened sole is not quite the right one to get me walking smoothly and steadily, and I do still lurch quite drastically, particularly at speed, but I am sure that I would be worse off in bare feet.

Fortunately, there are very few plate-glass windows on the route from my room to the cafe, so although I dunted my head quite severely a few times as I went along, I was never in any danger of causing expensive damage to other people's property. I have thought about trying to find an insurance policy to cover me in the event of such an accident occurring, but visiting a broker, even with purely exploratory intentions, seems a waste of time while paying a premium of any amount at all is still totally beyond my means.

The cafe was almost empty when I went in, the only customers being a couple of old folk drinking tea in the window seat. (Sometimes people were given their beverages free if they would sit in the window and make the place look busy.) I went right over to the counter by the till and rapped on it with my knuckles.

Good morning Joe! I cried.

What do you want? said Joe, without turning from his greasy griddle.

Let me think Joe, I said. Hmm, I know, make it egg today, if you please.

What kind of egg? he said.

Joe, you joke! I laughed, Hen's egg of course!

No, but scrambled or fried, he said, scraping with his metal lifter at something burnt stuck to the griddle.

Scrambled sounds good, I said.

Coming up, he said, Take a seat.

I scanned the cafe: I had my pick of the tables, except for the one in the window, but Joe didn't like me sitting there anyway: he said it would put folk off coming in if they saw me. I chose one quite close to the counter, and as soon as I had slid in to the table, I re-started our conversation.

You know Joe, I was having an interesting discussion with a young person earlier on, I said.

Oh aye, he said.

Yes, I said. I happened to pass some remark about glancing at something, and she corrected me – or at least she thought she was correcting me – by saying that what I really meant was chancing at something. Now the rights and wrongs of her correction are irrelevant for the moment (all I'll say is, does 'chancing at' something sound very correct to you? I don't think so), but the important thing is this: in my own country, such a correction would never be made, never. This correction brought home to me once again how I have travelled far, far from home. In my country, the language spoken is such a cosmopolitan one – that is it is spoken not just in my country but in lots of other countries around the world also – and my country is such a cosmopolitan one – that is there are so many visitors there speaking other languages and our own language in so many different styles, accents and dialects – that we are completely accustomed to great variety in the way people speak. So we never correct people who speak different to ourselves. But here, this is a small country, and the number of people who speak the language, and the number of people who visit here, these numbers are so small that . . . that people have this idea that there is a proper way to speak, a correct way: an only way! And hence if anyone deviates at all they get slapped down, corrected in the public street as to their manner of conversing. It is incredible, and in fact I am now at the stage where I can laugh at it! Yes, I actually find it funny!

Here's your scrambled-egg roll, said Joe. He'd come round from behind the counter and was sliding the plate across the table towards me. That's your pay. And I've given you a fried-egg roll as well. That's like a kind of bonus. A golden handshake.

That's very kind Joe, I said, Come and sit down and talk.

Eh, I won't bother actually, he said and stayed standing, above and to the side of me. So do you see what I'm getting at with the extra roll and that?

Further explication would be appreciated, I said, eating.

He cleared his throat. Well, you know these handbills you've been giving out . . .

And I have Joe, I said, The full bundle every day.

The thing is, he continued, I've been thinking about it, and they're not actually doing much good. He paused, and watched as the old couple left the window seat and went out the door. We were now alone in the cafe. I've been thinking it's maybe not very good publicity having my leaflets handed out by a cripple.

I put down the roll I was biting into. What do you mean? I said.

You're not doing it any more, he said, The job's cancelled.

But if I don't give out leaflets you won't pay me, you won't give me my hot filled roll in the morning . . . He nodded, and looked at his fingernails. So what am I going to eat? I shouted.

He moved away from the table. That's up to you, he said, So, eh, goodbye. He walked swiftly over to behind the counter, bent down out of sight, and started making a rattling noise with plates and pans or something.

I couldn't finish my food, I couldn't chew what was already in my mouth, my mouth was all dried out. I could feel moisture gathering in my eyes though. After a few moments of sitting there, dazed, I got up and left the cafe as quickly as I could. Outside, I crossed the street, hardly looking out for traffic at all, and started the walk down the tenement-lined street at the far end of which my room lay.

There were innumerable thoughts rushing around in my brain, but they were going at such a tremendous speed, and swirling round and round in such tight circles, that I was conscious only of a dark gurgling hole, a ferocious whirlpool that was swallowing up all my attempts at rational mental activity. And for some reason my lurch seemed to be very bad, almost the worst I ever remember it being: I struck my head off the rough stone of the tenement wall very hard and very frequently, but could in no way control my self-destructive behaviour.

By the time I reached the entrance to my stair, I had to lean back against the door-frame to steady myself. I heard myself breathing very loudly and raggedly, and when I put a hand up to wipe sweat from my brow, I found that I was bleeding profusely from all along one side of my head. The only thing to be done was to go up to my room immediately, lie down and close my eyes and ears for as long as possible.

I turned to enter the stair, but for some reason stopped as I went to push the door open. I looked back at the pile of binbags at the edge of the pavement, which had still not been collected: the jigsaw pieces had disappeared. Some parent must have spotted them, thought their offspring would enjoy the challenge of putting the puzzle together, even in its damp and damaged state, and have grovelled around in the gutter collecting all the available pieces, before taking them home to dry out, perhaps in a large flat pan over a low gas.

But for me, even that possibility was now closed. I stepped round the rubbish and past a parked motorcycle into the roadway. Swiftly I walked half-way across, turned a right angle, and began to proceed in a straight line on top of the dotted white paintmarks on the tarmac there. I reasoned that if I stuck to the precise middle of the road, equidistant from the tenements on either side of the street, neither of them would be able to influence me with their dangerous gravity. My reasoning seemed to be correct. Certainly, I walked on in this manner for quite some time.

Dying and Being Alive

The first thing that comes into his head when he wakes in the morning is death, and the fear of death is with him all of the day.

One night he was sitting on the settee watching telly, his two wee boys playing with lego on the carpet behind him. His gaze drifted away from the screen for a moment, then he started, looked around the room, and shouted on the kids.

Gordon, Darren, come here.

I'm here Daddy.

Me too.

Aye, but come round here though.

Och . . .

Come here!

The boys came round from behind the settee, and stood in front of him in their pyjamas. He took hold of their hands.

Look at me, he said. The boys raised their eyes to his. Then he said, What are you going to do once you're dead?

They looked at him. He raised his eyebrows, cocked his head on one side, gazing at each of them in turn.

Eh, what can you do? said the bigger boy after a while.

He looked at the boy, nodding slowly, seeming to consider his answer. Then he turned to the younger boy, leant closer to him and said, Well Darren, how about you?

Darren pulled away slightly, looked over his father's shoulder towards the kitchen door. His eyes were beginning to pucker up and fill with tears. Mummy! he called.

Wheesht, wheesht! said his father, letting go their hands, but the kitchen door was already opening, and the boys' mother took a step in.

What's up honey? she said.

Nothing, said Gordon.

It's Daddy, said Darren, He's asking me questions . . .

Hey, come on son . . . The father stretched out to pat Darren on the head, but the boy jerked away and ran over behind his mother.

Keith, she said, What've you been saying to them?

Nothing! he said, Nothing at all. He fidgeted with the TV remote-control. Well, except . . . He looked up, shrugged. Nothing.

He said what would we do when we died, said Gordon.

Och Keith . . .

I was just trying to get them thinking, you ken. He let out a short laugh. It's good to face up to things.

Not at the age of six and four though!

Well . . . it has to be sooner or later. He turned back to the telly, turned the volume up slightly.

She stared down at him for a few seconds, her lips moving against each other, then she said, Come on boys, time for bed.

When the kids were settled, she came back into the lounge, then passed through into the kitchen. She reappeared five minutes later with two cups of coffee and a couple of butteries on pieces of kitchen-towel.

I stuck these under the grill for a minute, she said, Freshen them up a bit.

Aye, very good, he said. He wasn't actually looking at the TV now, but at a spot on the carpet just in front of it.

Keith, she said.

Hmm.

I wish you wouldn't talk to the kids like that. Especially just before they go off to bed. Keith, are you listening?

What? Aye, aye.

Well, I mean to say. You'll be giving them bad dreams.

He snorted, turned towards her. Bad dreams Lesley? I wish it *was* all bloody bad dreams!

She looked into his eyes for a few seconds. Have you been worrying about them making a mistake again? You getting buried and then waking up?

Christ, not just getting buried, he said, That would be bad enough. But imagine waking up and finding yourself being created, I mean cremated: imagine yourself being burned to death! The flames licking up the coffin walls, you banging and shouting as the air gets hotter, but your screams covered up by the roaring of the furnace! Jesus Christ almighty, it makes my blood run cold . . .

He was almost shouting now, and beads of sweat were beginning to form on his forehead and slug down the sides of his nose.

But Keith, she said, You're just not being sensible. I mean I'm sure they do loads of tests and everything, I mean they make sure you really are, you know, dead.

The autopsy! he cried, That's almost worse: lying out there on a cold stone slab, some guy in a white coat slicing you open – slicing you right up the middle! – then cutting out all your innards, your heart and your lungs! And sometimes they even saw off the top of your head and poke around in your brain! He wiped his mouth with the back of his hand. Imagine lying there and feeling all that!

You're just being stupid now, said Lesley, shaking her head, You'll be dead: you won't feel a thing!

I might.

No you won't: that's the whole point of being dead. God, Keith, sometimes you're just so . . . Jesus! She picked up her coffee.

I'm not saying it's definite, he said. I'm just saying it's possible, a strong possibility. I mean nobody *really* knows, because you can't really know till you actually die. But I have this theory. I've been thinking about it a lot, and my theory is: you feel everything after you die, everything.

He leant over towards her, clutched the arm of the settee. His eyes were bulging, and sweat was making his face glisten all over in the grey light of the TV.

After I die, he said, I'm going to feel every little thing they do to me. That scares me: the fear of dying and being alive.

Loaves and Fishes, Nah

Look I'm sorry Mr Angusson, but the fact is that new claims take a certain time to process, and it doesn't matter I'm afraid how much money you have at the moment, or how little money, but once your forms go into the system, they will certainly be coming out the other end at some point.

Not well-paid not well-treated these clerks, don't lose the rag does no good anyway, hated by one and all, yin and y'all, you fucking eight-grand-a-year pen-pushing bastard, key-pushing these days I suppose: some rob you with a six-gun, some with a silicon chip.

Aye, but the point is, it's not a question of having a little money just, it's a question of having no money at all: I've nothing left, nothing.

Lying bastard, I've got thirty-seven pence in my pocket, keep the hand out of there he'll hear the jingling, but don't look like you're not putting your hand there on purpose, fuck's sake a drop of sweat on the brow, don't wipe it wiping looks guilty, aye but so does sweating.

Well there is the possibility of applying for a hardship loan of up to fifty pounds; we could probably get that through to you by the end of next week.

He's no fucking idea, no idea at all.

Nah, don't bother with any of the loans business, I'd only have to pay it back; the actual supplementary, that's the main thing, I'll hold out for that. Five weeks I've been waiting now, a day or two more won't kill me. Probably.

Is thirty-seven pence enough for food for two days? Aye, if you're a cat: half pint of milk, one tin co-op own-brand minced cow brain cat sludge. If you're male, Scottish, twelve stone odd, I DOUBT IT. But there's always the bright side, think of this forthcoming foodless period as the ideal opportunity to start that diet you've been promising since Xmas, slim off those turkey burgers on the DHSS guaranteed weight-loss regime.

Well what I'm saying Mr Angusson is, it might actually be more than a day or two still; because you have been working recently, you see, you are in fact a low-priority claim.

Jesus fucking H. Corbett Christ, murder murder murder.

Three weeks at fifty quid a week and now I'm a low bloody priority, I mean to say! Not much wonder folk . . .

STOP, don't say it, don't mention not declaring work, even to admit (maybe) that you've heard (possibly) about the existence of such a crime could result in immediate severance of benefit. But I'm not getting any! Okay, jugular then. Anyway, I have declared it, aye *this* time, but that last time was a year ago, aye but dole clerks are like elephants: big fucking ears and small brains. And the memory. And the grey wrinkly skin. From now on I shall call you Nelly.

It is unfortunate that your employment was terminated at an earlier date than originally envisaged, but this office has no formal connection in fact with the scheme that . . .

The clerk is havering, my mind is wandering. Now my eyes; the desk between us is blank and empty: desks are always empty in these booths, in case of violent struggles, clerks thrown bodily through the air, crashing into piles of purple, white and shite-coloured forms, valiant claimant fists sending paper-clips, staplers and red biros flying willy-nilly. William Nilly OBE, inventor of the DHSS interview booth with patent grille in the protective glass barrier at precisely non-mouth height, so to make the pen-pusher hear involves shouting the details of one's miserable state at the top of one's miserable voice. Graffiti: I died waiting 29/5/86. The unknown claimant. His national insurance number liveth for ever more. Monuments raised outside every broo in the land.

. . . your B1 form, your P45, your UB40 . . .

On the cubicle wall by his left ear, a piece of A4 taped up, typewriting on it. At the back of the cubicle a door to somewhere, the bowels of the computer, full of shite haha. His hair is very thin, the worry of the job, poor sod I don't think. The paper, the A4 notice, notice the notice: DISTRIBUTION OF EEC FOOD. Please pass on revised times for distribution to claimants. In line with other areas throughout Edinburgh, times now synchronised for Leith benefit office area as 10 a.m. to 12 noon every Thursday till further notice. Venue as before: Salvation Army Hall, Bangor Street. Hmm. Thursday: today. What's the . . . five to ten!

. . . when a decision is reached a form A14N will explain in full . . .

Eh, excuse me. It's just, eh . . .

Yes?

Eh well, I'm going to have to get going now.

Well . . .

Arise slowly and crawl.

I mean I can see you're pulling your weight for me there so, eh, thanks for that – keep it up! – but as I say . . .

Don't look at the watch, that looks like previous appointments, that looks like not available for work.

Well if you're clear now on the procedures . . .

Aye, that's great, ta very much. Bye!

Open the door and out, out and away, he doesn't mind, he doesn't care: time for a cup of tea before the next victim. Hope it's that lassie with the screaming infants ya bas. Through the waiting-room: those about to, we salute you. Somebody reading a book for fuck's sake, bad move, looks like a student: get to the back of the queue wanker, make way for the genuine article, you'll get a grant cheque in three months anyway, whadya needa giro for? Totally unjustified assumptions there, totally unfair one is being, but who can blame one? I blame society. Down the stair and out into the rain. Which has now stopped. I blame sobriety: if I could be drunk more often, or maybe all the time . . . but in this day and age thirty-seven pence purchases absolutely no alcoholic beverage of any amount or kind whatsoever, except for those wee bottles of Dutch lager well there you go my point proven, except in France or Spain of course where you can take your billycan along to the vineyard and they'll pour out the vino for you straight from the fucking tap, what a place, and no need for a roof over your head either: sleep rough without your extremities turning blue.

Bangor Street, Bangor Street, easy: round here, along North Junction, across the roundabout, looking out for the maniac juggernauts of West Bowling Green Street: what a name, I ask you who called it that? Someone with a sense of humour. Or a very long memory. West Bowel Movement Street I would say. Then across there and along Great Junction Street, and it's not far along, opposite the hospital I think. Jesus, the time the bottom fell off that teapot and the tea was fresh made and it went all over Aileen's leg, and the blisters came up in seconds. Her sitting on the edge of the bath with her leg in cold water, then I suggest going to the hospital, it being just ten minutes away, so off we went: me, Leith resident of eight months' duration, proudly showing off the shortcut via The Quilts, not knowing the hospital had stopped dealing with accidents and emergencies three weeks before. The notice by the door. Fuck's sake. Cuts. No dosh for a taxi, but enough for a bus: all the way to the centre of town, a very long journey, tears coming out of her eyes, not running down her face but spurting straight out, the pressure, the pain.

Across the bridge, Leith's Super Cinema on the gable end: if only. No need for a bus up town, special matinées for the unemployed (packed-out) three jamjars a ticket. Now there's a thing, jam, jam tomorrow, what's that all about? Sixty a jar therefore one-eighty a ticket, that's not cheap, though of course you'd get to eat the jam, but then if you weren't going to buy it anyway it's still not a saving. Like *free tea-towel with every fifty pot-noodle lids sent*, folk fall for that! And then they moan about the Tories.

There it is, cross. Bangor Road, not Bangor Street – shit! – so is this it then? Aye, no question, another DHSS fuck-up just, here's the Sally Army and here's the queue. I walk the line. Being in a queue gives a licence to stare at anyone passing by, always, always, like guys in a bus queue staring at women as they pass, But why, ah now, that's a good question, and there must be a good answer to it but not now not now. Not so long, fifty maybe, and would you fucking believe it (yes I fucking would) the whole lot of them are pensioners, well the whole lot bar two, two other doleys I think. It's a total disgrace this situation: not the pensioners getting told, but us not getting told. If I hadn't been in for an interview, and if I hadn't spotted the notice . . . and it's a good job it was today and not tomorrow I was in. I should've taken it up with the bastard: hey you, mister figure juggler, what's the scam on the free grub, eh? You were meant to tell me the fucking details, that's a dereliction of duty, that's grounds for me having a word with your superior! No fucking chance: he'd probably get a medal for saving money. And I'd have my claim kicked around a few weeks longer for having an unhelpful attitude. Anyway it's best to be in near the start, so no time for talking. And here's the end.

The doors open yet doll?

Fuck's sake, the very exact fucking precise second I join the queue an old dear appears with a trolley out of nowhere, directly into my place.

I don't think so, ten they're meant to be letting us in, eh no?

Aye that's it, ten, I heard about it at the lunch club.

Hih, aye, same with me.

I would've thought there would've been more folk than this here; I was reading in the paper that at one place in Glasgow three-and-a-half thousand folk turned out! They had to call the police, and there was near a riot when they ran out of food. But that's Glaswegians for you: a bittie lacking in civilisation.

Voices raising, bags being picked up, feet shuffling.

I think that's them opening the door now.

About time too . . . hold on son, where's your bag?

What, do you have to have a bag?

Aye! Well, no, you don't have to have one, but it makes it easier to carry home, saves you getting it wet if the rain comes on again.

I was just going to stick it in my mouth, keep it dry in there.

Here, listen doll, don't be daft, I'll give you one of my carriers, I won't need more than two.

And she has approximately five hundred in her trolley: well-prepared for any unexpectedly large avalanche of the European food mountain in her direction.

That's great, thanks very much.

Don't mention it son, here we go look.

I wish I'd brought me trolley, good for cleaving a passage through the heathen hordes. Follow in her wake, towards the Hall of Distribution. When was the last time I was inside a religious institution? Who cares! Jesus cares, my son. And so does the EEC: the feeding of the five thousand hungry Leithers, loaves and fishes, nah, what're we getting? Boxes on trestle tables all round the hall and, here's the commissionaire.

Unemployed is it son?

Aye.

Can I see your UB40?

Aye.

Not a commissionaire, it's just the peaked cap and the uniform makes him look like he should be chucking folk out of the pictures, Leith's Super Cinema, instead of chucking them into the non-works canteen.

Over there son, table three.

Here we go, free food for the masses: socialism in action! No, the opposite. A female commissionaire and a plain-clothes assistant behind the table, the nice one and the nasty one routine maybe?

Unemployed is it son?

Aye.

Can I have your card?

Aye.

Take my card, take my whole life too, cause I can't help getting my lunch from you. What's this she's written on it?

Is that a carrier you've got there son? See it over. Ina, check off: milk, two pints semi-skimmed; butter, one pound charity blend; cheddar cheese, eighteen oz. approx. There you go son.

Ya beauty missus! Praise the lord and the member states.

Back out the way you came in son. Now sir, have you got your pension book please?

I can't breathe, I'm dying, the excitement is too much for me, I haven't been so happy since the scheme was stopped by the Health and Safety. Fresh air, quick, fresh air and open spaces, let's have a look at the loot. Out the hall, down the corridor, folk still streaming in, and there's the fourth non-pensioner of the day, a record I think Norris, yes Boris, scrounging bastards the lot of them. Outside and the rain's on again: thank you Jesus for Mrs Tartantrolley the baglady and . . . and here she is, on the road outside the hall, shaking a lump of cheese at somebody in the queue.

You dirty bugger you, you cheating swine! Oh hello son, see I tellt you the bag would be handy, you stinking thief!

Something the matter?

Aye, I'll say there's something the matter: see her there, that bisom's been in already, she was in front of me, and now she's going back in there again for more, the greedy old hog! It would drive you gyte!

Surely they'd recognise her face?

There's been that many old folk in the day, doll, she'll probably get away with it. A young one like you would be spotted, but not her the old bitch.

But they were writing something on the pension books and that, was that not a mark to show you'd had your share-out?

Aye, but look at it doll, get your card out.

Angusson, P.D. NJ 43 9696 B. Thurs Feb 5th and every second Thurs thereafter. Box 5. And now at the top edge in pencil: Leith, 25/3/87.

See son! They should never have given the food over to the Sally Army to give out, all that religion's gone to their heads: they've written it in pencil, the stupid ginks!

Hmm.

So you could just rub it out . . . smudge it away with a bit of spit on your finger, and then go in for more?

Aye exactly, it's a bloody disgrace. I even heard of some old body that had a motor, and he was going to one depot, like Leith, getting his portion there, then rubbing out the mark, jumping in his car and going off to Muirhouse community centre! Then on to Drylaw or somewhere . . . all over the town in the one morning! It's a sin what these Christians have been doing: pencils!

Hmm. Hmm again. Thirty-seven pence in my pocket. Hmm. Four pence for a roll, or seven pence for two rolls if it's the old grandad behind the counter and I nip out quick while he's still trying to count. Cheese sandwiches Jesus, with butter! Which would leave thirty pence, which would be almost the right amount for the stages, not too much too little for . . .

Listen missus, thanks again for the carrier, but time's getting on, I've got to be somewhere by twelve. So, eh, see you!

Bye son.

Top speed up to the end of Bangor Road, glance right along Great Junction Street: yes, there's a red bus coming! Past the fish van, quick, to the bus stop at the end of the bridge. Here it comes. Thank you God, a 7 for Surgeon's Halls, North Leith and in big letters: MUIRHOUSE. Wave it down: hold out the arm, carrier bag of milk, butter and cheese swinging there, and look the driver in the eye as you ask for a thirty.

The Druids Shite It,
Fail to Show

Colin was out in front, shouting the lead for the songs, clapping his hands, and the rest of the crew were behind him in a line across the road, chatting away, smoking, slagging each other off, and now and then joining in with Colin bawling, BOUNCY BOUNCY BOUNCY BOUNCY DYCE DYCE DYCE!

Back a bit, not bouncing or singing, sweating, Billy and Ray were following on, each of them lugging two massive carriers of cans. With every step, the bags of booze were banging against their legs.

We should've brought our fucking shinguards, said Billy.

A fucking car would've been more like the fucking business, said Ray.

Stop talking and start walking! somebody shouted from up ahead.

FUCK YOU! shouted back Billy.

Cammie stopped and turned, hands spread. Okay lads, point fucking taken, just keep the fucking pubes on. I'll tell you what, right, give us a can each and the bags won't be so heavy.

Like fuck we will! said Ray. You think we've carried it this fucking far to have you cunts get stuck in while our fucking hands are full!

Aye, no fucking chance Cam, said Billy, We're near enough there now, so you can just fucking wait and suffer like the rest of us.

Cammie was smiling: Well, I reckon you better just shut your fucking moaning then . . .

I reckon you better just fuck off, Billy came in. I mean it wasn't my fucking idea to come away up here. I've been up here afore with that mad bastard, I kent it was a bugger of a walk. If you're peched out from walking it's fucking Colin you should be complaining to.

Cammie grinned and laughed, and walked faster for a few seconds till he joined up with the lads ahead again, joined up with the bunch of them and joined in with the singing, HELLO HELLO WE ARE THE BEACH END BOYS!

I tell you what, said Ray, We should never've agreed to fucking tossing a coin for this fucking job.

Tossing a quine, said Billy, Now that would've been more acceptable.

Ray laughed. Nah, he said, I mean we should just've worked out a rota system, fucking taken it in turns man. Christ, these handles are cutting into my skin like blades!

They'd left the edge of town behind by this time and had been making their way up a farm track for a while, clouds of stew rising up under their trainers, drifting back into the eyes and mouths of Ray and Billy coming up in the rear. And the two of them were also stubbing over ruts and potholes in the road.

Is it much fucking further is it? said Ray, breathing hard.

No, look, said Billy, and nodded up ahead to where the crew had come to a stop at a gate by the side of the track.

As Ray and Billy caught up with them, Colin was lifting a circle of twine off the stoup. He nodded at them. Come in to the body of the kirk, he said, then, as the gate started to swing open, he jumped onto the bottom bar and swung with it, pointing into the park and shouting, CHARGE! Fifty yards away, at the top end of the park, there was a clump of trees raised up on a grassy knowe.

The lads looked at each other, then Pidge said, Eh, is that all there is to it then? I mean where's the fucking mystic remains, eh?

What! said Colin, jumping down off the gate, Can you not feel strange forces in the air? Whoohoohoo!

Aye aye, Col's been on the magic mushers again, said Duggy.

Come on, let's get moving, said Colin. It's a mental place, that wee wood. Let's go! And he marched off across the dreels. There was a shrugging of shoulders, then folk started after him. Half-way across the park, Colin turned and shouted back, Don't forget the Country Code: shut the fucking gate!

Aye, better not let the sheep and that escape, said Beamer.

Right enough, you'll be needing them later on, said Cammie.

Everybody laughed, and then Pidge started singing, Sheep-shagging bastard, he's a sheep-shagging bastard! And everybody else started giving it laldie too, except Beamer, who was standing there going red in the face, and Billy, who had passed his bags of carry-out to Duggy and gone back to close the gate.

After a few minutes they were at the end of the park, and Colin climbed up onto the dyke surrounding the trees and turned back to face the crew, who were all shouting and laughing now, trying to nick cans from the carriers, looking up trying to make out what was on top of the mound amongst the trees. Colin threw his arms apart in a cutting movement, and when the noise only half-stopped, he shouted, Silent drill! Everyone shut up and looked at him, and he raised a finger to his lips, shushing them, then signalled with it for them to come up and over the dyke one by one. Cammie went first, then Pidge, Billy, Duggy handing the booze bags to Colin first, Ray next, doing the same, Beamer last, till they were all in over, and Colin louped down beside them. Through all this nobody opened their mouth to speak, and the sounds of the town were left far behind and below now; the only noises were the occasional clatter of an oil-rig chopper carried on the wind from the heleport a couple of miles away, and caw-coughing craws from some big black birds in the trees overhead.

Colin passed to the front of the crew and led them up the slope, through the trees and out into a slight dip in the ground which was followed by a clear grassy space with the big grey jagged stones ranged around its edges. Colin held up a hand, and the others stopped in the middle of the stone circle.

Lads, said Colin, These are the Devil Stanes . . .

None of the Dyce Casual Crew moved or spoke at all. They stood and looked round at the tall flat slabs, some of them even taller and broader than Duggy, rising straight out of the earth, others looking shorter, leaning at various angles, half tipped over by tree roots or something. A couple were completely couped and partly grown over with grass and red moss. The hoodies were keckling up above, the wind was guttering through holes in the dyke and branches, and the crew was in total silence.

SHITING IT LADS? shouted Colin suddenly and immediately everyone was talking and laughing and stepping from foot to foot, walking about the clearing. A couple folk took off their jackets, and Ray hung his shell-top over one of the stones.

Crack open the bevvy! called Duggy, and a cheer went up as the carriers were emptied out onto the short grass, near to where someone had had a fire going fairly recently.

I'm fucking parched by the way, said Pidge, and he grabbed at the can that Duggy had just opened.

Get your own you cunt, said Duggy, turning away. There's plenty for everyfuckingbody.

It is hot though, eh? said Beamer.

Hot enough to make you beam, said Ray. He put on a cheesy grin and slapped at his cheeks.

I reckon we should've gone down to the beach, said Beamer.

I'm fucking fed-up of the carnies, said Ray.

Aye, but I'm not talking about them, am I: I'm saying it's hot enough to get going in the water, ken.

A few folk laughed. Shite! shouted Cammie from the other side of the circle.

Feel this fucking heat man, Beamer went on. It would've been grand mucking about in the sea, and we could've got the bus straight there, instead of climbing all these fucking hills.

Cut the fucking peenging, said Colin. Christ, it was only one wee fucking hill we had to climb: if you're not fit for that . . . Jesus!

All the lads were looking at Beamer, who was starting to go even redder in the face. Colin spoke again:

Anyway, the sea won't be hot enough for swimming. It doesn't heat up, that's the problem with the bastarding sea around here, it just doesn't fucking heat up: no matter how hot the weather is, the water's still cold enough to freeze your chugs off. If you had any, you peenging fucking poofjuice!

Beamer took a big swallow of lager, then he said, Still, we could've given it a go. And if it was too nippy, we could've gone to the carnies as a last resort.

A few groans went up.

I just can't be arsed with that place, said Ray, shaking his head. I used to like the shows, but I'm just fucking . . . fed up of them these days.

Tell you what Beamer, said Colin. Next time we're down there, we'll go to that Test Your Fist machine and draw your face on the fucking punch ball.

Everybody laughed. Profits'll soar, said Pidge.

Aye, we'll get one of your old floppy hats and stick that on top, said Cammie. Nobody'll ken the difference! Big and round and red as fuck: is it the ball or is it Beamer's head?

I had to buy a new hat this week, said Beamer.

Ah-ha! Changing the fucking subject you cunt! said Cammie.

No, I did though, they only last about three fucking games, then they're so muckit you can just forget about them.

Aye, you're right enough, said Ray. He had taken off his hat and was twirling it round on one finger of his non-drinking hand. If you try and wash them they end up looking like shite, all frayed and white and that: the red just comes flooding out.

Blood! said Pidge.

You'd ken about that right enough Pidge, said Colin. Hey, Ray, Billy, you missed yourselves yesterday, you should've seen this cunt! Jesus, speak about blood . . .

What're you talking about? said Billy from the far side of the circle where he was sitting and drinking, leaning back on one of the big stones.

You could've made a black pudding out of Pidge's spillings yesterday, said Cammie.

Colin jumped up from behind his pile of cans, and started jumping about amongst the crew and their carry-out, dancing about in the middle of the circle.

It was fucking MAGIC man, I'm telling you! he said, stomping on the grass at Billy's feet. Me and Pidge and Cammie and Duggy, we came out of Tannadice, right – after our historic victory – and there was this massive fucking escort waiting, pigs on horses and everything. Right away! I thought, and we decided we'd give that the fucking swerve. There'd been no fun in the ground, ken, and we didn't fancy going straight back to the fucking station and home.

You could've got off at Arbroath or somewhere, said Billy.

Wise up, said Pidge. We're in the middle of fucking Castle Street Dundee, and you're talking about Arbroath! Smokie Soccer Crew versus Tayside Trendies? No competition man!

Colin cleared his throat, looked at Billy and Pidge, then went on, So we're outside this pub, Reflections or something, and there's fuck all going on, right, there's nobody in the town but a few old scarfers. And we were more or less going to call it a day — eh Cam? — when there was this roaring and cheering, and we looked around and there were about twenty of the fuckers, piling out the swing doors of this bar . . . half the cunts still with glasses in their hands!

So did you run for it?

We didn't have time to run! We didn't have time to fucking turn around! One minute I was thinking the day was a wipe-out, the next thing I kent I was on the floor with some jute bastard kicking my head in!

And see me? said Pidge, Well I was furthest away, so I made a break for it.

Fucking bottled it, said Cammie.

Too fucking right, said Pidge, Tactical retreat I'd call it.

I bet Duggy never ran, said Ray.

No way I never.

Duggy never runs, said Billy, He's no brains. Everybody laughed.

Aye, and you've no balls Billy-boy.

Stop fucking bargling and get on with the fucking story, said Beamer.

Me and Cammie were on the ground, said Colin, And Duggy as well, we were just fucking outnumbered, we'd no chance. So, they've been putting the boot into us for a while, and then they see Pidge bombing away down the road, and one of them shouts, After him, don't let him away!

They thought I was the leader.

Now there's a fucking joke, eh! Anyway, it was a magic laugh, the three of us were left behind, a bit worse for wear and tear but basically A-okay, so we get up, brush ourselves down . . .

Aye, you didn't rush to come and help me, did you?

We thought you'd got clean away, said Colin, turning away to wink at Duggy and Cammie.

Pidge snorted. Actually I was getting put clean through a window at the time!

What! said Billy. Everyone was laughing and cheering.

Fucking classic! shouted Duggy.

Did you not stand up to them? said Ray.

Aye, but only for about three seconds! Then they had me down, started to kick me and that, and then one of them, this big orange paisley top on, he says, Hold on lads, through the window with the cunt! And they drag me across the street, lift me up, swing me like a bag of tatties: A one! A two! A three! And the next thing I ken I'm in a fucking coma.

Fainted more like, muttered Cammie.

What?

Nothing.

Here's me lying on the floor with all this blood in my eyes, and broken glass and records all over the place: they'd chucked me through the window of the fucking Virgin Megastore!

Billy laughed.

Were you lifted? said Ray.

Och, one of them turned up at the hospital and speirt all the usual shite, but what could they do me for: head-butting a plate-glass window? I was the innocent victim.

Makes a change, eh! said Colin.

I'll tell you who gave me a real grilling though: my mother! I came into the house about half-ten: two black eyes – as you see –

stitches all over the shop, my clothes all torn and covered in blood, and she looks me up and down and says, What time do you call this? Half-ten, I say. And where've you been till this time of night? Dundee Infirmary. WHAT? she screams, and she makes to clout me! Would've taken half my stitches out!

You didn't run from the Tayside Trendies, but you ducked your own ma, eh? Billy was laughing.

Beamer joined in. I can just see it, he said. Here son, what's that ambulance doing out in the road? Och, they gave me a hurl up from Dundee Mum, I said you'd pay the fare!

So you lost a lot of blood did you?

Too right I did, Ray. The doctors told me, Son, get out there and drink at least five pints immediately, or else your body's going to shrivel up like a dried-out johnny.

What does Adidas stand for? said Duggy.

Folk stopped laughing, there was a short silence.

What? said Cammie.

A durex is dead after sex!

No, but what was the question though?

Hih, I bet they told you to drink Guinness, eh Pidge?

Nah, red kola they said Ray, Guinness is the wrong colour.

But it's good for you though, I mean it's the most healthy drink you can get, it builds you up. That's how they give it to blood donors.

Everybody looked at Ray.

Away and shite, said Colin.

Nah, it's right enough, said Ray. Cause my mother goes to the blood transfusion, and she says she aye gets a half pint of Guinness afterwards: it fills up your veins again I suppose.

You can sell your blood in America, said Cammie. I saw a programme about it.

You can sell your spunk as well, said Beamer.

What?

Fuck off Beamboy!

You're joking man!

It's true, you sell it to a sperm bank. I read it.

Who'd want to buy your spunk anyway Beamer? said Colin.

I'm not saying mine just, but anybody's.

What, even some AIDS-ridden Jambo?

Well, I suppose they do tests Col . . .

Aye, I can just see it, said Colin. Now sir, are you an HIV positive by any chance? You are? Well, that's fine. Hold on though . . . Hearts supporter? FUCK OFF!

What Beamer's saying is right enough, said Billy. I mean it's good to know: if you're really hard up you can always go and get paid a few quid for wanking into a test-tube. Or a two-litre beaker in my case!

Fuck off! everybody shouted.

I still don't see what they do with it once they've got it though, said Pidge.

Well, said Billy, You ken Tunnock's Tea Cakes . . . ?

Everybody laughed.

They say it's good for the skin, said Billy. I read that somewhere, gets rid of spots and that.

Ho ho, so that would explain why your Sandra hasn't had any plooks lately, said Colin.

Cammie sat up from where he was lying on the grass, knocking a few empty cans aside. I can just see you Billy, he said. Here Sandra, want to try some of my new face cream? He held his hand under his nose, sniffed at it, stared at the palm as if examining something there, then started to pat it over his cheeks and forehead.

Aye, said Colin, And the next stage is: Hey Sandra, I hear it's very good for mouth ulcers as well!

Everyone was laughing, except for Billy, and they were licking their lips at him, sticking their tongues out, and making jerk-off movements with their hands up at their mouths. Billy jumped to his feet.

Here, hold on a minute, he said. Just fucking . . . just, just fuck off you bastards! There was more laughter. Shut it cunts! This is my girlfriend you're fucking slagging here!

Who mentioned slags? shouted Duggy. Right enough, slag's the word!

He let out a shout of laughter, but already Billy had leapt over in front of him, was bringing his leg back away to kick, leaning into it with the weight of his body. Colin was on his feet too, and as Billy began to swing, Colin was across and shoving him off his balance, Billy hytering away, Colin striding after him, pushing him down and onto his back on the short grass, standing over him, arms at his sides but fists clenched.

Stop right fucking there Billy boy! You watch who you're lifting your feet to, or I'll be lifting my hand to you: you'll be fucking stabbed you cunt . . .

Billy sat up, tried to get to his feet, but Colin raised his right foot, stuck his trainer right under Billy's nose. Billy could've grabbed it, twisted Colin to the ground, but he just looked at it, stopped rising, and then Colin placed his foot on Billy's shoulder, slowly leant forward on that leg, till Billy was forced to lie back again and flat out on the ground.

Billy's eyes were closed. His chest was heaving up and down. He opened his eyes, looked straight up into Colin's face.

Aye, fair enough, he said. But I can't have just anycunt going around miscalling my dame.

That's the point man Billy, that's the fucking point! You thick fucker! Aye, *anycunt* badmouthing Sandra fair enough, give them a belt across the fucking chops. Aye, *any*cunt. But not Duggy, nah, not any of the crew . . . your own fucking mob man! That's enemy-within stuff that is, that's the end of the Dyce Casual Crew if we start fighting amongst ourfuckingselves.

Billy lifted his head slightly and began to look slowly round the circle. Colin sniffed:

Tell him I'm right Cammie.

Well I would say you were right actually, to be honest.

Too right you're right, said Duggy. I mean if we're going to start battering each other we might . . .

Shut your gob, said Colin. Don't go fucking stirring it now, I'm trying to get your hash sorted out here.

He glowered around at Duggy and then the others as they sat or lay around drinking and smoking. He shook his shoulders, kind of shivering, then stepped away from Billy, moved over to where he'd left his can before the trouble. He paused, then bent to pick up the can, and swallowed the contents.

There's some more Kestrels over here, said Pidge.

Colin lowered the can from his lips, crumpled it in his hand, then chucked it onto the pile of empties that was growing in the centre of the circle. He was looking into the trees. Suddenly he turned back to Billy.

Come here with me man. Aye, Billy, come on.

Who, me?

Aye, you.

What, can I get up now?

Just shut it and get over here, okay? Colin moved away towards the edge of the clearing.

Billy sat up, leant back on his arms for a second, shaking his head, then stood up and followed Colin. The others watched them for a few moments, then started moving as well. Pidge and Cammie crawled over and grabbed a couple more cans each from where the carriers had been couped; Duggy davered out between two of the stones, down as far as the dyke surrounding the circle, then slowly walked further round the side of the knowe, gradually working his way up towards the top again; Beamer and Ray tagged after Colin to the far side of the circle. Here there was a massive brute of a stone, big as three of the others put together, and it was lying on its side inbetween two upright stones, touching them at each end. It was flat on the top, and Colin was leaning his elbow on it, staring at Billy and flicking his eyes over the rest of them as they approached. Billy stopped a couple of feet in front of him, hands in the pockets of his jeans; Beamer and Ray were slightly behind Billy; Pidge and Cammie had got to their feet and were drinking and watching from a short distance away; the sound of Duggy fighting through branches and bracken was coming closer.

Listen, said Colin, and slapped his hand on the flat top of the big stone. See these bastards here, they're called the Devil Stanes, as I said before. A few of the others nodded. But. Who kens who put them here?

Eh, the devil? said Cammie.

Colin raised his eyes slowly to the sky, sighed, and said, Nah, they only got the name cause the farmers were ignorant feartie bastards a hundred-odd years ago. So not much has changed: I mean look at Duggy's father.

Duggy had been struggling up the back of the mound. Now he reached the top, and leant over the big stone, peching hard. What's that you're saying about my da? he said, looking up.

I was just talking about who put these stones here, said Colin.

Well it wasn't my da, said Duggy. His ground only comes as far round as the quarry, not up to here.

Colin looked at Duggy for a moment, then shook his head, curled his top lip in a kind of sarcastic smile. Well I'm glad we've got that sorted out, he said.

Was it the Picts? said Ray.

Not a bad guess Raymie, said Colin, But still completely fucking wrong. Nah, these things were here years before the Picts came along. These are Stone-Age stones, these are, fucking ancient history! These go back to the days of the druids – fucking two thousand BC man!

Everyone looked around at the circle. Colin waited a few seconds, then slapped his palm on the flat stone again, and nodded at it. Come on Billy, he said, Get up on here a minute.

What?

You heard me.

Eh?

Billy. Get up on this stone for a minute, I'm needing to show the lads something.

Billy kicked at a lump of grass a few times, then shrugged his shoulders. Fine by me, he said. He leant back against the side of the big stone, placed his hands on the edge of it behind him, elbows jabbing into the air. Fine by me, he said again. Then he straightened his arms and pulled himself up and back, scrabbling with his heels on the rough side of the stone at the same time. Then he was there, sitting on top of the big flat stone, his feet dangling a good eighteen inches off the ground. He looked around at the rest of the crew, smiling.

Now lie down, said Colin.

Billy snapped his head round, mouth open. What? he shouted. The others were laughing, apart from Colin. Colin was looking at Billy, unsmiling. Then he scratched his head, took a step back, and began to walk slowly round to the right, round the upright stone, and in behind the back of the flat one.

Shift! he said, and elbowed Duggy away from where he was leaning. Duggy wandered round to the other side, where Beamer and Ray were standing; Pidge and Cammie came closer too. All of them were looking at Col. Billy turned his head too.

Can I get down now? he said.

Don't move, said Colin quietly. Now listen. Back in the Stone Age, right, when the druids were on the go, and they put up this stone circle here, how many of them do you think it took? He glanced around, but nobody made to answer. Well I'll tell you for nothing: it wasn't a couple of mates that got drunk one night and decided to cart the buggers up here just for a laugh. No fucking way. It was a big job. Look at the size of this thing! He spread his arms out along the length of the flat stone; his fingertips were still a couple of feet away from the upright stones at each end. See that? Must weigh twenty ton at least – more! And they'd no fucking JCBs in them days.

And all these others as well, said Pidge, looking round at the smaller stones that made up the circle.

Must've taken a hell of a lot of druids to hump these things all the way up here, said Beamer.

Exactly! cried Colin, and smacked both his hands down. Team work, that's what it was! The Druid Mental Crew in action: fifty lads pushing from behind, another fifty pulling with ropes, all the way up the fucking brae! Sweaty work, Christ aye, but they stuck in, they had the fucking dedication, dedication to howk them out of the ground God knows where, drag them away up here, then plant them in the ground again!

Sounds pretty daft to me, said Duggy. They'd've saved themselves a lot of bother if they'd just set them up in a circle wherever they found them.

Aye, or at least they could've stuck them down by the river or something, said Ray. I mean it was bad enough coming up here with two bags of carry-out.

Ah well, that's the whole point, said Colin. Hih, Billy, lie down a minute, will you?

I tellt you: no.

Oh, okay. Anyway, they had to put the circle up here, cause there was a lot of mental violence going on, and you had to be able to see the country all around, to make sure nobody was sneaking up on your ceremonies and that.

Ceremonies? said Pidge. What, you mean like devil worship and that? Black Sabbath fans were they?

The devil wasn't even invented then, said Beamer. Is that not right man? It was the sun and the moon and that they worshipped, eh? We did it in history, mind Col?

Colin glowered at him, then cleared his throat and went on, Aye, that's another reason for having the circle up here. They had to have a good view of the stars and the sunset and stuff, so they'd ken when to do their various ceremonies, and their HUMAN SACRIFICE!

As he shouted, Colin jumped forward and grabbed Billy's shoulders, and pulled him down backwards. Billy's head thunked onto the stone. Jesus fuck! he shouted, and began to struggle to sit up, and to clutch at the back of his head. But Colin was holding both his arms, pinning his shoulders down.

Grab his fucking feet, said Colin.

Nobody moved, except Billy, who began to thrash his legs about.

CAMMIE! PIDGE! GET A HOLD OF HIS FUCKING FEET! shouted Colin.

The two of them moved forward.

Stop waving your legs about a minute, said Pidge.

Billy made a spluttering noise half-way between a laugh and a snort and some watery bogies shot out his nose onto his top lip, then ran down his cheeks, one dripple each side. He stopped kicking.

Hold him down, said Colin. Now, he said, Move him round so he's lying longways.

Billy's body went very stiff, all his muscles tightening, his legs and arms stretching straight out, but he wasn't struggling any more. They half-lifted and half-dragged him till he was lying out along the length of the flat stone, his head touching one upright stone and his feet just short of the other. His eyes were staring straight upwards. Colin leant over Billy's face and grinned down at him. Then he pursed his lips, pushed them together and out in a kissing movement.

You wouldn't, said Billy.

Wouldn't what? said Colin, smiling.

You haven't even got your blade with you. Why should you?

Don't you worry about me and my friend Mr Stanley, said Colin. We can look after ourselves okay. He laughed quietly, and looked up at the others. They nodded and grinned as they saw him glancing round, then went back to frowning, looking worried. Duggy, Beamer, Ray, said Colin. Come in close. They shuffled forward.

What's the score Col? said Pidge. How long've we got to hold him down for?

Not long, said Col. Just till I've finished. The corners of his mouth were upturned, the teeth showing, but the skin around his eyes was smooth and unpuckered. I've got something to say to you, you see, all of you, and Billy especially. Listen. Colin shifted his hands off Billy's shoulders, lifting one free into the air, and moving the other over to hold Billy's throat. This squabble theday, he said, The wee ruckus between Duggy and Billy here, well, we can't have that kind of thing going on in the Dyce Casual

Crew. He shook his head. The only folk who get anything done in this world are the folk that stick together, that work together. Like the fucking druids dragging these rocks up the fucking hill. Now if they'd been fighting amongst themselves, they'd never've done nothing. Agreed? Now. What was this fight about theday?

Duggy started slagging my dame . . .

SHUT UP! shouted Colin, and brought his free hand down to press along with the other on Billy's throat. LISTEN! This fight, and a couple of others recently, they've all been caused by one thing and one thing only. And what's that? Women, the fucking hairies've been at the back of it all.

There was a stirring of noise amongst the lads.

Aye, like you just on Friday, Pidge. We were supposed to be discussing tactics for yesterday, and what happens? You piss off to the pictures with – what's her name?

Eh, Colleen. Aye.

Colleen, you go to the pictures with Colleen. Okay, that's fine, no law against that, I mean she's a tasty bit of stuff, nobody's denying it. But: you went out with her on Thursday night as well! Now then, that's just totally out of order. Two nights in a row!

Christ, that's as good as married, said Billy.

Colin ignored him. It's simple, he said. Either you go out with her or with the boys, simple as that. You can't do both.

Pidge shrugged. I ken, usually, he said. But I was just getting her warmed up on the Thursday, ken? I mean she was pretty randy-radge already: just about sucking my tongue out of its socket, just about swallowing my fucking head! And on Friday she says, Do you want to come back to my place then? My folks are out . . . And I say, So nobody's in, eh? And she says, Aye, nobody except my wee brother and my big sister looking after him. But I mean, if it hadn't been for them I reckon . . .

Pidge, said Colin, You've proved my point. Once you get stuck on some lassie you're finished: you become a totally boring bastard, dancing up and down like her fucking yo-yo. Save it! We're not interested in your sex life! He paused, staring at Pidge, breathing heavily.

Sex, said Billy.

Shut up you, said Colin.

No, it's interesting, said Billy in a husky voice, his throat still constricted. Never mind Pidge though. Come on Col and tell us about your sex life.

Don't fucking start, said Colin. Don't, just don't . . .

Ach, don't be shy man, come on: the full juicy details: names and places Col, points out of ten, let's have it!

No! Fuck . . . what . . . Colin's eyelids were trembling, and one corner of his mouth was twitching up into his cheek.

If you're too modest, Col, I'll just have to tell the lads all about it myself . . .

Colin's head jerked back. His lips were moving, but no sound was coming out. He glanced down at Billy, then quickly jerked his head away again, and froze. He slowly closed his eyes, held them clenched shut for ten seconds, then opened them again, opened them very wide.

Billy raised his arms from his sides and moved his hands up around Colin's wrists, as if to prise the fingers away from his throat. But before Billy touched them, Colin loosened his grasp and lifted his hands up and away. He lifted them up to his head, rested them on top of it for a moment, then dragged them down over his face and rubbed his eyes with his fingertips.

Billy sat up. Immediately, Cammie and Pidge let go of his ankles and stepped off backwards. Billy swung round till his legs were hanging over the side of the stone, the same side Colin was standing at, then he slid forward on the arse of his jeans and dropped onto the ground beside Colin.

Colin had let his hands fall from his face, but he wasn't looking at anyone. He stared at the top of the stone where Billy had been lying.

Billy turned and leant over the stone, and spoke. I think what wee Col here is trying to say is this: he's no chance of getting a ride for at least three years – I mean look at him, he's a scrotty wee runt – and *we've* all got to live like monks till *his* balls drop and he gives us the nod, Okay to get your hole now lads! Well fuck that for a game of soldiers! Billy laughed. I'm fucked if I'm going to live like a fucking druid, no sex and carrying boulders all over the fucking shop! I tell you Col, if the druids are so fucking magic and clever, where are they theday, eh? Tell me that? Why are they not here now telling us to get the fuck out of their stone circle, off of their patch? Here's why: cause they're fucking extinct, they died out man! And why? Cause they were too knackered from dragging standing stones about to shag their birds when they got home. They never fucking grew up! And that's not going to happen to me. I'm off.

Billy looked at Colin for a few seconds, then stepped away from him, round the side of the stone and into the middle of the circle. He stopped. I'm going down the High Street, he said. Anybody coming? Nobody moved. Billy shook his head. Well fuck the lot of you, he said. You'll be down sooner or fucking later. He turned and strode off, out the far side of the circle, down the slope and over the dyke. The others watched as he walked away across the park.

Ray cleared his throat. Actually, I think I'll go with him, he said.

Eh, if you're going . . . I'll chum you down, said Beamer.

Colin focused on the crew for the first time, glowered round at them all. No one spoke. Ray and Beamer picked up their jackets and followed after Billy. As they started to climb over the dyke, Duggy shuffled his feet and took a couple of steps in the direction they'd headed, but almost immediately he stopped, turned, took a couple of steps back. He glanced over in Colin's direction, then looked away at a tree growing out of the side of the knowe; it had been half blown-over at some point, and its trunk was jammed at an angle against the next tree down the slope. Its roots were half rugged out of the earth, looking dried-up and grey hanging there in the air.

Are you going then? said Colin.

Duggy started. Who, me? he said. Colin was staring at him. He shrugged, nodded, then shook his head. Nah, Billy's a wanker, he said. I'll stay here. I mean there must be a few cans still to be drunk . . .

Have a look, said Colin.

Duggy went over to where the carriers had been couped out, picked up a couple of cans there, then got a few more from the far side of the circle, where someone had made a second stockpile when they first arrived. He came back over, and set the cans up in a row on top of the flat stone. There were five of them.

Well, said Colin, Is anybody else pissing off?

Not me, said Duggy. Cammie and Pidge shook their heads.

Well that's one each then, said Colin.

And one extra, said Pidge.

I was just fucking coming to that, said Colin.

Well, who gets it? said Cammie. Do we share it out, get a gulp each like? I mean that would be fair after what you were saying about teamwork and that.

Ken this, said Colin, I'm glad those three cunts've buggered off. I've been worried about them for a while. They were getting weak, losing their bottle. And if we're going to be the toughest in battle, the hardest mob in Aberdeen — and that means in the country — we can't have any slackers. If we're going to keep our self-respect, keep our name as the mentallest team around, it has to be all or nothing.

So who gets the extra can? said Duggy.

I do, said Colin. Any complaints?

Shoebox

He said, What do you think about when we're having sex?

What do you mean?

I mean, when we're having sex, what do you think about?

She looked into space for a few seconds. Nothing, I don't think about anything.

Nothing? Come on . . . !

No, honestly, I don't. I don't think you're meant to think; I think it's more of a feeling thing. I mean if you were thinking about something, you couldn't really be enjoying yourself very much, could you? She scratched herself somewhere under the covers, then nodded. Yes, I would say it's a bad thing to be thinking during sex.

Oh aye?

Aye.

Hih. So why were you smiling back then?

When?

He turned over towards her, propped his head up, looked at her. Back then, when I first asked you.

I wasn't smiling!

Aye you were, I saw you! Jesus, your thoughts must've been

pretty dirty before you could smile like that: you were just about drooling over the sheets!

She rolled her eyes. That's cause I'm starving, she said. Away and make some breakfast.

What, me? He sat up. Me, the man of the house doing the cooking? Up and do it yourself woman: what else are you good for!

Fuck off! She lay back with her hands behind her head on the pillow. What else are *you* good for? Not much, judging by last night's performance.

Huh! He slid out from under the blankets and walked round to the end of the bed, where he started pulling his clothes out of the tangled pile lying there. After a while he said, That's not what you were saying last night.

I don't remember saying anything last night.

Well that says it all, doesn't it. He pulled on his tee-shirt and tucked it into his jeans, grinning down at her.

Well if it makes you happy to think that . . .

Hmm. And what would make you happy, like?

Getting some breakfast before I starve to death! She flung her arms out across the bed and sucked her cheeks in, eyes crossed.

He laughed. Two minutes, okay, and I'll get it. He stuck his feet into his trainers and went over to the door; as he paused to take it off the snib he said, Hey, shove on Radio Forth and we can listen to the phone-in show while we're eating. She yawned in reply, and he went out the door and shut it behind him. His footsteps went away down the corridor towards the toilet.

A couple of minutes later, the door opened again and he stepped in. She was still lying in bed, her back to him; the radio wasn't on. Hey, he said.

She rolled over, looked at him. What?

Mystical sights in the lavvy!

What?

He went over and sat down on the bed. Well, I was standing there having a pee, right, as you do . . .

No I don't.

You're just a lazy bugger though. Anyway, you ken how somebody's put in one of those blue rinse things? Well, I was standing there, and I was looking down at this blue water in the pan, and my yellow stuff going into it, and I suddenly thought: Jesus, this looks just like the Northern Lights . . .

Whaaat?

I ken, amazing, eh? The pee was going in, and you could see it going in yellowish, and then it would sort of fall down, it would turn greenish and it would fall down through the blue water in short of sheets, no, curtains, greeny curtains waving about and shimmering. Aye, that's how it was. And I tell you, it was just like the Northern Lights: beautiful!

She had propped herself up on one elbow. What a load of shite!

No! That would've ruined the effect completely!

She sighed, blinking slowly. Anyway, how do you ken what the Northern Lights look like? You've never seen them.

Aye I have.

No you haven't.

Ah, you're forgetting where I was born and raised quine. I saw them hundreds of times when I was a kid. We watched them instead of having a telly, in fact.

She laughed, fell back on the bed.

Well, I saw them a few times, he went on. And they looked just like that there; made me feel quite nostalgic in fact. They call them the heavenly dancers . . .

Aberdeen, she called out over his singing, The biggest public pisspot in the country.

He stopped the song. You insult my place of birth, he said,

putting on an offended look. I'm afraid I must ask you to step outside and . . . make the toast.

She rolled out of bed and began to get dressed. Okay, she said, But only cause I'm wasting away here waiting for you to do it.

Why else?

She smiled at him, stuck up two fingers, and left the room.

He listened to her walking away, then laughed to himself and lay back across the bed, putting his hands behind his head as she had done earlier and laughing again. Then he sighed, smiling.

The door banged open and she strode into the room. Shit! There's no milk!

So? He sat up. We've had it black before.

There's no bread either.

What? There were at least two slices there last night! Has somebody nicked it? I wouldn't put it past that bastard next door . . .

No, shut up, listen: it's mouldy, that's all.

He shrugged. Cut the bad bits off then.

It's all fucking bad bits! she shouted. If I cut the bad bits off we'll be left with two toasted crumbs for our Sunday breakfast!

He creased his forehead. What've we got then?

She leaned back against the wall, her eyes closed. Some lentils.

And?

That's about it really. There's that Chinese seaweed you bought. Pity you hadn't bought some kippers instead. Mind you they'd smell pretty bad by now seeing as you've had the bloody stuff for six months and never used it once.

I'm just waiting to find a recipe, he said quietly.

Aye, okay, okay. But meanwhile could you think up some way to get our breakfast out of lentils, seaweed and scrapings off the floor!

He thought for a moment, then, Couldn't we borrow

something from somebody else's cupboard? They wouldn't miss a couple of slices and a wee bit of cheese.

What's this? Two seconds ago you were ready to strangle him next door for taking two mouldy heels, and now you're away to nick bread off of him! She looked down at her feet. Anyway, he doesn't have any, I already checked.

Ach . . . shite. He sighed, shook his head, and slowly looked up at her. We'll have to go across to the shop, he said at last.

She cleared her throat. Aye, I suppose so.

He got up off the bed, and slowly walked over and out the door. She picked up her coat and followed him: down the corridor and out the flatdoor into the stair, down two flights then out onto the street, across the cobbled roadway and onto the pavement in front of Majid's.

You get the milk, she said. They went in.

He made his way to the counter, squeezing an orange in a tray of fruit on top of the freezer as he passed. There was a groan from the backshop, and the sound of a heavy body struggling up from a spring-busted armchair.

Morning Mr Majid, he called out.

Mr Majid appeared through the bead-curtain behind his counter. Oh hello, he said, It's you.

Well it was the last time I looked.

Mr Majid lifted the corners of his mouth slightly, reached under the counter and brought out a pack of B&H and a box of matches. He lit a fag, inhaled on it deeply, coughed.

Nasty habit, the boy said.

Mr Majid coughed again. At least I get them wholesale. The boy laughed. Mr Majid looked at him for a few seconds then said, So what can I do you for?

The boy bent down to the side of the counter and picked up a pint of milk from the crate there.

Thirty-three, said Mr Majid.

And have you got any matches?

Wee box?

Aye: do fine. A box of Bluebells was put down beside the milk. How much is that so far?

Forty-three.

The boy took money out of his pocket, dumped it on the counter, and slid the coins across to Mr Majid as he counted: Twenty, five, five, ten, one, one, one. He looked at what he was left with. What have you got for seventeen? Mr Majid shrugged, waved his non-smoking hand around the shop. The boy looked at the shelves that went as high as the ceiling, the boxes of fruit and veg ranged along the bottom of them, and the freezer units and sweet display-racks in the middle of the floor. The girl was pottering about by the babyfoods. The boy shouted over his shoulder, What do you want for seventeen pence?

I don't know, she replied. Something chocolate.

A Mars bar, Mr Majid?

Twenty.

Two Milky Ways?

Ten each.

A Twix then?

He took a long drag, looking at the boy over the top of his specs. Nineteen, he said.

Not seventeen?

He blew out a jet of smoke. Okay, you can owe me.

Ach, that's great, said the boy. Ta very much.

The next time you're in . . .

Aye, sure thing, said the boy, picking up the milk, matches and Twix.

The girl opened the shop door and called, Bye for now, as she went out. The boy started to walk after her.

Mr Majid stubbed his fag out under the counter somewhere. Have a nice day, he said, and, as the boy left the shop, went back through the bead curtain.

Outside, the girl was already on the other pavement, looking back, waiting for the boy. He crossed over to her slowly, and as he caught up with her she headed for their stairdoor. Once inside, they let it swing to behind them, then immediately they ran: along the passageway, up both flights of stairs, through the flatdoor, down the corridor and into their room. She collapsed on the bed, him on the floor, and they were both laughing away, gasping for breath in between. After half a minute they calmed down.

Well, he said, What did you get?

She sat up on the bed and started pulling things out of the pockets of her coat. Streaky bacon, marge, half a dozen eggs . . .

Eggs! Jesus, how did you manage them?

I have my methods . . . Now then: tin of tuna, beans . . . hold on, what's this? Processed peas? Shit, I meant to get beans; must've picked up the wrong tin.

Never mind, never mind. Anything else? I mean did you get bread or anything?

She reached inside her coat and from under her arm pulled out a small brown loaf. She held it up to him on the palms of her hands, grinning.

Brilliant, he said, High in fibre. Health-conscious even now.

That little extra for quality goods is always worth it.

Little extra? Jesus, did you see that? Thirty-three for a pint of milk: it's criminal! He slapped his hand down on the floor.

Ha! He probably has to put his prices up to cover for the amount of stuff folk thieve off him.

What, so if I took all this back he'd give me the milk for thirty? Right away!

Well, this is where my theory falls down . . . She flopped out on her back. He leant forward, grabbed her ankles, and started to pull her off the bed. She laughed. Let go! Mind the eggs!

He stopped pulling. *My* theory is, he said, You should go and get started on a big pan of scrambled eggs, I'll stick the bacon under the grill, then we'll stuff our faces with that and have the Twix for pudding. What do you reckon?

I reckon barrie. And still, say, tuna sandwiches for tea.

Or maybe we could save the tuna for tomorrow? I mean we'll be all right on Tuesday: we'll be able to stock up then . . .

Stock up? she said, To hell with that! Let's just go out somewhere, that Chinese place by the Playhouse, it's good and dear: we'll spend the fucking lot, eat till we can't stuff another crumb down!

Eat the whole eighty quid? Impossible: we'd explode!

Well if there was anything left, we'd leave a tip.

Ha, tips! Jesus aye! And a taxi home. And live off our fat for a fortnight . . .

They laughed for a moment, her sitting on the edge of the bed, him kneeling in front of her. Suddenly she slid down and onto her knees too, put her head in his lap, circled her arms round the bottom of his back; she wasn't laughing anymore. She was whispering something, her jaw clenched. Jesus, Jesus, Jesus . . . She jerked against his body. She was shaking.

After a few seconds he started stroking her hair. Then he stopped and gazed down at her. Do you want to know what I think about when we're having sex? he said.

Jesus . . . She sniffed, nodded her head against his leg. Okay.

He stroked her hair with one hand again, the other resting on the small of her back, fingertips under the top of her jeans. I don't suppose I do think things really; it's more like I see them. Like sometimes I see myself sort of flying, no, more like bouncing: leaping about over the city. It's night, and there are lights in the windows, but I'm outside. And I'm floating about above it all: I land on the top of a roof and I just give a wee push off and away I float. I can jump through the air for miles, above all the buildings and people below, floating around for ever . . .

Mmmm.

And sometimes when I go inside you, for the first time maybe, or when I've been in before but then come out and then I go in again, I feel like I'm walking into a room – aye, that's it – it's all dark, and then I see this door and it's bright inside and I go into the room.

What's in the room?

Nothing, it's just . . . light, there's light in it. But it's empty, an empty room, full of light, and I go in.

There was silence for half a minute. His hand stopped moving on her hair. Then she stirred, moving slightly so she was lying on the floor at his side. He leant back on one arm, stretched his legs out, looked down at her. Her eyes were open, red-rimmed, staring at something: the milk and matches on the floor behind him.

I've just remembered something I was thinking too, she said, Something I was seeing. It was just when you said you saw things, suddenly I remembered. It was last night. Mind how, quite near the end, you were holding me from behind? We were lying on our sides and you had one arm round under my head and down across here. She placed an arm across her chest. And your other arm was over the top and you were rubbing me there as you went in and out. And I remember . . . I was staring at the wall there, it was good, but I was staring at the wall in the dark, and I'm sure my eyes were still open, but I saw something. Somehow I saw something. She paused, breathing.

What? he said after a moment, What was it you saw?

It was the inside of a shoebox. It was all sort of opened up: I could see right in from the end, it was black inside. It was black outside too, but the edges of the box were there, I saw them. Somehow I knew that's what it was: a shoebox.

He didn't say anything. He looked across at the wall on her side of the bed.

What do you think it means? she said.

Eh . . . He lifted her head from his lap. Hold on, he said, I'm getting pins and needles. He swung his legs out from under her and got to his feet, then stepped through the scattered food and away. He crossed to the window and looked out over the roofs and chimneys.

Well, she said, What does it mean?

He stared out of the window, unblinking, then slowly leant forward so his forehead was resting on the glass. I don't know, he said at last.

Don't you? she said. I do.

Jesus Fuckeroo

My cisterns are totally fucked, their insides are rotten with rust. But will the town pay to fix or replace them? Will they buckies!

I was leaning by the door the other day when this old guy came out, looking a bit stunned. What's up old timer? I said to him.

Jesus fuckeroo! he replied.

I looked him up and down. As bad as that, eh?

I think I'm pishing blood, he said, and his voice was shaky.

Do you want a seat? I asked him.

No, he said, I just had one. And when I looked down, after, the water was red with blood.

This is where I clicked: there was no blood involved, it was rust from the cistern, stirred up in the flush and staining the pan . . . those fucking decrepit iron cisterns up to their tricks again! I could hardly keep the smile off my face.

Has anyone kicked your kidneys lately? I asked the old boy.

He looked at me, closed his eyes for a second like he was trying to think, then, No, he said, Not that I can recall.

How about your guts, any punches to the guts theday?

No, he said, Not at all that I've noticed.

I glanced around to check no one was near, then whispered in the hairs of his lug, How about your chugs, old man? Has anyone bounced on your balls lately?

He looked really shocked, he took a step back, the whole of his face was shaking. Do you think that could do it? he said.

Christ aye, I replied, looking serious. But the state of his face, the worry, his eyes folded up under tatters of skin . . . I just couldn't help it, I let out a laugh.

I don't think it's funny, he said.

Och grandad, I told him, I've been having you on. I wiped at my eyes with my fingers. It's just rust in the cistern gives water that look: you're fit as a fiddle, my friend, I bet you can pee straighter than I can!

Jesus fuckeroo, he said. You bastard.

Tongue

At one minute to two, Dugald came in the back door. There was no one about. He took his white coat down off its hook, put it on, and rolled the sleeves up above his elbows. Then he reached up for the blue-striped apron, placed the loop over his head and under the collar of the coat, and drew the cords right round his back and began to tie a bow in front of his belly. There was the sound of the venetian blinds being drawn up in the frontshop, and the snib being taken off the door. The apron ties were greasy with blood and fat, they were hard to get into a knot that would hold; Dugald leant back against the bench, sighed, looked down at his fingers amongst the string.

Is that you Kennedy?

Dugald looked up. It was Eleanor shouting through from the frontshop. No, it's me, he said.

Dugald?

Aye.

Well son, did you have a good dinner theday?

Aye, it was fine, I had fish pie and . . . The bell over the shop door rang.

Afternoon Mrs Rae! said Eleanor.

The apron was tied. Dugald smoothed his hands down over the

stiff blue cloth, made sure his coat sleeves were rolled up tight, then looked around the backshop. There was a tray of rolled pork on the sidebench, and beside it another tray, with briskets in it, waiting to be boned and rolled. On the draining-board by the sink was a basin full of sausage skins getting their brine soaked out in fresh water. Before dinner, Dugald had been mixing the sausage spices into the minced pork and beef; there were a couple of places where cuts on his hands still nipped from the spices or the chemicals they were blended with. Later on Kenn would be bringing out the sausage machine. Maybe Dugald would get a go at filling the skins this afternoon, or maybe tying the links; he'd watched Kenn do it twice now, and it looked difficult, but not impossible: circle, nip, twist, pull through a loop, nip, twist, and repeat. And three weeks into a career as a butcher seemed to be high time to be learning how to do sausages.

Through in the frontshop, Eleanor was saying goodbye to Mrs Rae. After the door closed, Dugald heard her walk through to the small office where she did the books and took freezer orders over the phone. She switched on the radio, Radio Two, but almost immediately the shop door opened again.

Dugald looked at his watch. He checked his sleeves, then gazed around the benches, the bandsaw, the metal trays of meat. It was a cold day, no flies, so the trays could be left out of the chill if necessary. He started to unroll his left sleeve, then stopped and rolled it up again. He sighed. He couldn't stand about doing nothing all afternoon. But he hadn't been told what to do yet. He went over to the sink and washed his hands under the hot tap, with plenty of soap from the dispenser. As he was drying them on the rotary towel, the back door opened and someone came in, boiching and hawking: Kenn. He didn't come through into the backshop straight away, but stayed by the open door for a few seconds, till there was the sound of him bringing a big gob of phlegm up his throat and spitting it out on the chuckies in the back yard. Then he closed the door and came ben.

Aye aye Kenn, said Dugald, pushing his sleeves up his arms.

Aye lad, said Kenn, walking quickly right through the backshop. Afternoon Mr Gilbert! he called as he paused in the front. I hope she's keeping you happy . . .

Fairly that butcher! The old man laughed.

The noise of the fans in the big walk-in chill filled the shop. Not too happy mind, Kenn shouted over it. You have to watch the likes of him Nell, the old ones are the worst! The chill door banged shut. There was a short pause, then Eleanor and Mr Gilbert started talking again.

Dugald looked around. Still nobody had told him what to do.

There was the sound of the fans again, and now Kenn was coming back, staggering slightly under the weight of a big foreleg of beef. He had to step sideways to get it through the passageway between the front and back shops, and he grunted as he turned full on to his bench and prepared to flip the foreleg up and into the proper position for cutting. Dugald, he said.

Dugald looked at him. His face was red, and there was sweat on his forehead. Aye?

The big lump of beef smashed down on the bench, setting the hooks jingling on the metal bar above it. Get the chill door, said Kenn, picking up his knife.

Dugald walked through into the frontshop, squeezed past Eleanor at the scales, and went to close the chill. As he stood looking in for a moment at the rows of lambs and pigs hanging by hooks through their ankle sinews, and the shelves of boiled ham, potted head and offal, he heard Mr Gilbert say, So this is your new laddie is it Mrs Butcher?

Aye, this is Dugald, said Eleanor.

He closed the chill door and passed along the rear of the counter. He nodded at Mr Gilbert.

I used to have a dog called Dugald, said the old man. Named him after that one on the telly. Hee hee! He was a scrunty wee tyke! He started laughing. Dugald's face was going red; he looked at the floor as he passed Eleanor, and went quickly towards the backshop. As he went through the passage, Mr Gilbert was laughing and coughing and wiping water away from his eyes and nose with the back of his hand. Dugald the dog! he cried again, and coughed deep down in his guts.

Kenn was bent over the beef, running his knife down a seam. He looked up as Dugald came in. Choke to death you old bugger! he said loudly. Dugald jumped slightly, but Kenn had already turned back to the foreleg and was still talking. See him? he said, In here at least twenty minutes, blethering away keeping Nell from her accounts, and all he's bought is a quarter of slicey and one mealy jimmy. It makes my blood boil!

I ken, said Dugald.

What?

I said I ken. That he never buys much like.

Oh. Aye. I thought you were talking to me.

Dugald leant back on the sidebench and checked his sleeves. Kenn stared at him for a few seconds, then lifted down the steel off its hook and started to stroke his knife along it, long slow movements, one side of the knife then the other, rotating the steel a little each time too. All the while he was looking at Dugald. Dugald looked at the point of the knife as it moved towards him and back, towards him and back. After half a minute the knife stopped, rested on the steel.

Well hash on then, said Kenn. I don't pay you to stand around doing bugger all!

The butcher turned back to his work, and Dugald stood up, looked about the room, and wiped his hands down the front of his apron. He opened his mouth, but shut it again without saying anything; his gaze came to rest on the big mincing machine in the corner of the room. He stepped over to the sink, pulled out a basin from under it, and filled it with hot water and a squirt of soap. Then he wrung a clout out under the tap and carried it and the basin over to the mincer. He gave the outside of the machine a dicht and then started swabbing down the big meat funnel on top. Suddenly Dugald was aware that Kenn had stopped working. He rubbed hard at a small patch of dried blood on the metal.

For God's sake man, what are you doing? said Kenn, and banged his knife down on the wooden bench-top.

Dugald half turned, dropped the clout into the basin of water. I was just eh . . . well, I thought the machine could . . . eh . . .

It's not half past two yet, we'll probably have to put three or four more loads through afore lowsing-time: don't piss about washing it the now!

Dugald carried the basin over to the sink, emptied it, and rinsed the clout. He started to wash his hands.

Get on with the bloody work! said Kenn. It's Tuesday afternoon, so get on with the Tuesday-afternoon jobs! Christ, you've been here three weeks now, you should be learning the routine by this time!

Dugald nodded. His face was going red again. As he stretched to dry his hands on the roller towel, Kenn hawked, then came across and spat a big greener over Dugald's shoulder and into the sink.

Routine? said Dugald. I never realised, I mean you never told me . . . Come to think of it, I suppose you would need some kind of . . .

You would need some kind of kick up the arse, said Kenn,

going back to his bench. Now hold your tongue and get on with the work.

Dugald gave a start, glanced at Kenn's back as he set about the foreleg again. His face was still red, but the beginnings of a grin were appearing there too. He left the sink and went through to the frontshop. Eleanor had just seen old Mr Gilbert out the door. Dugald went over and opened the chill. Well Mrs Butcher, he said, I suppose it's about time I started the tongue.

Eleanor laughed. Aye, I suppose it is, *Mr* Butcher, she said.

Dugald went into the chill and slid a blue plastic bucket forward from the back of the bottom shelf. Inside, soaking in water made cloudy by blood and dissolved fat, were three ox tongues. He lifted the bucket to the floor, crouched down over it, and thrust his hand into the icy water. He reached down till he touched meat. The tops of the tongues were incredibly rough: sandpapery near the tip, and with rows of buds like match-heads towards the rear. The undersides of the tongues were smooth, like muscle, apart from at the rear end, the thick end, where there was torn flesh, ragged ribbons of tissue, as if the tongues had been ripped out of their sockets, ripped out by hand, not cut by knives. Dugald circled his hand round one of the tongues and lifted it out of the water, looking at the purply blotches like birthmarks across it, and feeling at the same time the roughness of the top on his palm, and the smoothness of the underside where his fingers pressed in to hold it.

He let the tongue slip back into the water, then hefted up the bucket and walked out of the chill with it, shutting the door behind him with a kick of his heel. He walked slowly through to the backshop, not spilling any of the water, lifted the bucket up to the sink, and teemed it.

Kenn was watching him. Do you mind what to do? he said.

Aye, no bother, said Dugald. Kenn raised his eyebrows. I get the scrubbing brush, and I scrub off all the blood and grassy feech . . .

Then you get the pickle-mix . . .

Then I get the mix, dissolve three scoops in the pan and . . .

Ach you've got it, said Kenn. You don't need me telling you, you ken it fine. Good man.

Dugald took the brush out from under the sink, set the cold tap running, and started work.

Lucky to be Alive

On the way to the bar I passed a table where somebody was saying, See him there, and them there? They live in pubs, it's a well-known fact: sleeping and eating and everything . . .

This was almost completely true, except we didn't do all our sleeping in pubs, only part of it, only short bursts. In fact we didn't do much of it anywhere: sleep is excellent for waking out of into a hangover, but not much good for anything else. We avoided it for as long as possible by taking fairly large quantities of speed and not having any beds in the flat we rented – we sold them shortly after moving in.

A few rounds later we headed back to the flat and crashed out in the smaller of the two rooms. Toad immediately skinned up and within ten minutes the air was heavy and thick and worth breathing for once.

We should smoke in here more often, I said.

Fine by me, said Benny.

Aye, we ken what's fine by you you clarty cunt, said Toad.

We all laughed at this: usually we used the big room to sit around and smoke in, but two or three nights before Benny had come awake in the early hours, somehow imagined he was walking to the lavvy, and dropped a shite in the corner by the window. It was only when he found there wasn't any paper to hand that he realised he'd fucked up pretty badly, and he went away to the small room for the rest of the night, leaving the two of us to wake up to the smell of whisky skitters a couple of hours later. Toad said to Benny he had two choices: either clean up his mess or get the fuck out of the flat. Benny pointed out that if he left the flat, then the two of us would have *no* choice: we'd have to clean it up. We should just wait, he said, till it dried out properly, and then we could sweep it up no bother if we got a brush and shovel from somewhere. It sounded like he had some experience of this type of situation, so since then we'd been using the small room for everything. And it was a great room to smoke in: we were all getting well relaxed.

At least, Benny and Toad were getting relaxed. I was trying to, but something was wrong. For starters, you shouldn't have to fucking try to relax, it doesn't make sense. But all the muscles in my body seemed to be cramping up: my stomach muscles were taking these sort of spasms, jerking each other in opposite directions, and as they did my other muscles were going rigid, I found myself stretching my limbs out, tensing my whole body, trying to stop my stomach from tying itself in a knot. Also I was shivering, I could actually hear my teeth clattering together, and I was cold, cold as hell – except every now and then there would be a feeling of terrible heat spreading out from my stomach to my extremities, as if I'd swallowed a red-hot stone and waves of heat were rippling out through my body.

Somebody was offering me a toke, but I couldn't answer: my jaw was rigid and chattering at the same time. Toad and Benny started laughing: they were pointing at me and laughing their fucking heads off, ha ha fucking ha.

The next thing was I was waking up half-way through a vomit. I was lying on my side and there was some bastard punching me in the guts: I was doubling up and spewing my ring onto the lino. Then I stopped vomiting, wiped my mouth, and listened to Benny and Toad snoring. Then suddenly I was puking again: there was nobody else in the room, it was some cunt inside me trying to boot his way out.

My guts were being twisted and wrung out like a wet rag: this was one of the worst vomits I could remember. But it was different, yes it was definitely different, because there was a smell, a foul smell, not just the reek of whisky and beer – though that was there too – but a smell of something rotten and foul and dead. It was very like a smell I knew from the days when I worked in a meat-products factory; one of my jobs was to clean out the large vat that held the liver and lights before they went on to be minced down for pâté and sausages and the like: and that was a bad smell, that was the worst. You had to hold your breath, do thirty seconds of hosing or mopping, then climb out and gulp down the fine clean air of the factory, before climbing back in for another half-minute. If you tried to stay in any longer than that it was like having rotten corpse-flesh shoved up your nostrils. And this smell coming from inside me was like that, except this time there was no chance to hold my breath. I wasn't in control of my lungs or my guts or anything at all: I would retch up some stuff, gasp for some air, then retch again . . . In fact I was fighting to get any breathing done at all in the gaps between boaks. But after a while it seemed to be over, and I went back to sleep.

Benny shook me awake. It was light. He was leaning over me, shaking me, saying something:

You alright mate? He shook me some more, then turned towards the door and shouted, Hey Toad, he's woke up, he's opening his eyes.

Toad came into the room and crouched down beside Benny. Rough night was it? he said.

I don't know, I said.

What's all this then? said Toad, and pointed to some half-dried-up puddles of black liquid on the lino and a black crusted stain down my shirt.

I don't know, I said. I sat up. My brain was pulsing inside my skull: it was too big and I could feel it pressing, crushing itself against the inside of my head. Jesus I need a drink, I said.

I think you should stick to milk, said Benny, You've been puking up fucking blood man.

I looked at him, then at the puddles of black stuff. Oh aye, I said.

No listen, said Toad, Not milk, that won't do: he'd only be spewing up yoghurt next.

Aye, that'd be right, I said, Cause rennet comes from cows' stomachs, eh? One of their stomachs. Or maybe all of them. And you can use that, that is what you need, that is the thing for fucking yoghurt-making. Which I fucking hate by the way.

They were both looking at me. Then: Aye, fuck the milk, said Toad, I know just the stuff. I'll have to go out and get it though. There's a guy I know works in that whisky-blending place in Leith, and sometimes somebody'll go a bit radge and pour some of the raw whisky down them, before it's been diluted and that. So they have this special mixture they give them, some chemical that counteracts the alcohol, and it stops their insides from burning up completely.

So are you going to go and fucking get some then, said Benny, Or are you just going to fucking stand there?

Aye, I'm off, I'm off. You'll wait here till I get back, eh?

Well if we're not here, we'll be in round the corner, I said.

Aye, I think you better wait here though, said Toad.

Okay, I said, see you in there then.

After Toad left, me and Benny made our way round the corner. I had to persuade him: Have you never fucking puked man? I said.

Aye, I ken, he said, But that amount of blood . . . this could be serious.

Away and shite, I said. All I need is a pick-me-up and I'll be fine. A raw egg stirred into a large brandy! Aye, that's the stuff by Christ.

What, and die of salmonella? said Benny.

I laughed and we walked in and I ordered a vodka and tonic.

We sat at a table near the door to the bogs. The first mouthful burned like buggery on its way down, but after that the fizziness and the alcohol seemed to help. I liked the idea that the drink was completely clear, it seemed to be a good condition to be in: it was clean and clear and that was how I wanted to be too. I had the idea that if I drank enough vodka and tonic then maybe my whole body would fill up with it and there'd be no room for any badness or blood at all, just pure clear stuff inside me. And I was talking about this, and talking talking about other things as well, but only every now and then would I come to with a sort of a start and realise what I was saying: most of the time I wasn't hearing myself at all.

Dying wouldn't be too bad, as long as it was immediately after a really good fuck. If there was somebody good, really good . . . and just to look up and see eyes and a mouth and a nose, that's all you'd need; and some hair too, to see some hair, and then to do it. To have good sex and then die, to get hit by a bus on the way home – it would have to be pretty instant actually. What else is there? I mean why wait till you're fucking eighty to die when you've no chance of a fucking screw? At least at the age of twenty-six you have that possibility, the possibility of a really good fuck and then death immediately following. Or even a really good hug!

Jesus, your arms around another person, someone's arms round you, tight, so tight. Cause it's impossible to be happy all the time, to have a happy whole life, but you can be happy in bursts: with a really good hug you could be happy for . . . for half an hour maybe, and then that would be the best way, not to waste your time trying to get permanently happy, but just the next half-hour you are happy for, well immediately after, just fucking kill yourself.

Aye, it's a bummer, said Benny. But listen man: you've got a no bad life really, eh? I mean not working at some shitey job, nearly always plenty to drink: what more could you ask for?

Well exactly, fucking exactly, I said. What more can you ask for? I have no fucking idea, and that's the truth.

I stopped hearing myself, though maybe I was carrying on talking, till after a while Toad appeared.

Where have you been? I said.

Here, he said, Get this down you pronto. He held out a small lemonade bottle half-full of a yellowish liquid.

What's this? I said. It looks like some fucker's urine sample!

I got it off my mate at the blenders you daft cunt. And I told you you should have fucking stayed off the bevvy. Your stomach's probably in fucking tatters man, the drink'll be sloshing through the holes and into your innards, fucking eating them up. Come on, wise the fucking head.

I felt too tired to argue and I'd forgotten what we were arguing about; I took the bottle. I'll go ben the lavvy, I said, We don't want the fucking barkeep on our backs for having a carry-in on top of everything else.

I went into the bogs, sat down in the cubicle, and screwed the top off the bottle. I held the bottle up to the light for a minute and looked at the yellow stuff inside, then I drank it down.

I opened my eyes. There was a tube up my nose. For fuck's

sake! I tried to yank it out, but I couldn't: I couldn't lift my arms, they were too heavy or something. I shut my eyes again.

Later, I looked up and there was a woman in a white coat bending over me. Hello, she said, Welcome to the Western General.

What's going on? I said.

Your friends had to break the door down to get you out, she said. You could have choked on all that blood you were bringing up; you're lucky to be alive.

It's funny you should say that, I said, because I was saying the same thing to a mate of mine just a minute ago.

Yesterday, she said.

What a stroke of good luck it was to be born! I should be counting my blessings one by one by Christ! I started to laugh, but it turned into a coughing fit, and I was retching again from deep down. The woman pushed a silvery basin under my chin, and with the other hand supported the back of my head. And out it all came.